P9-ELG-220

WITHDRAWN

epic!

CAT NINJA

Gift of the Friends of
the Pleasant Hill Library

Written by
Matthew Cody

Illustrated by
Yehudi Mercado

Andrews McMeel
PUBLISHING®

For Meika Hashimoto, editor extraordinaire,
and Cat Ninja's unsung superhero
—MC

For Asher Warfield
—YM

Cat Ninja text and illustrations copyright © 2020 by
Epic! Creations, Inc. All rights reserved. Printed in China.
No part of this book may be used or reproduced in any manner
whatsoever without written permission except in the case of
reprints in the context of reviews.

Andrews McMeel Publishing
a division of Andrews McMeel Universal
1130 Walnut Street, Kansas City, Missouri 64106

www.andrewsmcmeel.com

Epic! Creations, Inc.
702 Marshall Street, Suite 280, Redwood City, California 94063

www.getepic.com

22 23 24 25 26 SDB 10 9 8 7 6 5 4 3

Paperback ISBN: 978-1-5248-6094-3
Hardback ISBN: 978-1-5248-6138-4

Library of Congress Control Number: 2020933940

Design by Dan Nordskog
Additional art assistance: Sophia Hoodis, Dave Wheeler,
Mary Bellamy, and John Padon

Made by:
King Yip (Dongguan) Printing & Packaging Factory Ltd.
Address and location of manufacturer:
Daning Administrative District, Humen Town
Dongguan Guangdong, China 523930
3rd Printing – 11/15/21

ATTENTION: SCHOOLS AND BUSINESSES
Andrews McMeel books are available at quantity discounts with
bulk purchase for educational, business, or sales promotional use.
For information, please e-mail the Andrews McMeel Publishing
Special Sales Department: specialsales@amuniversal.com.

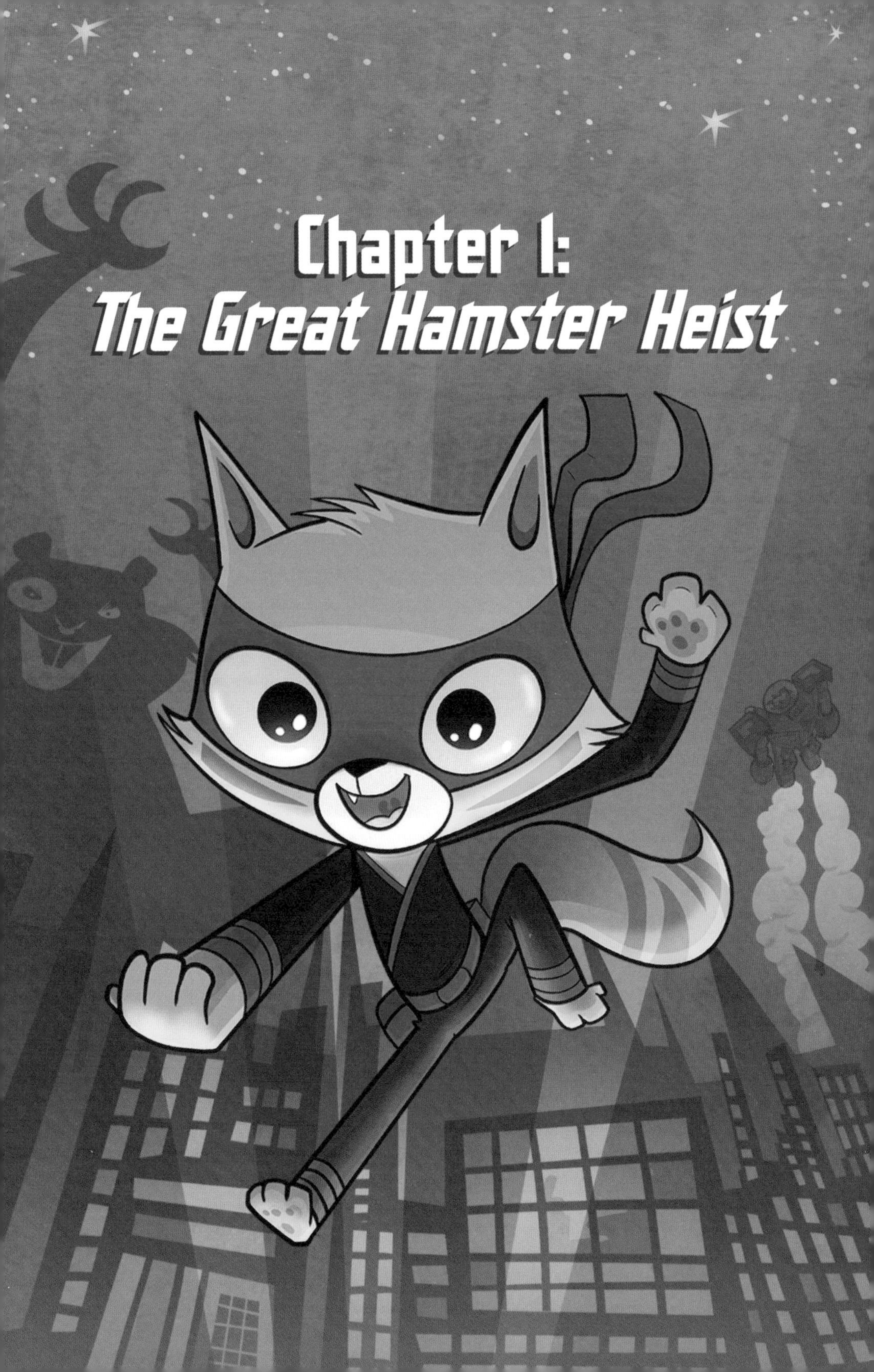
Chapter 1:
The Great Hamster Heist

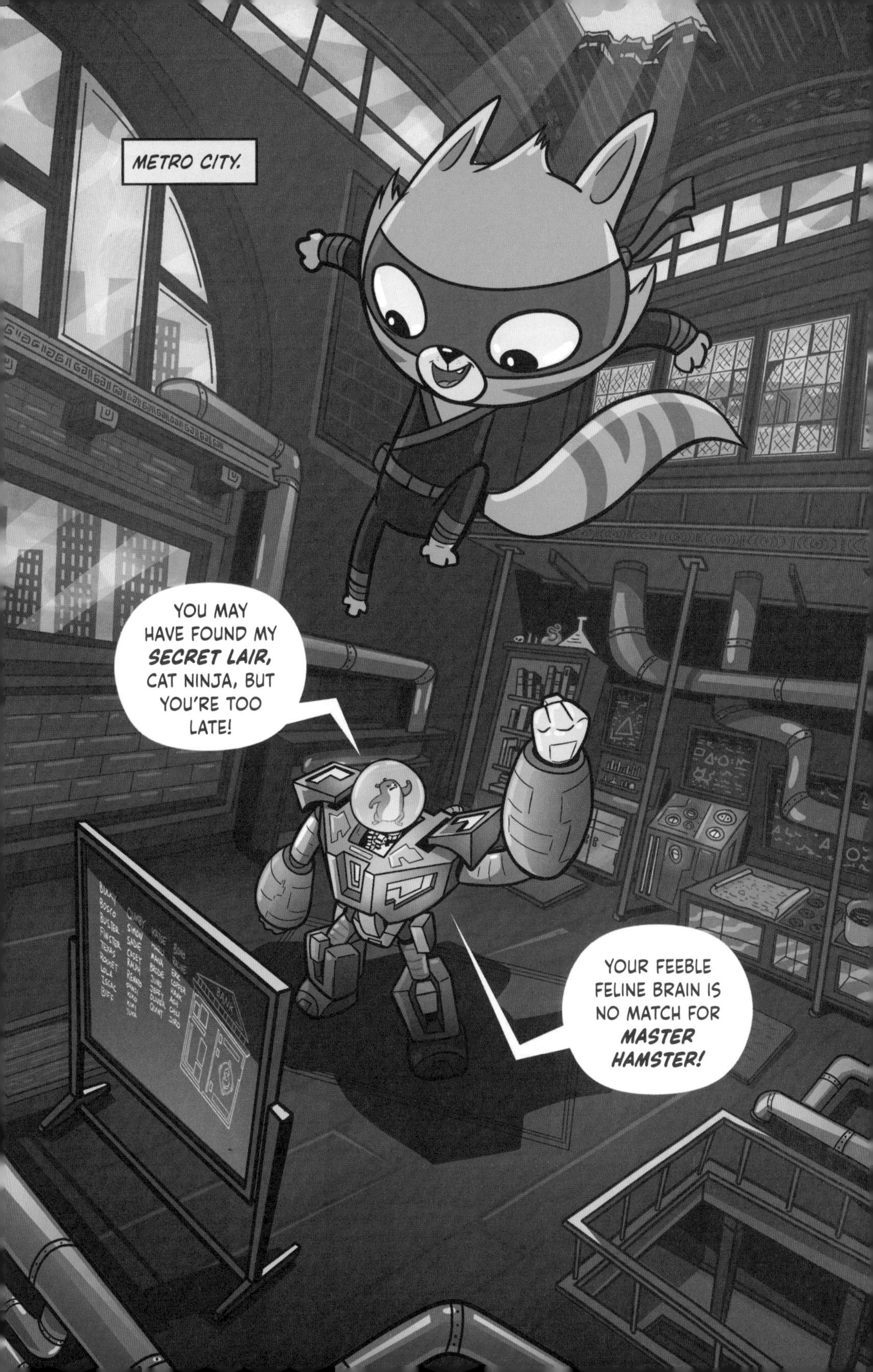
METRO CITY.
YOU MAY HAVE FOUND MY **SECRET LAIR,** CAT NINJA, BUT YOU'RE TOO LATE!
YOUR FEEBLE FELINE BRAIN IS NO MATCH FOR **MASTER HAMSTER!**

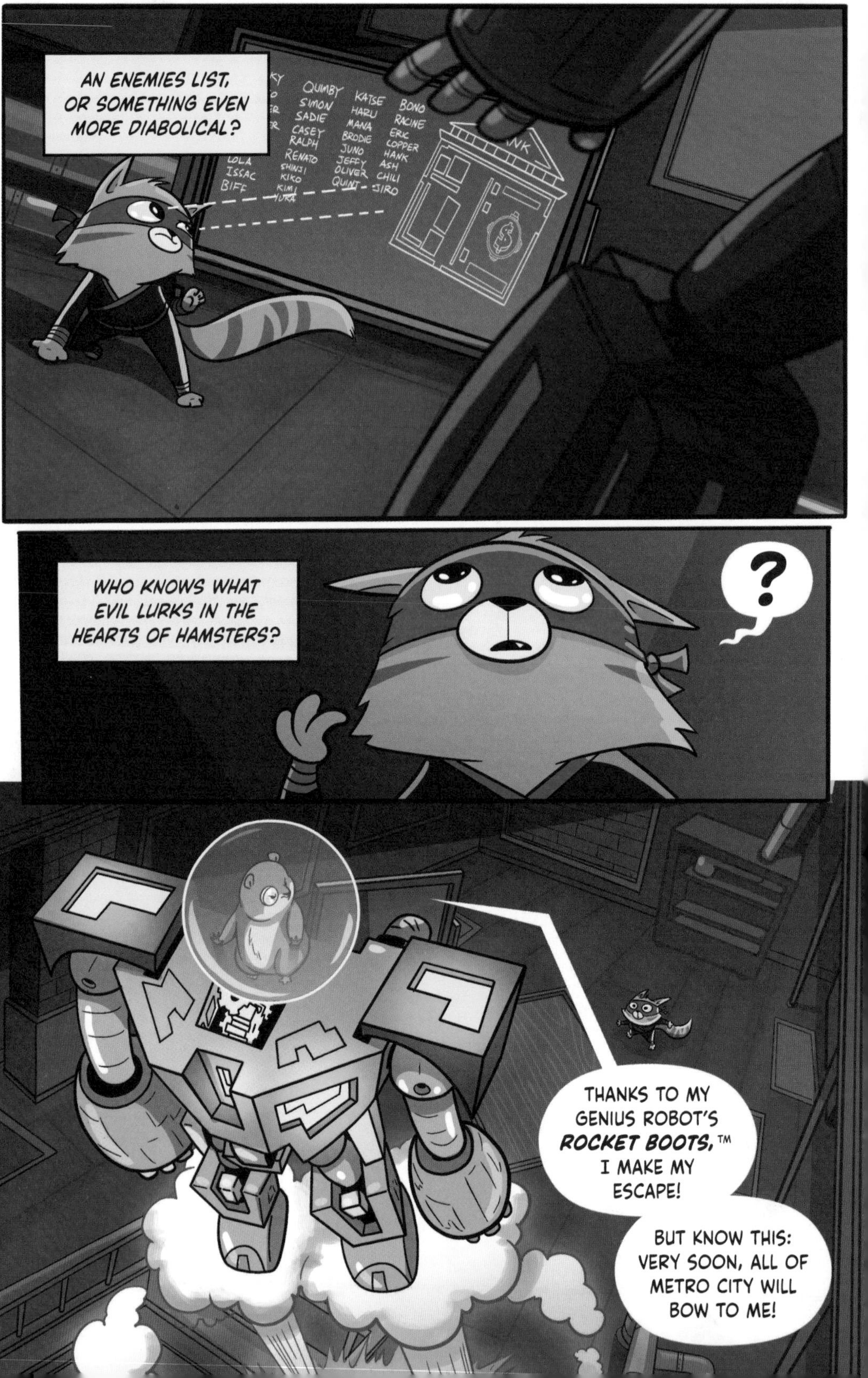
AN ENEMIES LIST, OR SOMETHING EVEN MORE DIABOLICAL?
QUIMBY SIMON SADIE CASEY RALPH RENATO SHINJI KIKO KIMI YURA
KATSE HARU MANA BRODIE JUNO JEFFY OLIVER QUINT
BONO RACINE ERIC COPPER HANK ASH CHILI JIRO
LOLA ISSAC BIFF
WHO KNOWS WHAT EVIL LURKS IN THE HEARTS OF HAMSTERS?
?
THANKS TO MY GENIUS ROBOT'S ROCKET BOOTS,™ I MAKE MY ESCAPE!
BUT KNOW THIS: VERY SOON, ALL OF METRO CITY WILL BOW TO ME!

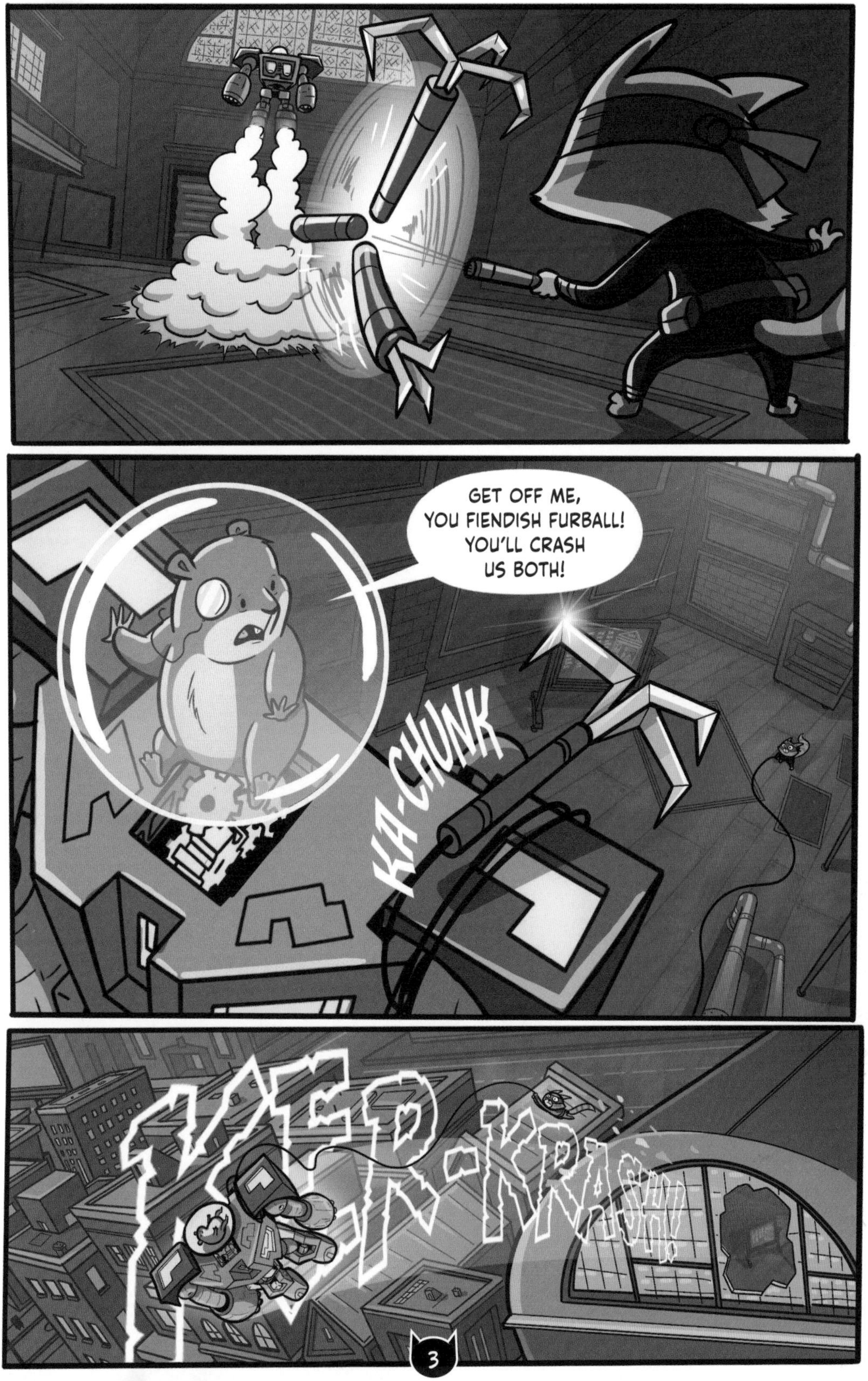
GET OFF ME, YOU FIENDISH FURBALL! YOU'LL CRASH US BOTH!
KA-CHUNK
KER-KRASH!

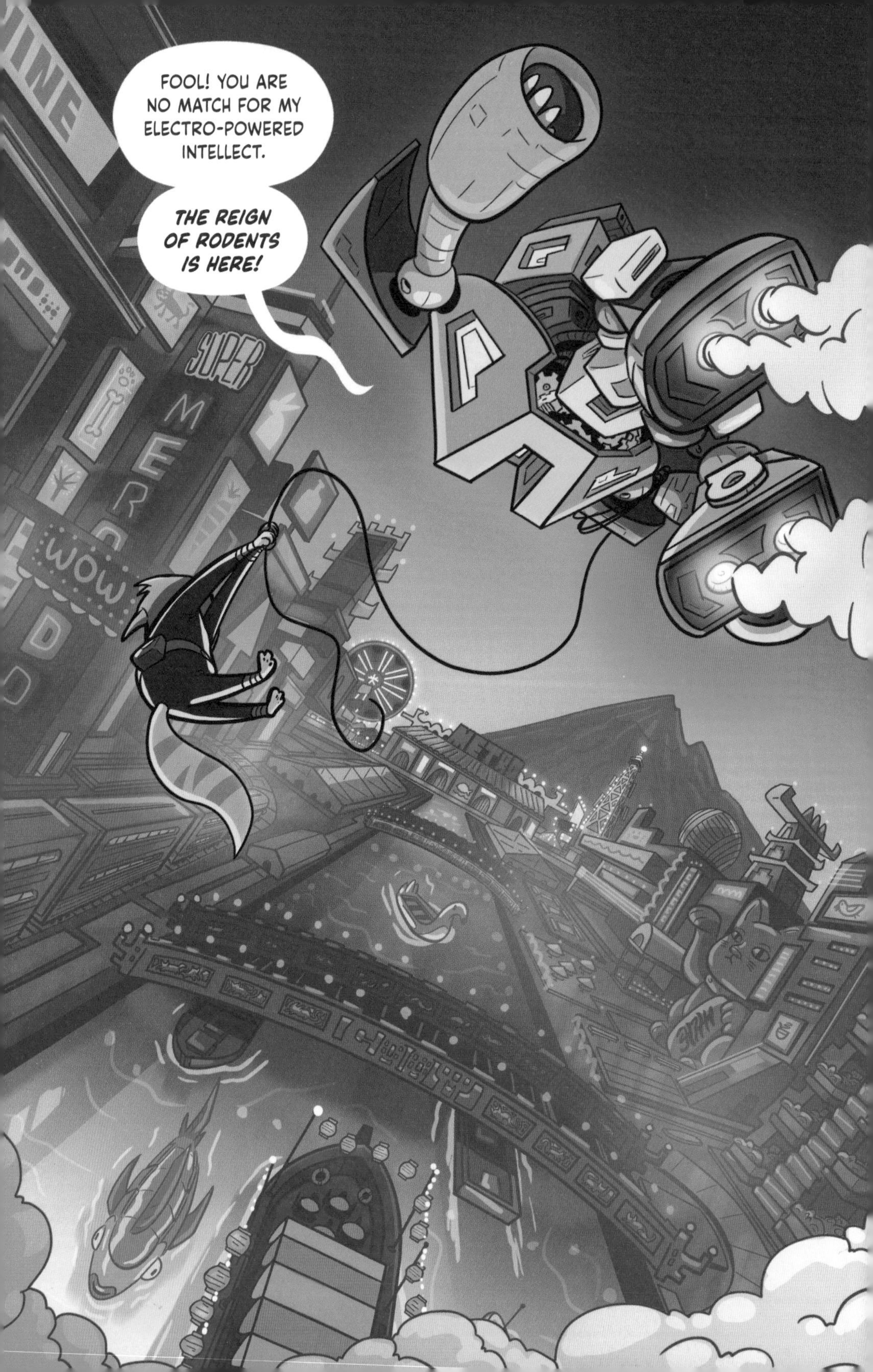
FOOL! YOU ARE NO MATCH FOR MY ELECTRO-POWERED INTELLECT.
THE REIGN OF RODENTS IS HERE!
SUPER
WOW
METRO

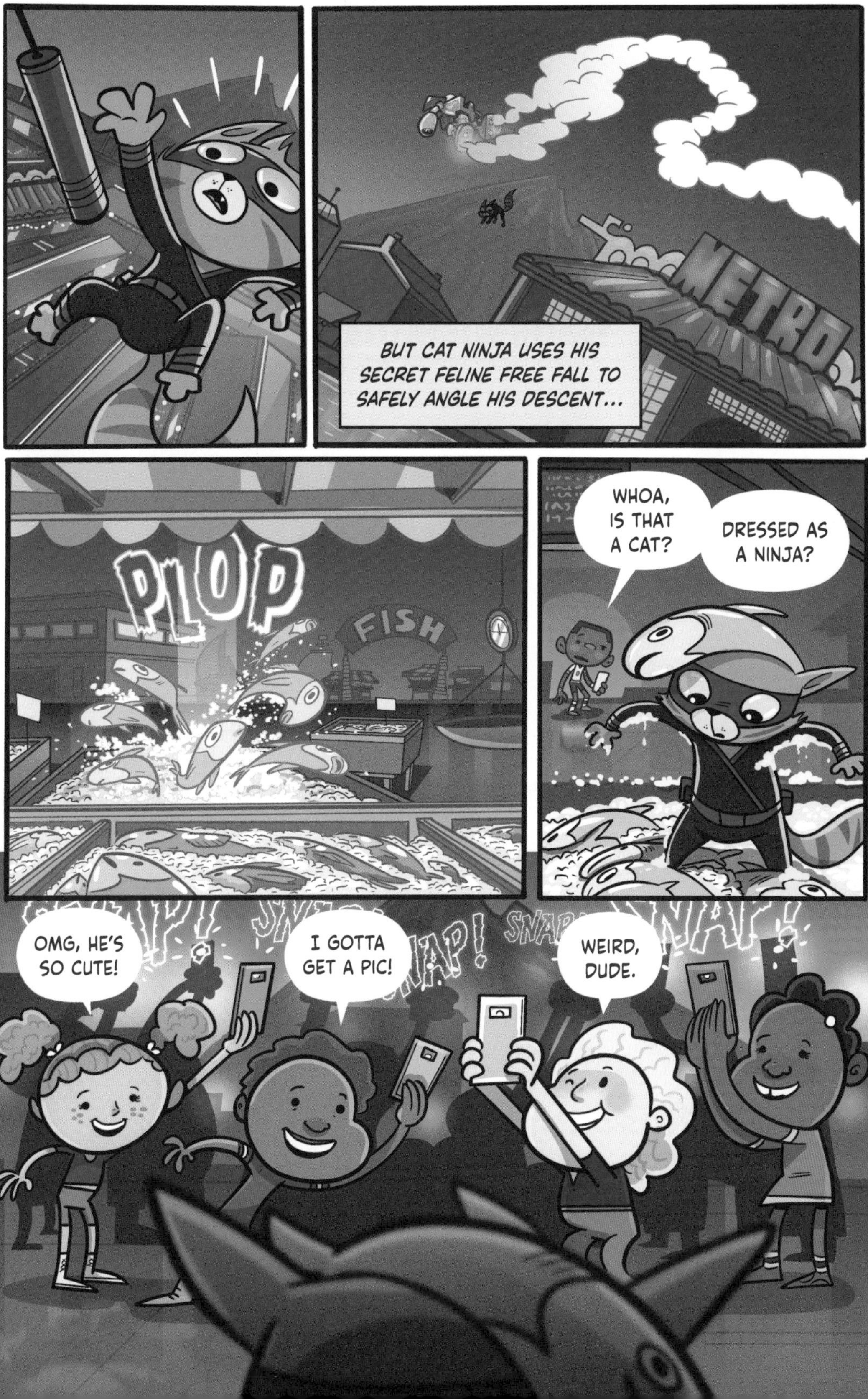
BUT CAT NINJA USES HIS SECRET FELINE FREE FALL TO SAFELY ANGLE HIS DESCENT...
METRO
PLOP
FISH
WHOA, IS THAT A CAT?
DRESSED AS A NINJA?
SNAP!
OMG, HE'S SO CUTE!
I GOTTA GET A PIC!
WEIRD, DUDE.

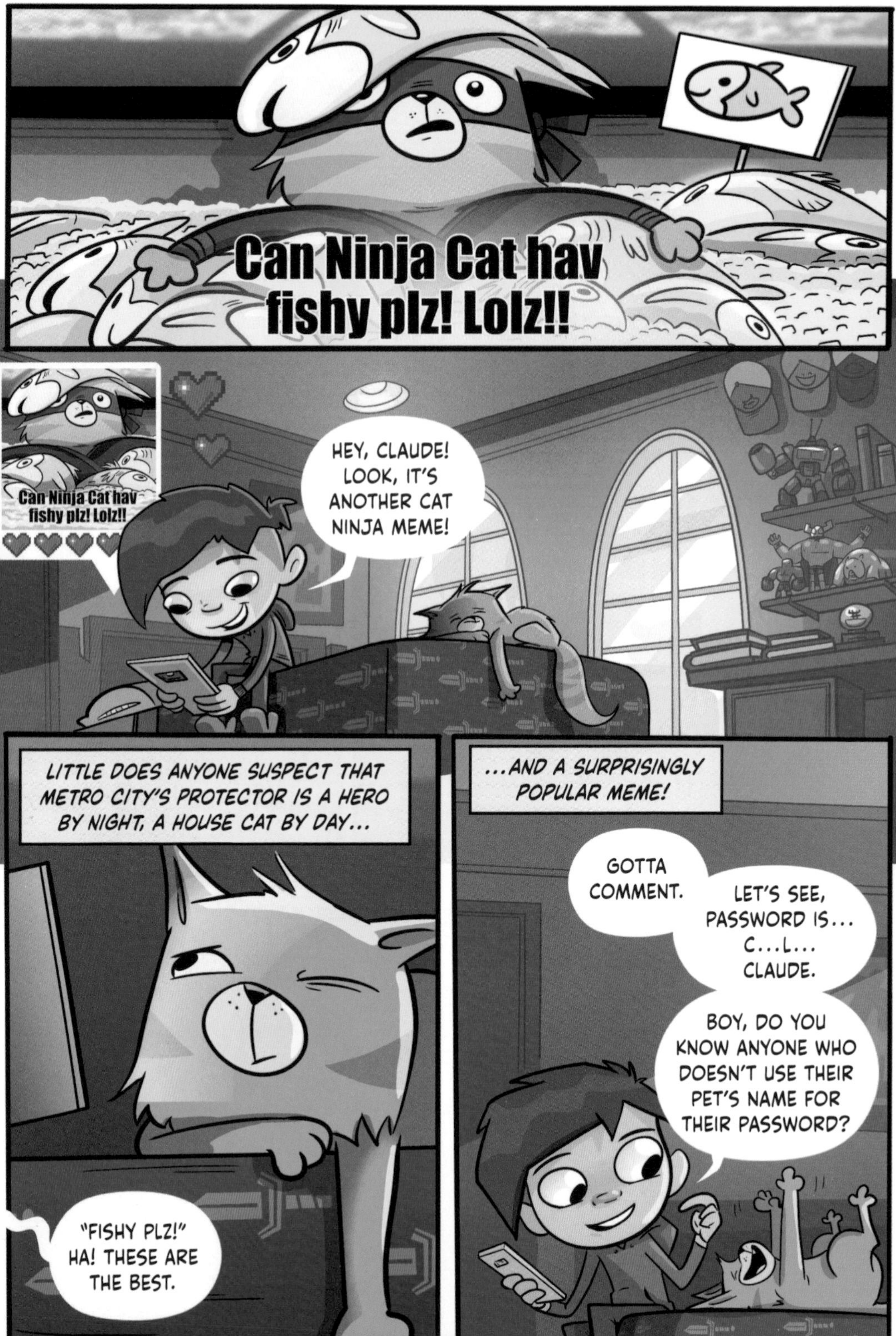
Can Ninja Cat hav fishy plz! Lolz!!
Can Ninja Cat hav fishy plz! Lolz!!
HEY, CLAUDE! LOOK, IT'S ANOTHER CAT NINJA MEME!
LITTLE DOES ANYONE SUSPECT THAT METRO CITY'S PROTECTOR IS A HERO BY NIGHT, A HOUSE CAT BY DAY...
"FISHY PLZ!" HA! THESE ARE THE BEST.
...AND A SURPRISINGLY POPULAR MEME!
GOTTA COMMENT.
LET'S SEE, PASSWORD IS... C...L... CLAUDE.
BOY, DO YOU KNOW ANYONE WHO DOESN'T USE THEIR PET'S NAME FOR THEIR PASSWORD?

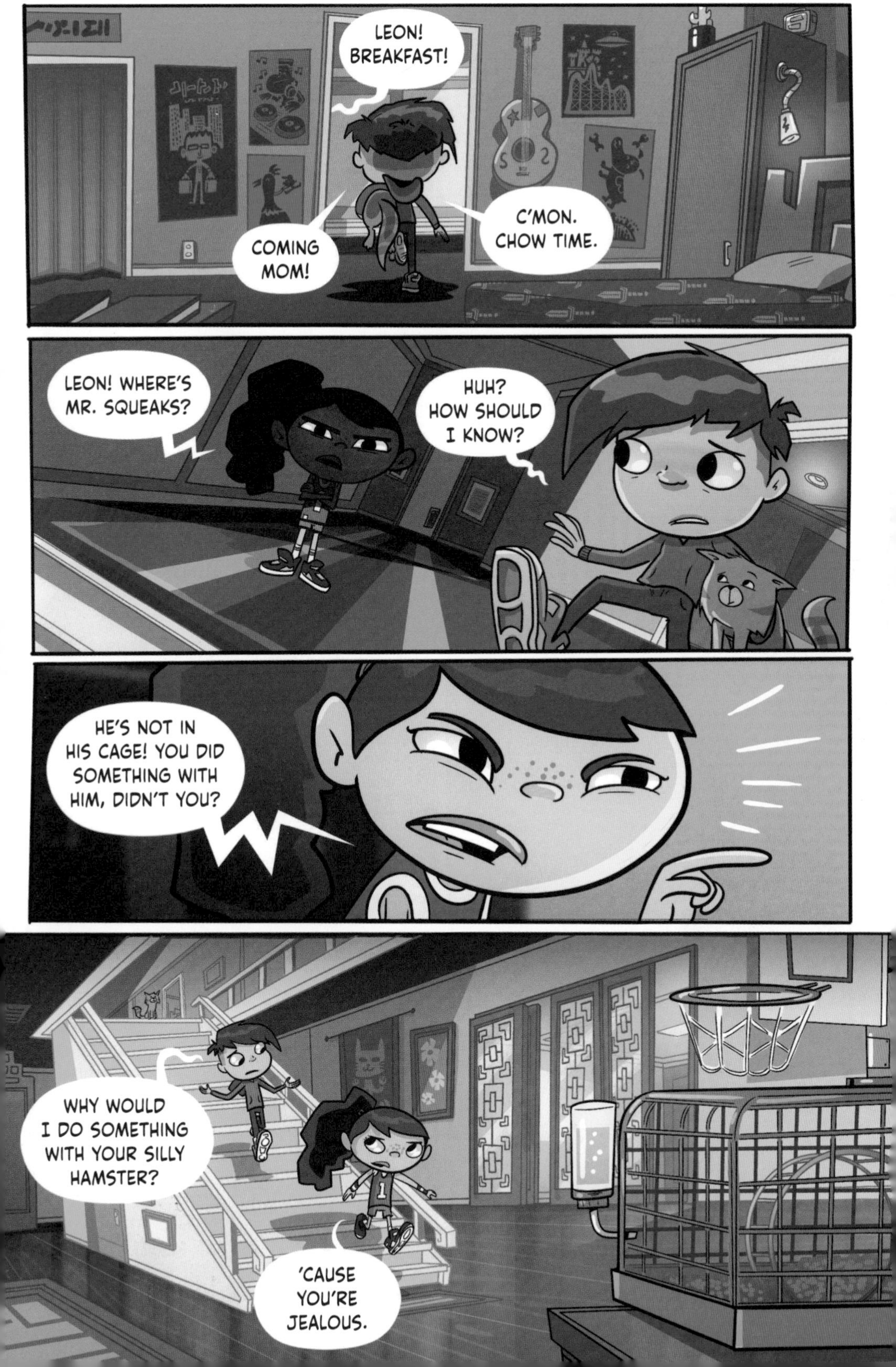
LEON! BREAKFAST!
COMING MOM!
C'MON. CHOW TIME.
LEON! WHERE'S MR. SQUEAKS?
HUH? HOW SHOULD I KNOW?
HE'S NOT IN HIS CAGE! YOU DID SOMETHING WITH HIM, DIDN'T YOU?
WHY WOULD I DO SOMETHING WITH YOUR SILLY HAMSTER?
'CAUSE YOU'RE JEALOUS.

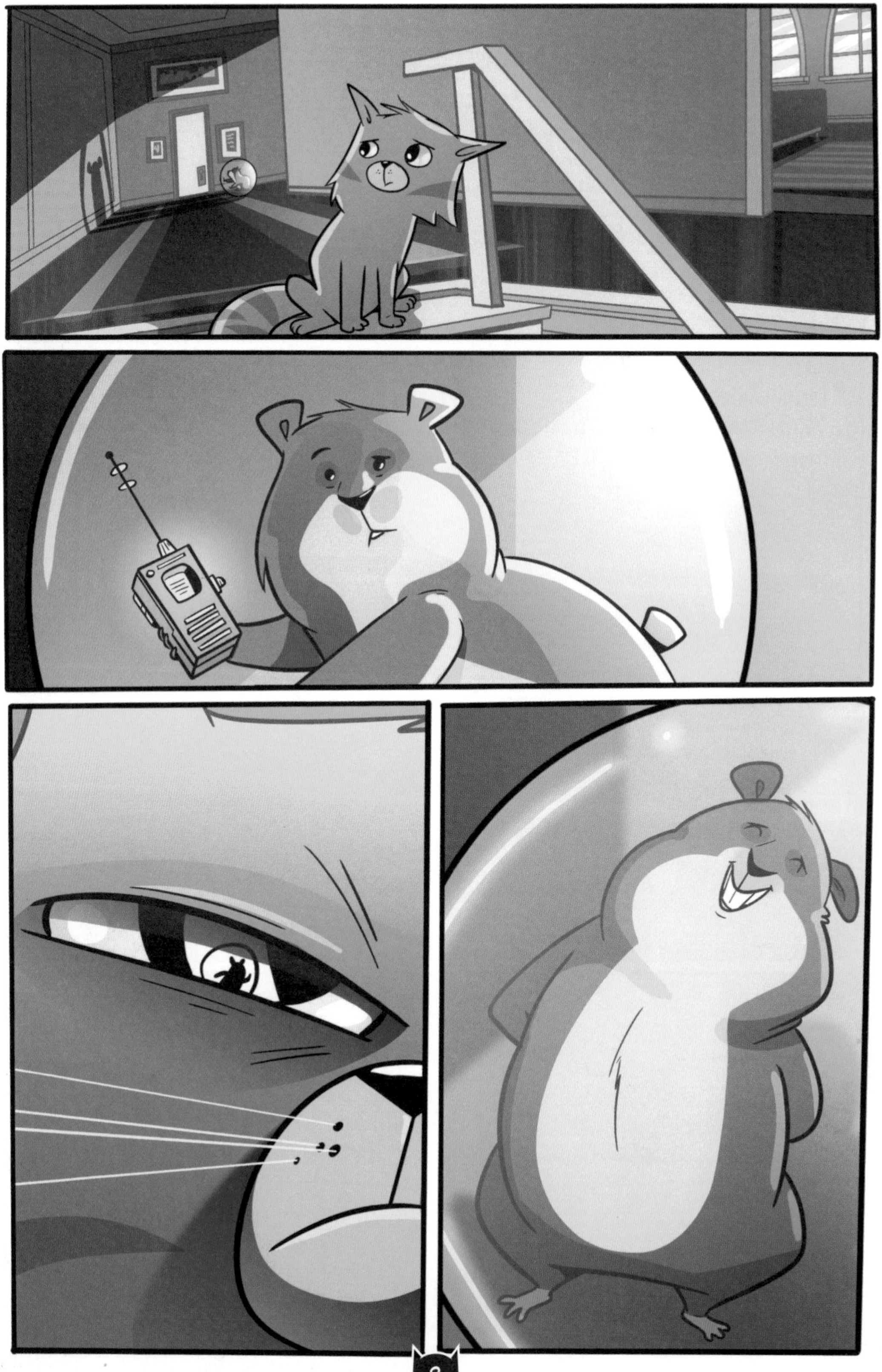

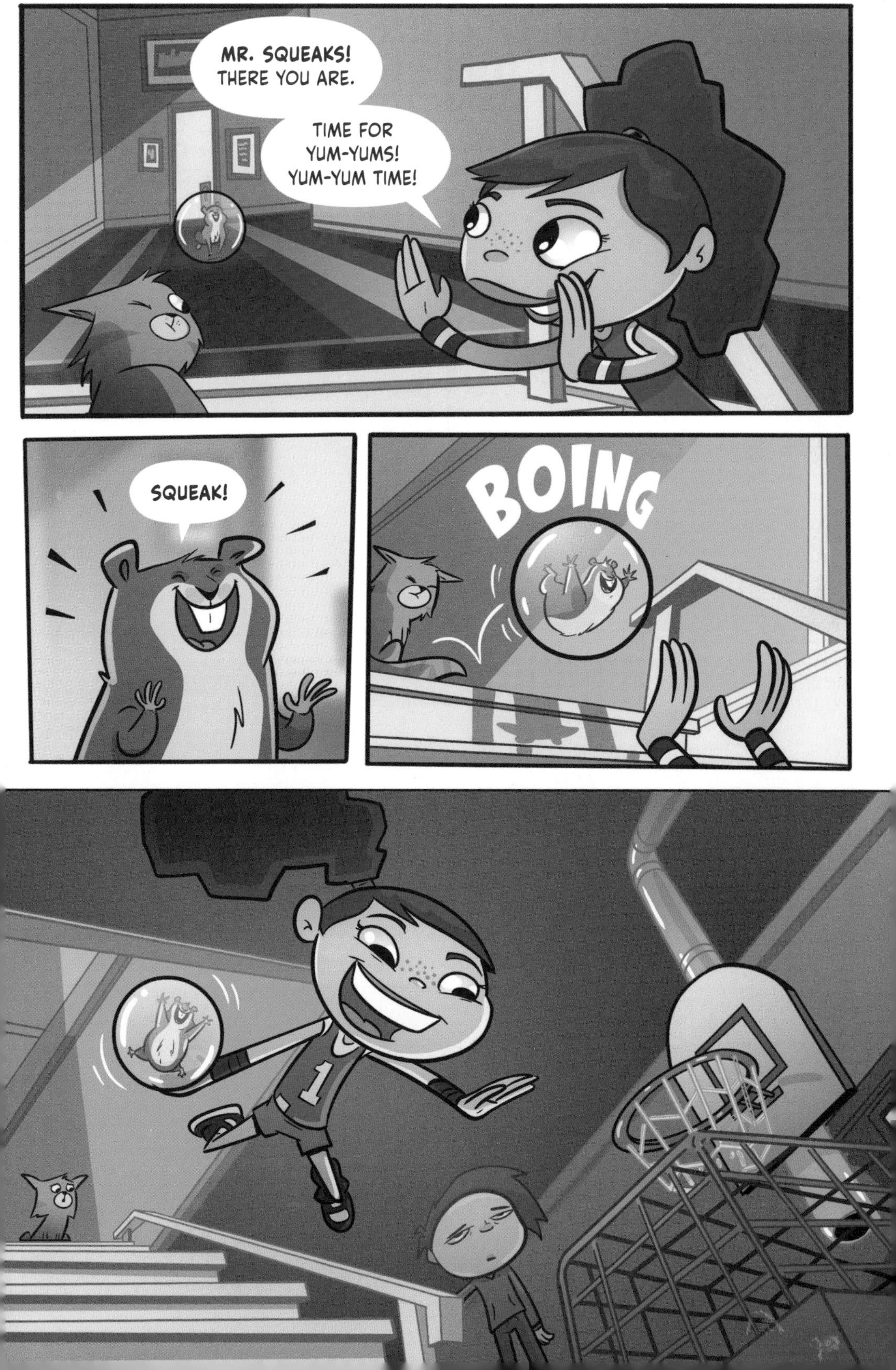
MR. SQUEAKS! THERE YOU ARE.
TIME FOR YUM-YUMS! YUM-YUM TIME!
SQUEAK!
BOING

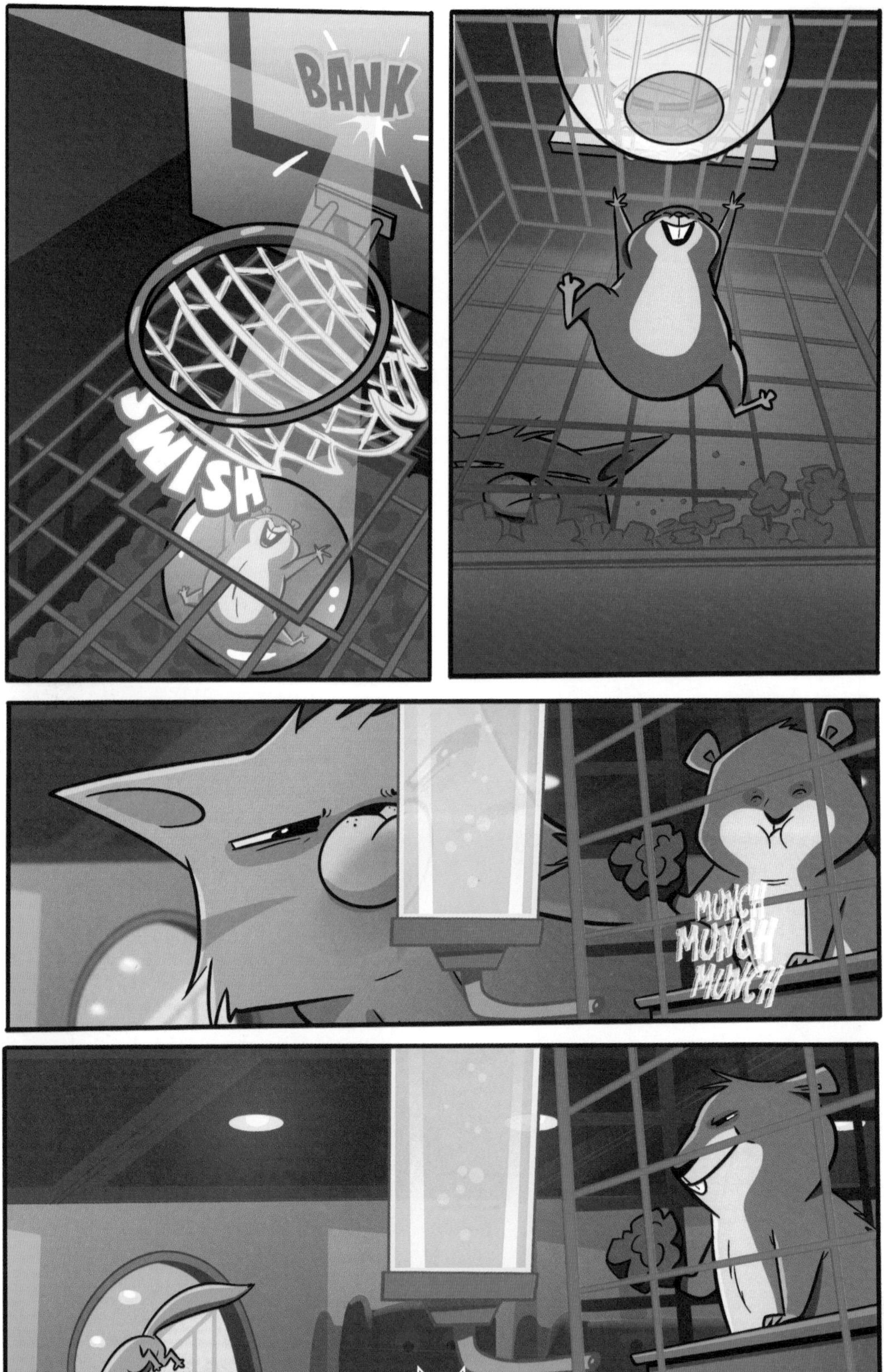
BANK
SWISH
MUNCH
MUNCH
MUNCH

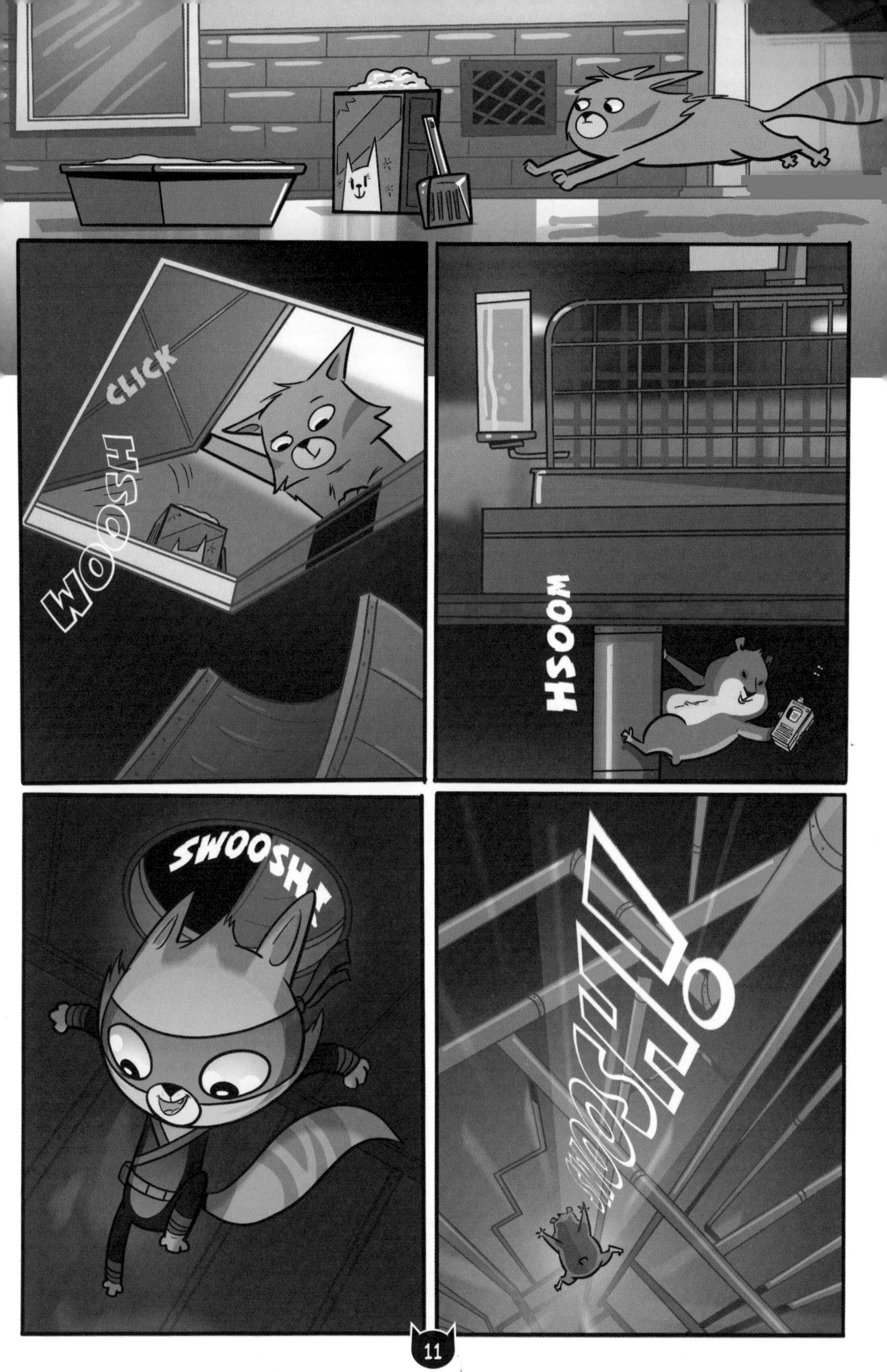
CLICK
WOOSH
WOOSH
SWOOSH!
SWOOSH!

Interlude: Origin Stories starring Cat Ninja and Master Hamster!

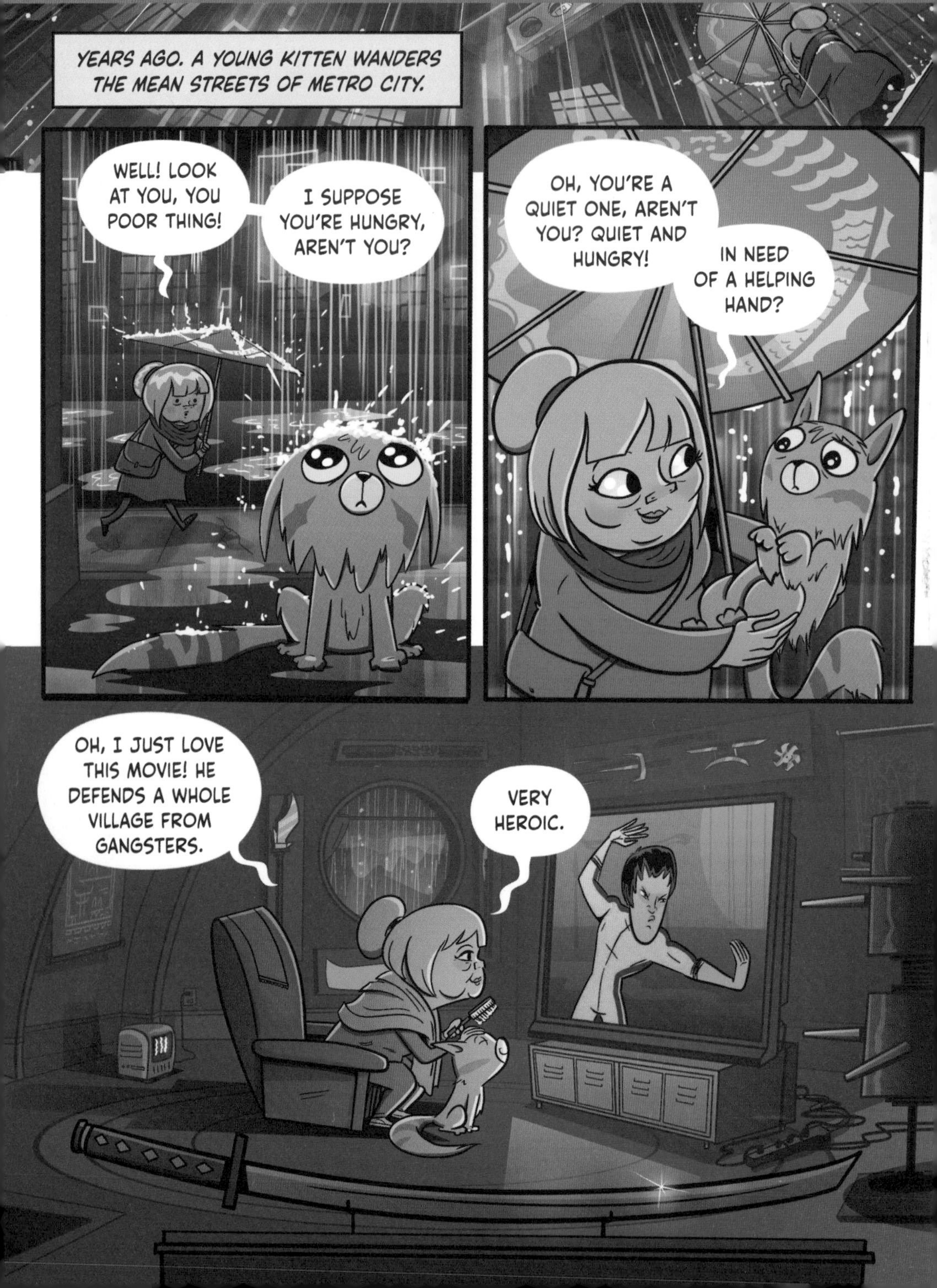
YEARS AGO. A YOUNG KITTEN WANDERS THE MEAN STREETS OF METRO CITY.
WELL! LOOK AT YOU, YOU POOR THING!
I SUPPOSE YOU'RE HUNGRY, AREN'T YOU?
OH, YOU'RE A QUIET ONE, AREN'T YOU? QUIET AND HUNGRY!
IN NEED OF A HELPING HAND?
OH, I JUST LOVE THIS MOVIE! HE DEFENDS A WHOLE VILLAGE FROM GANGSTERS.
VERY HEROIC.

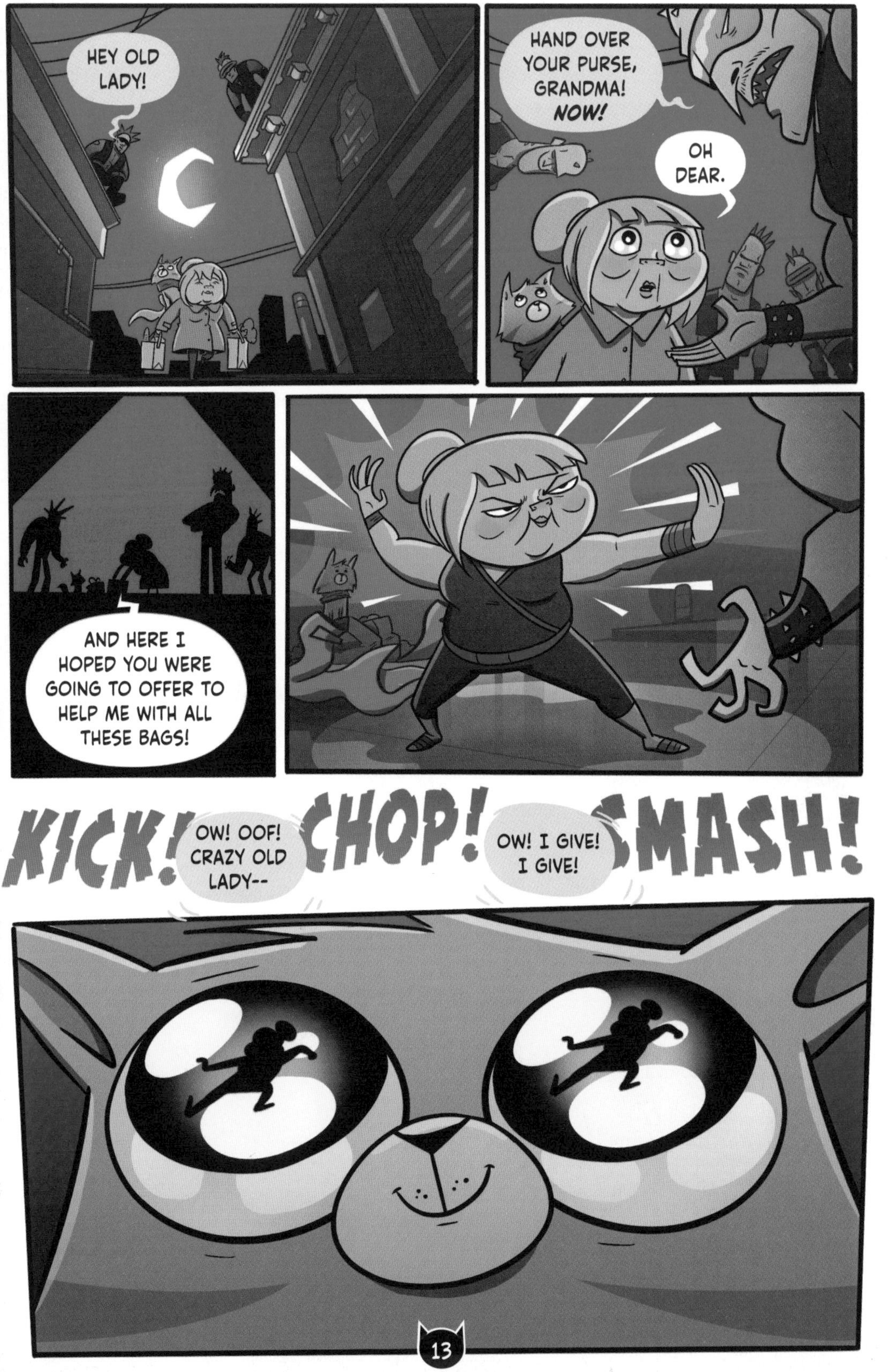
HEY OLD LADY!
HAND OVER YOUR PURSE, GRANDMA! **NOW!**
OH DEAR.
AND HERE I HOPED YOU WERE GOING TO OFFER TO HELP ME WITH ALL THESE BAGS!
KICK!
OW! OOF! CRAZY OLD LADY--
CHOP!
OW! I GIVE! I GIVE!
SMASH!

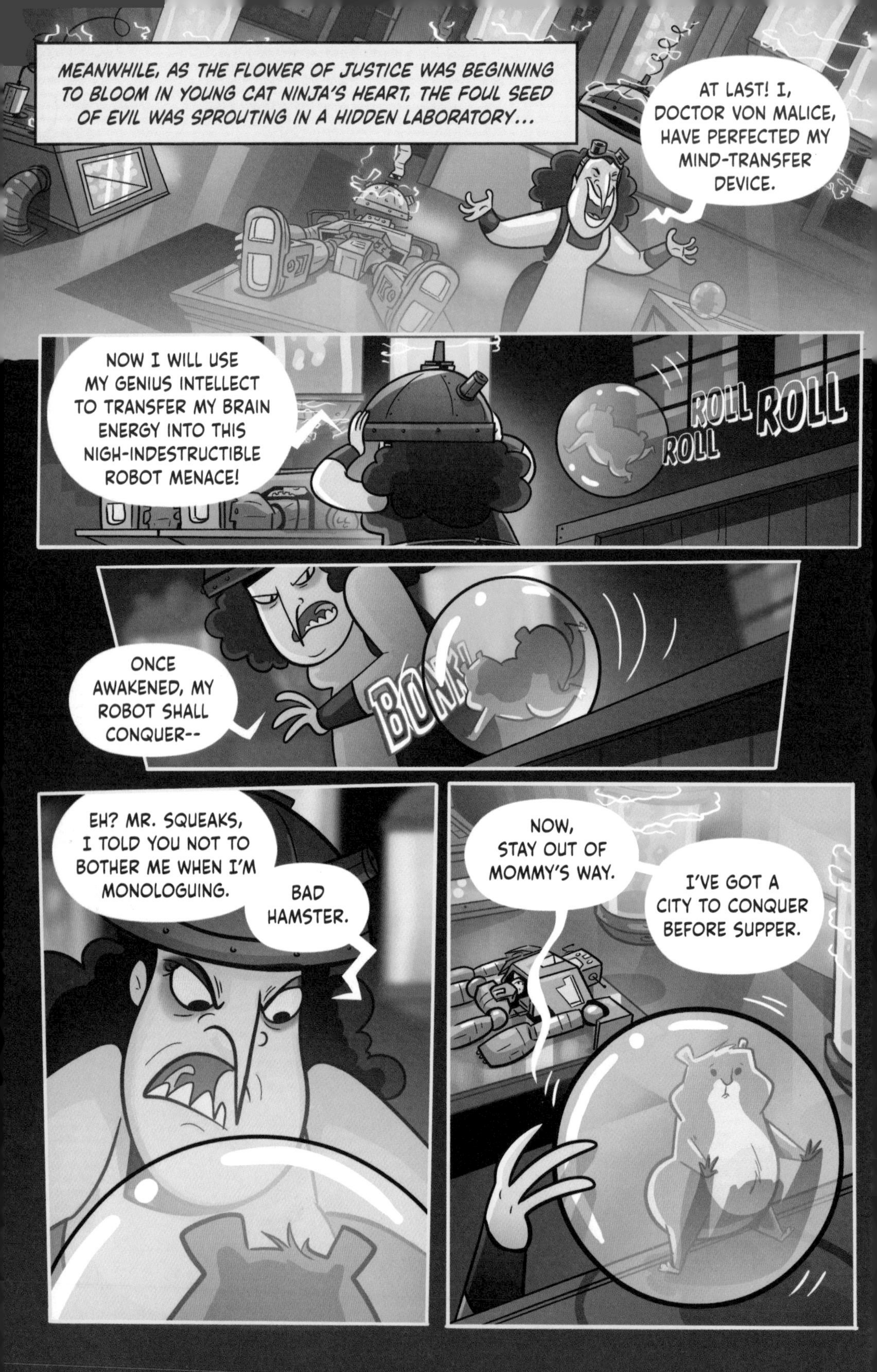
MEANWHILE, AS THE FLOWER OF JUSTICE WAS BEGINNING TO BLOOM IN YOUNG CAT NINJA'S HEART, THE FOUL SEED OF EVIL WAS SPROUTING IN A HIDDEN LABORATORY...
AT LAST! I, DOCTOR VON MALICE, HAVE PERFECTED MY MIND-TRANSFER DEVICE.
NOW I WILL USE MY GENIUS INTELLECT TO TRANSFER MY BRAIN ENERGY INTO THIS NIGH-INDESTRUCTIBLE ROBOT MENACE!
ROLL ROLL ROLL
ONCE AWAKENED, MY ROBOT SHALL CONQUER--
EH? MR. SQUEAKS, I TOLD YOU NOT TO BOTHER ME WHEN I'M MONOLOGUING.
BAD HAMSTER.
NOW, STAY OUT OF MOMMY'S WAY.
I'VE GOT A CITY TO CONQUER BEFORE SUPPER.

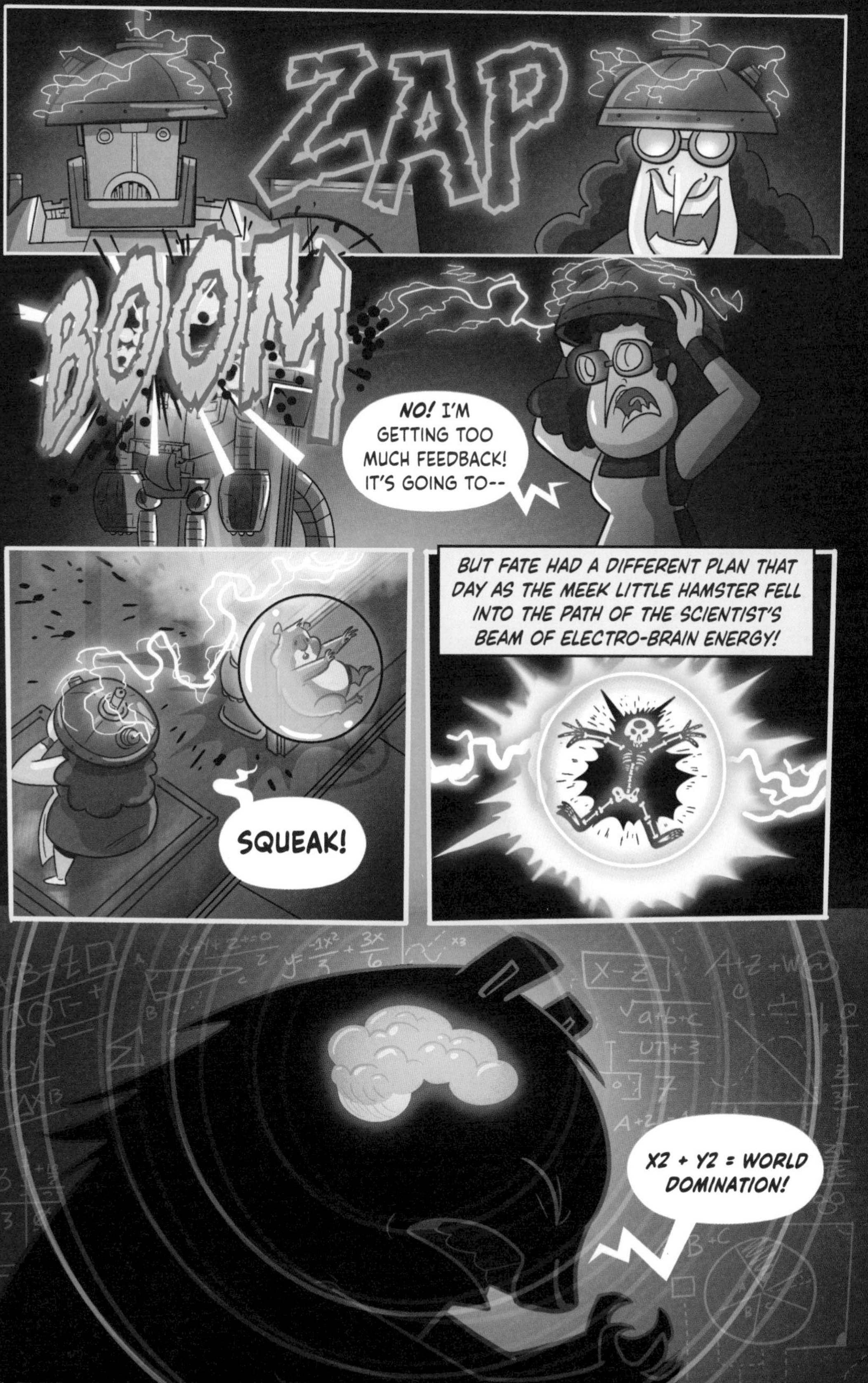
ZAP
BOOM
NO! I'M GETTING TOO MUCH FEEDBACK! IT'S GOING TO--
SQUEAK!
BUT FATE HAD A DIFFERENT PLAN THAT DAY AS THE MEEK LITTLE HAMSTER FELL INTO THE PATH OF THE SCIENTIST'S BEAM OF ELECTRO-BRAIN ENERGY!
X2 + Y2 = WORLD DOMINATION!

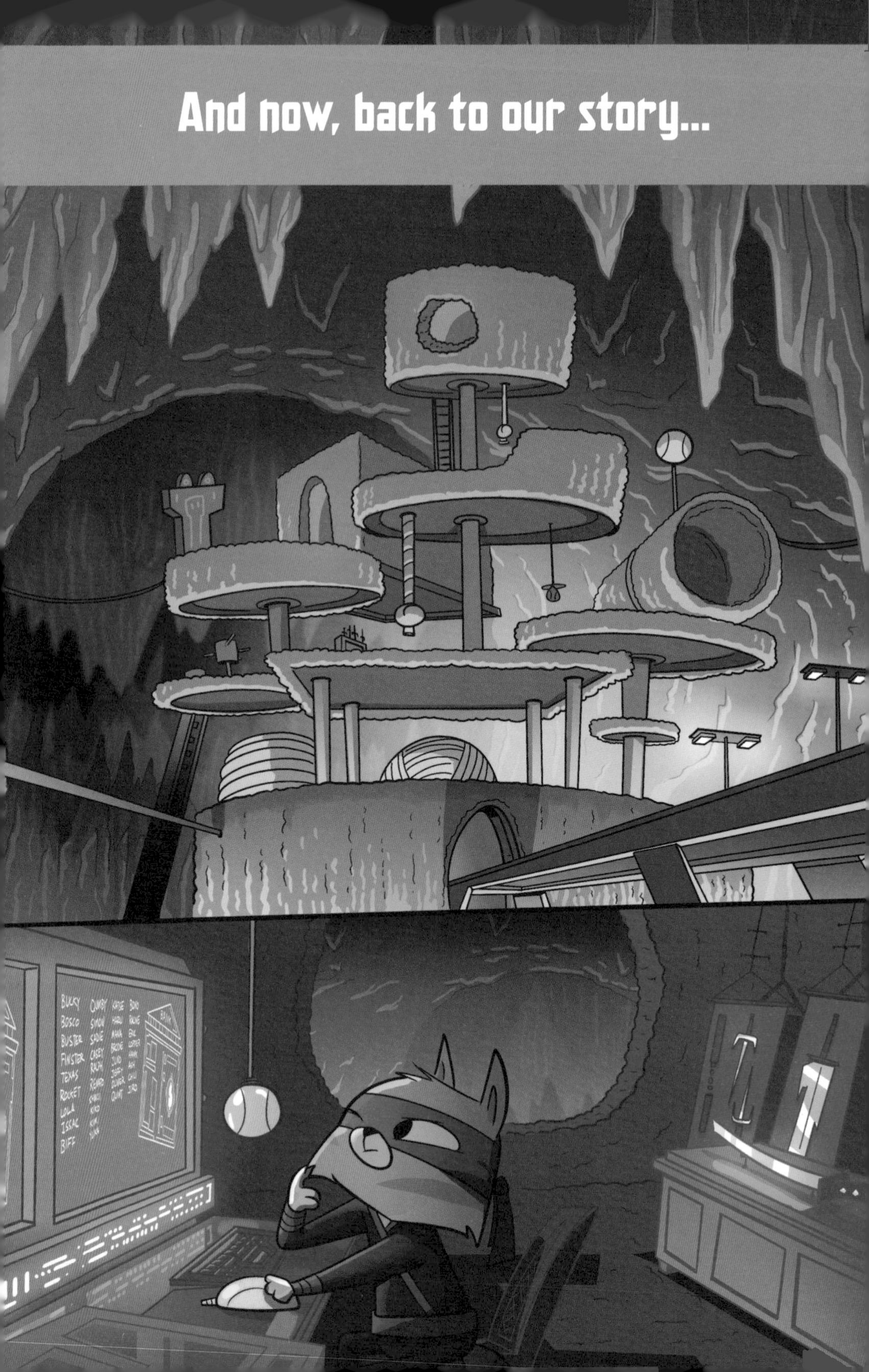
And now, back to our story...
BUCKY
BOSCO
BUSTER
FINSTER
TEXAS
ROCKET
LOLA
ISSAC
BIFF
QUIMBY
SIMON
SADIE
CASEY
RALPH
RENARD
KIKO
BRODIE
OLIVER
QUINT
BANK

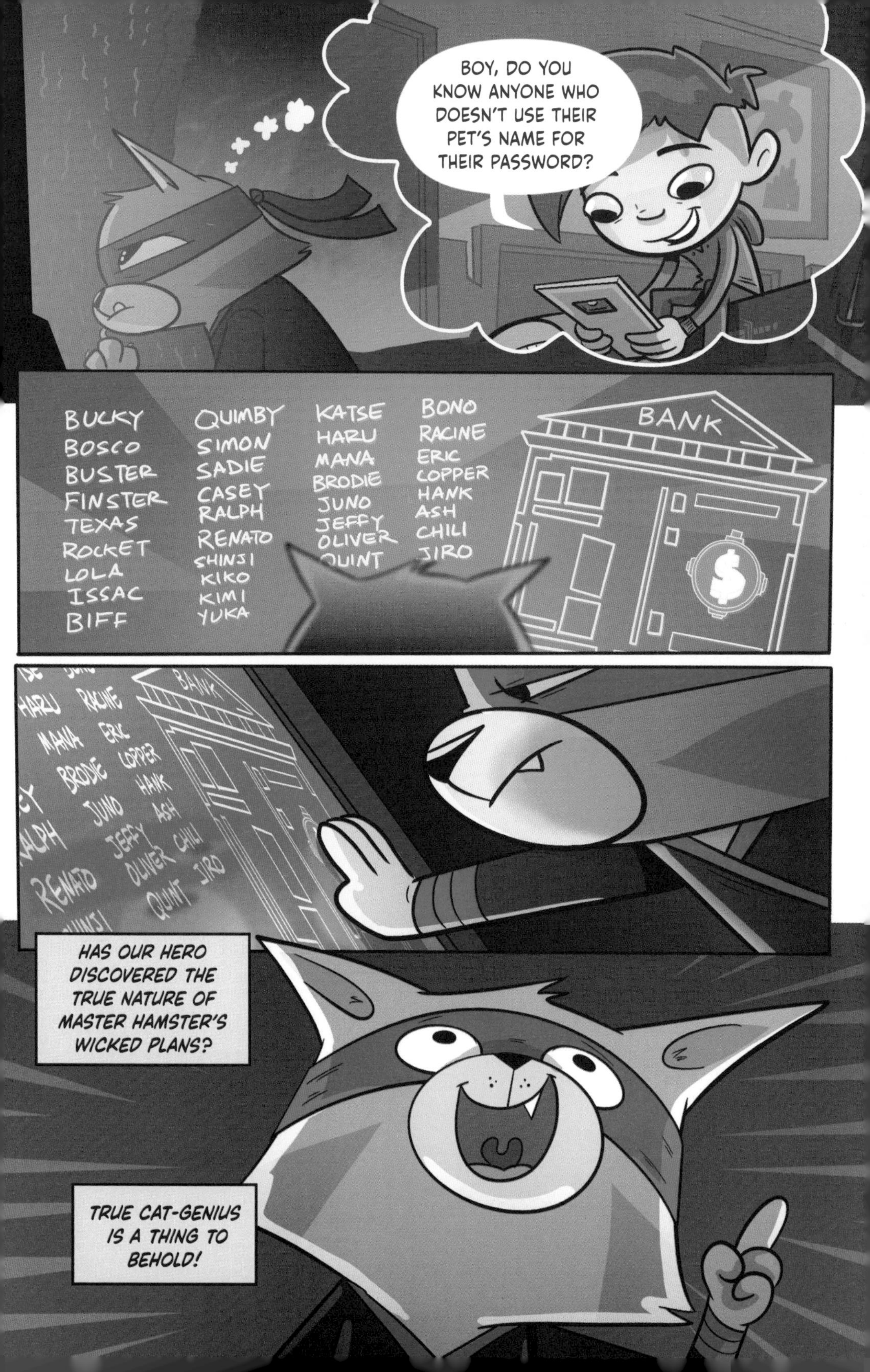
BOY, DO YOU KNOW ANYONE WHO DOESN'T USE THEIR PET'S NAME FOR THEIR PASSWORD?
BUCKY
BOSCO
BUSTER
FINSTER
TEXAS
ROCKET
LOLA
ISSAC
BIFF
QUIMBY
SIMON
SADIE
CASEY
RALPH
RENATO
SHINJI
KIKO
KIMI
YUKA
KATSE
HARU
MANA
BRODIE
JUNO
JEFFY
OLIVER
QUINT
BONO
RACINE
ERIC
COPPER
HANK
ASH
CHILI
JIRO
BANK
HAS OUR HERO DISCOVERED THE TRUE NATURE OF MASTER HAMSTER'S WICKED PLANS?
TRUE CAT-GENIUS IS A THING TO BEHOLD!

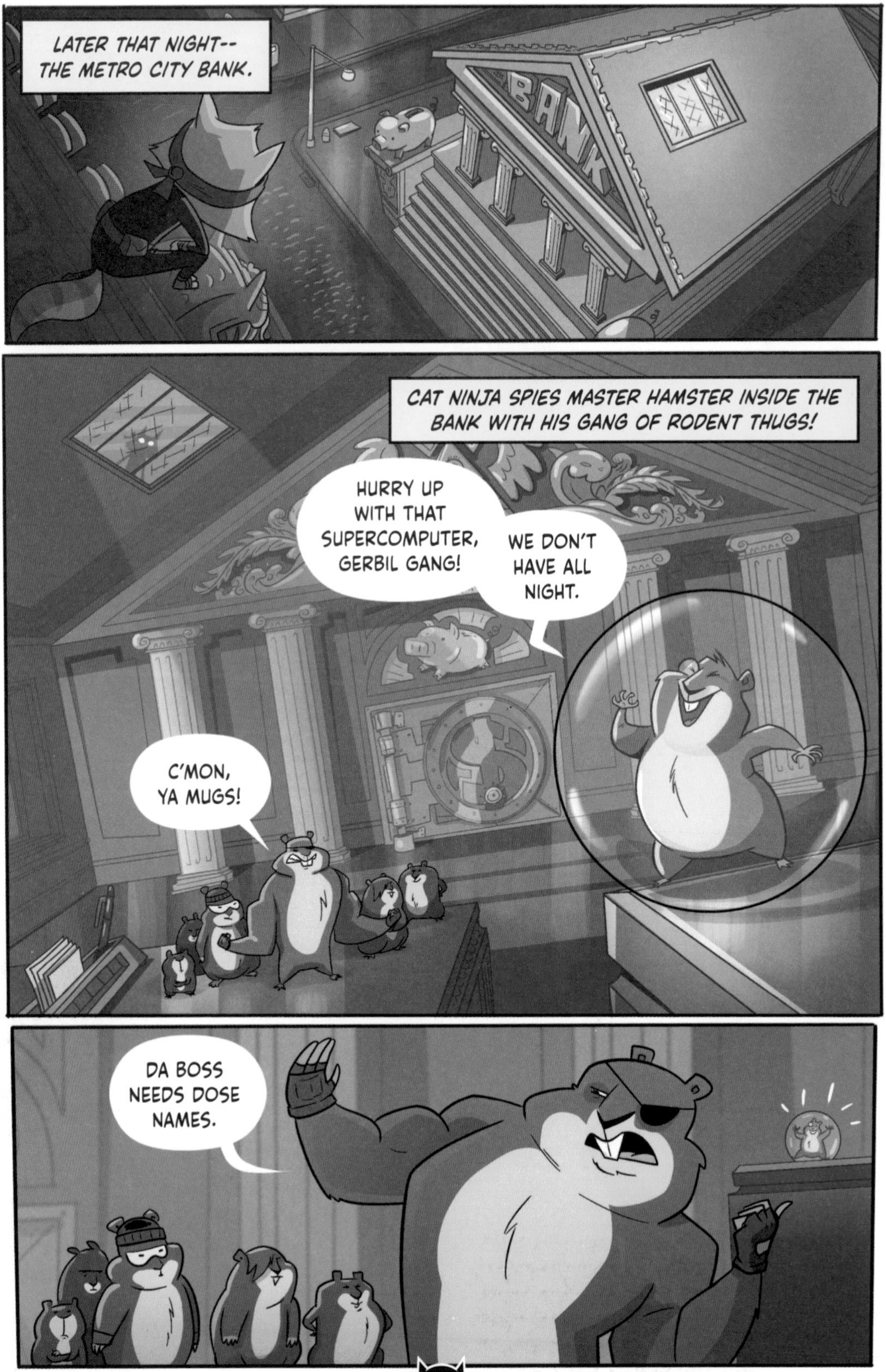
LATER THAT NIGHT--
THE METRO CITY BANK.
BANK
CAT NINJA SPIES MASTER HAMSTER INSIDE THE BANK WITH HIS GANG OF RODENT THUGS!
HURRY UP WITH THAT SUPERCOMPUTER, GERBIL GANG!
WE DON'T HAVE ALL NIGHT.
C'MON, YA MUGS!
DA BOSS NEEDS DOSE NAMES.

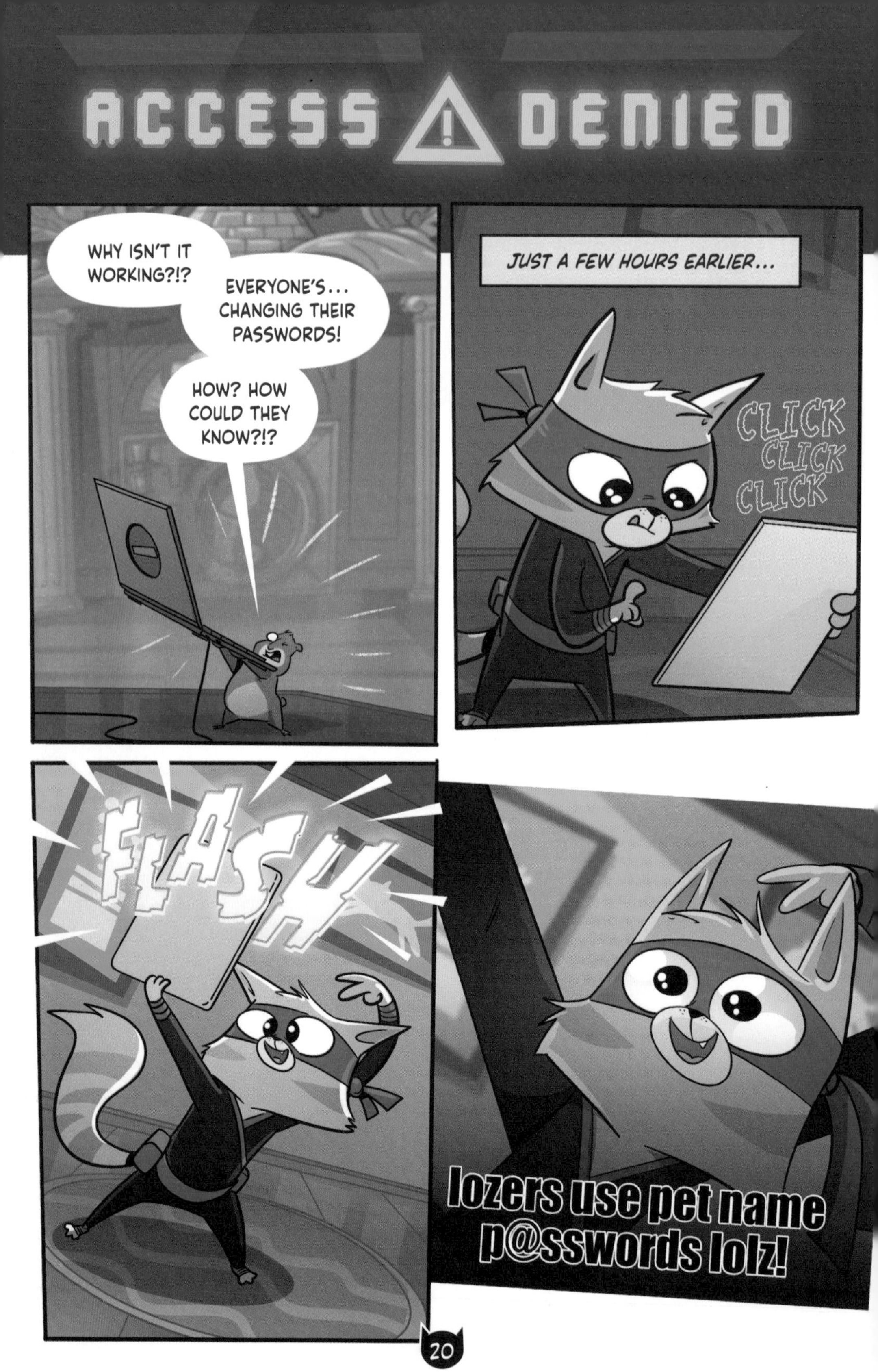
ACCESS DENIED
WHY ISN'T IT WORKING?!?
EVERYONE'S... CHANGING THEIR PASSWORDS!
HOW? HOW COULD THEY KNOW?!?
JUST A FEW HOURS EARLIER...
CLICK CLICK CLICK
FLASH
lozers use pet name p@sswords lolz!

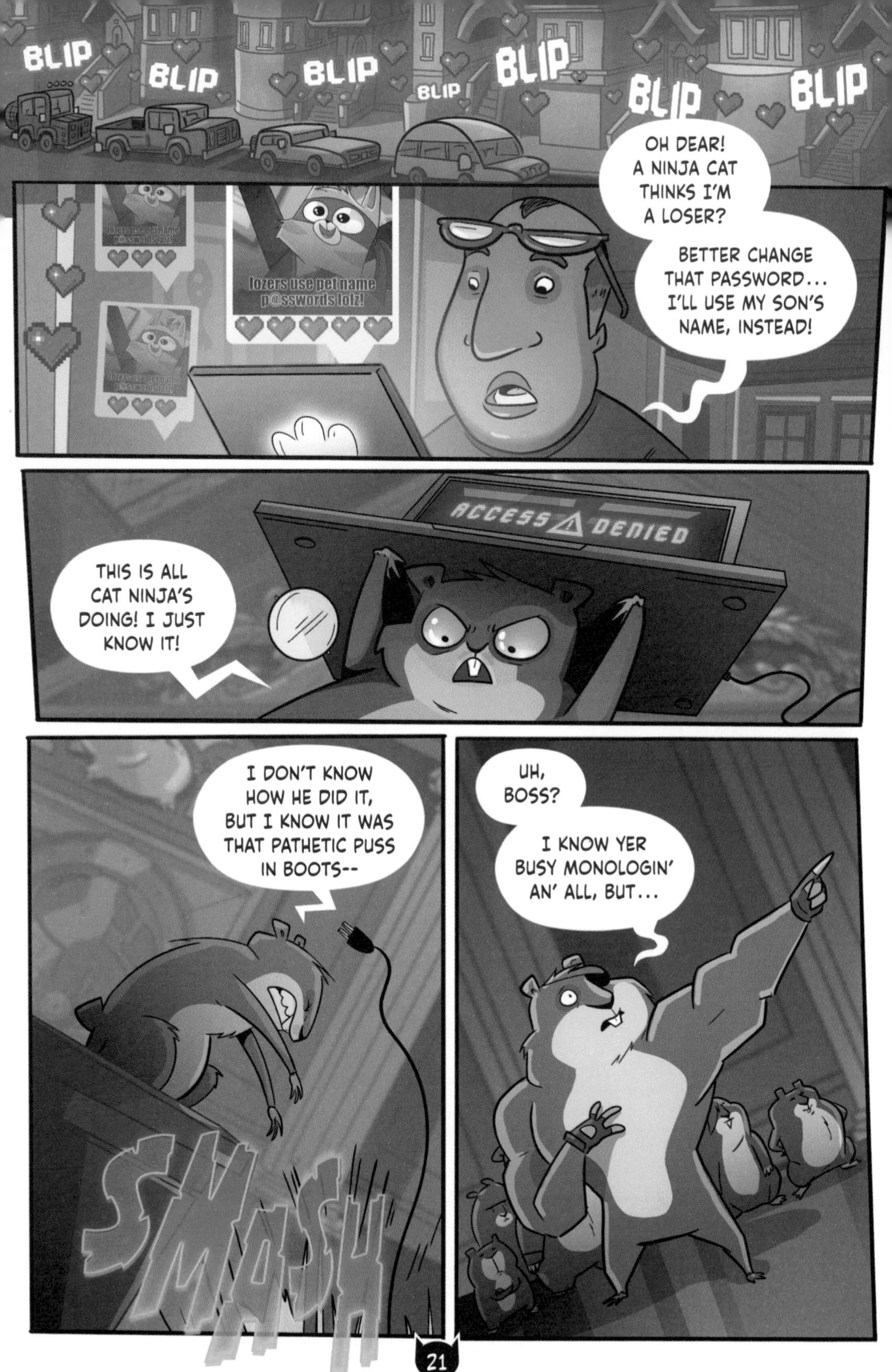
BLIP
BLIP
BLIP
BLIP
BLIP
BLIP
BLIP
OH DEAR! A NINJA CAT THINKS I'M A LOSER?
BETTER CHANGE THAT PASSWORD... I'LL USE MY SON'S NAME, INSTEAD!
lozers use pet name p@sswords lolz!
ACCESS DENIED
THIS IS ALL CAT NINJA'S DOING! I JUST KNOW IT!
I DON'T KNOW HOW HE DID IT, BUT I KNOW IT WAS THAT PATHETIC PUSS IN BOOTS--
SMASH
UH, BOSS?
I KNOW YER BUSY MONOLOGIN' AN' ALL, BUT...

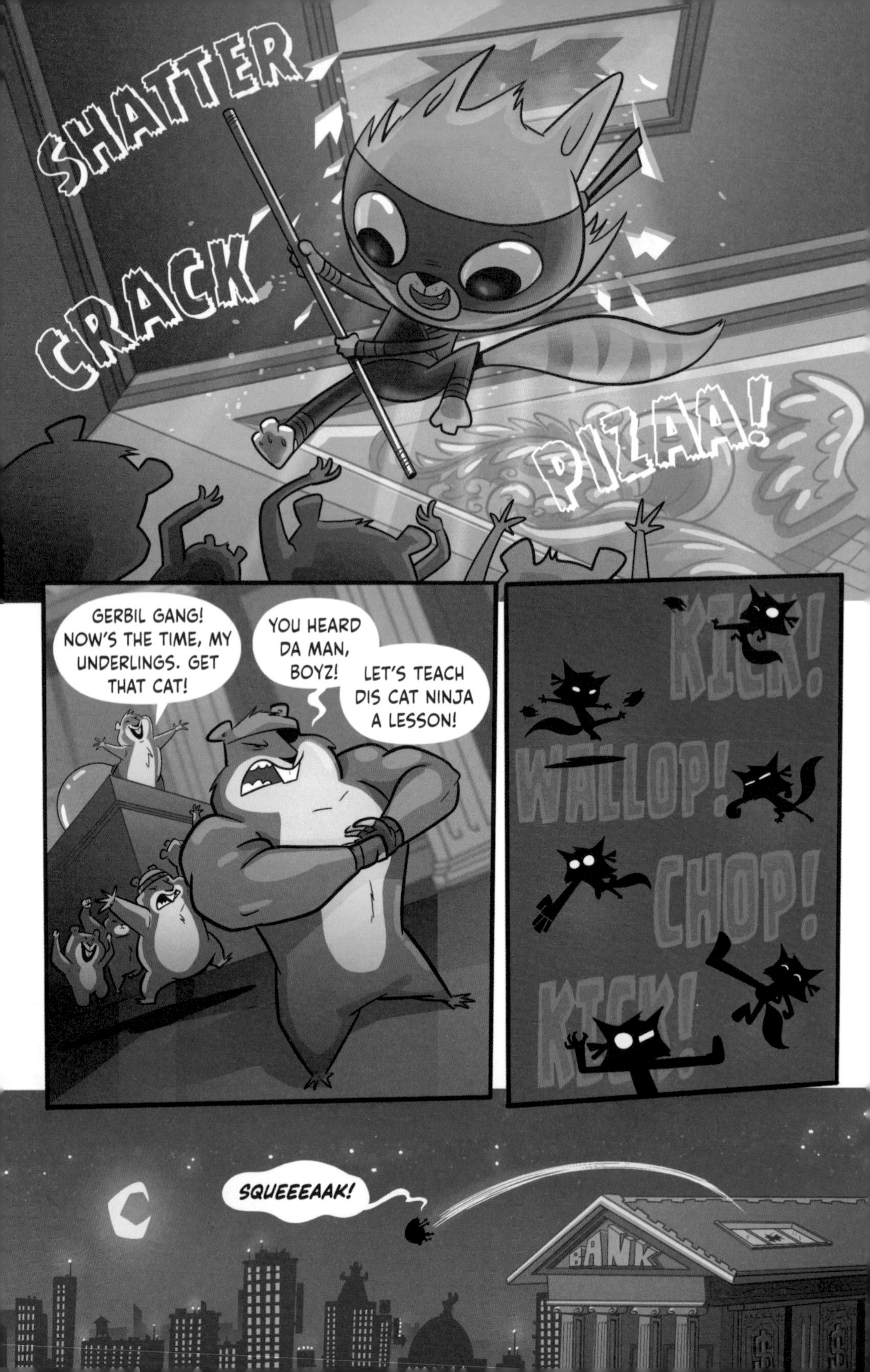

SHATTER
CRACK
PIZAA!
GERBIL GANG! NOW'S THE TIME, MY UNDERLINGS. GET THAT CAT!
YOU HEARD DA MAN, BOYZ!
LET'S TEACH DIS CAT NINJA A LESSON!
KICK!
WALLOP!
CHOP!
KICK!
SQUEEEAAK!
BANK

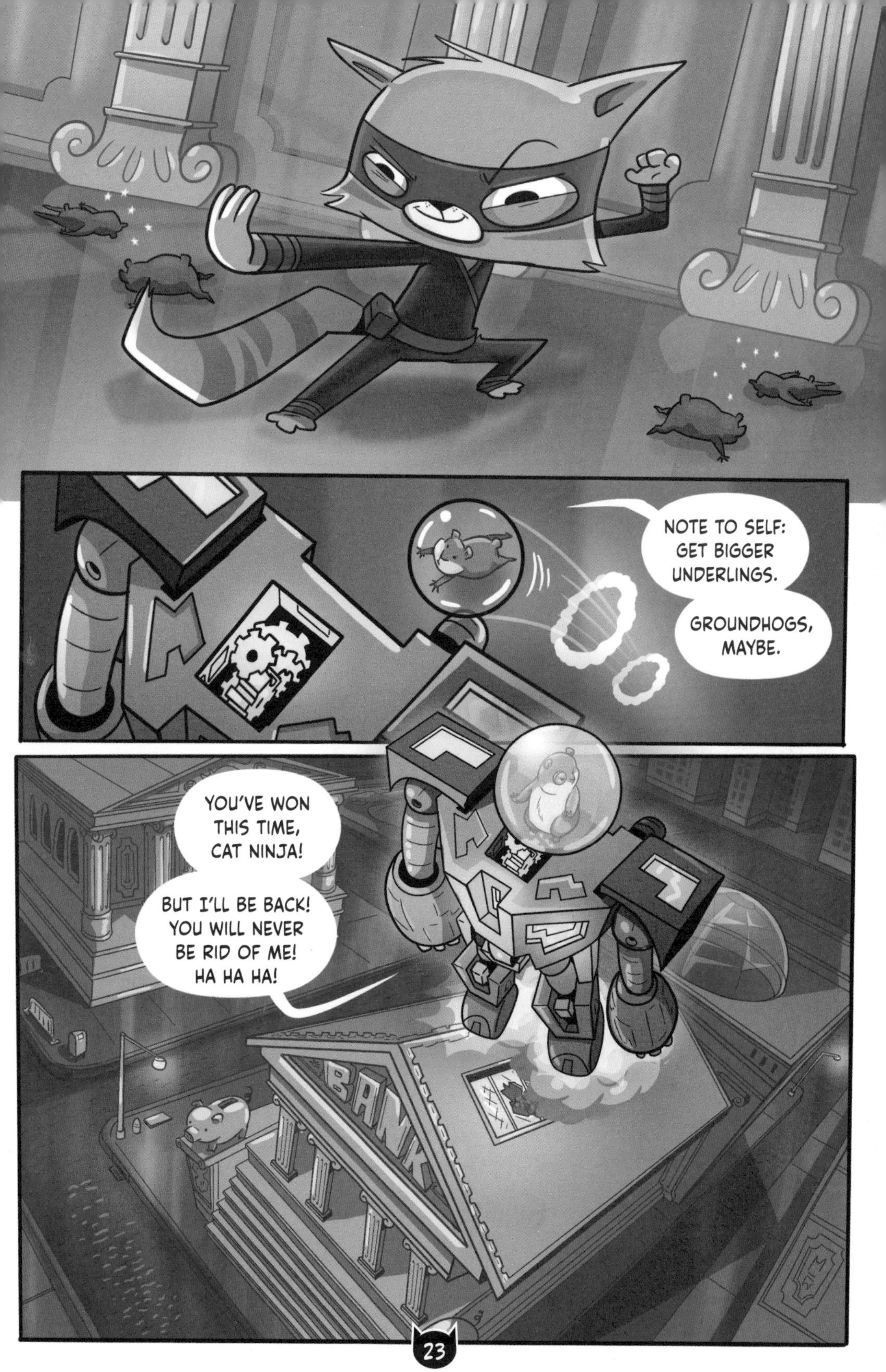
NOTE TO SELF: GET BIGGER UNDERLINGS.
GROUNDHOGS, MAYBE.
YOU'VE WON THIS TIME, CAT NINJA!
BUT I'LL BE BACK! YOU WILL NEVER BE RID OF ME! HA HA HA!
BANK

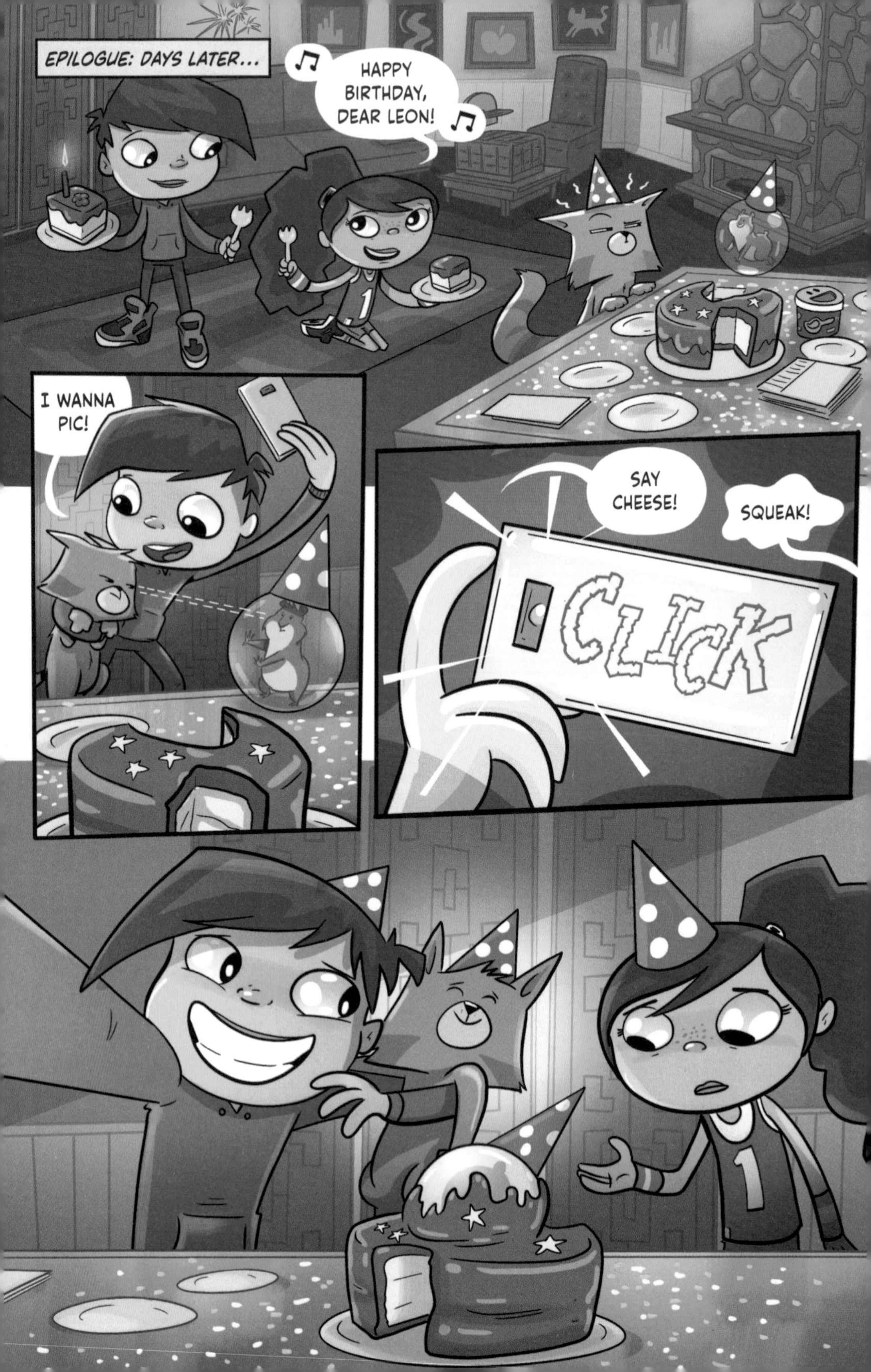
EPILOGUE: DAYS LATER...
♫ HAPPY BIRTHDAY, DEAR LEON! ♫
I WANNA PIC!
SAY CHEESE!
SQUEAK!
CLICK

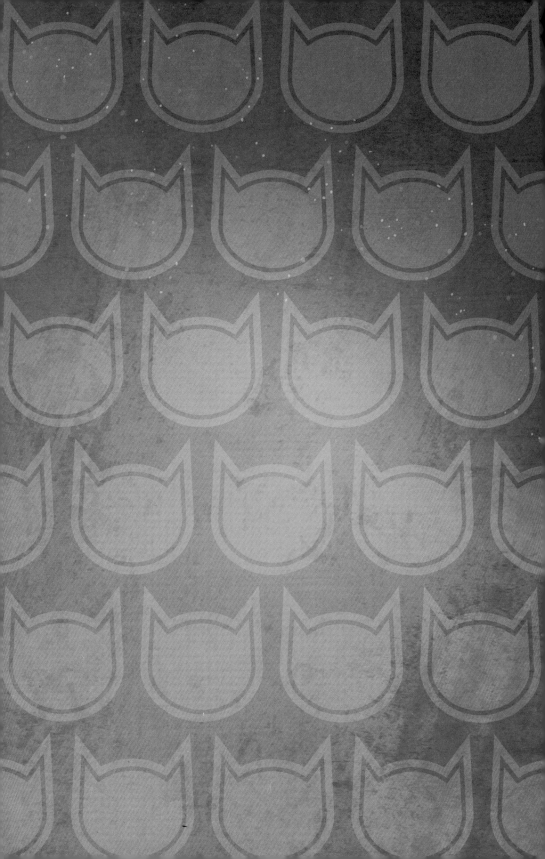

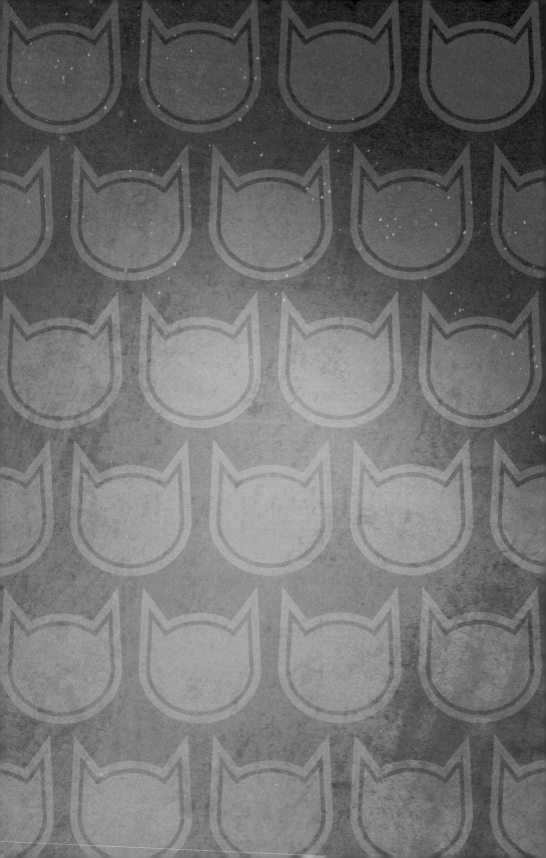

Chapter 2:
Le Chat Noir!

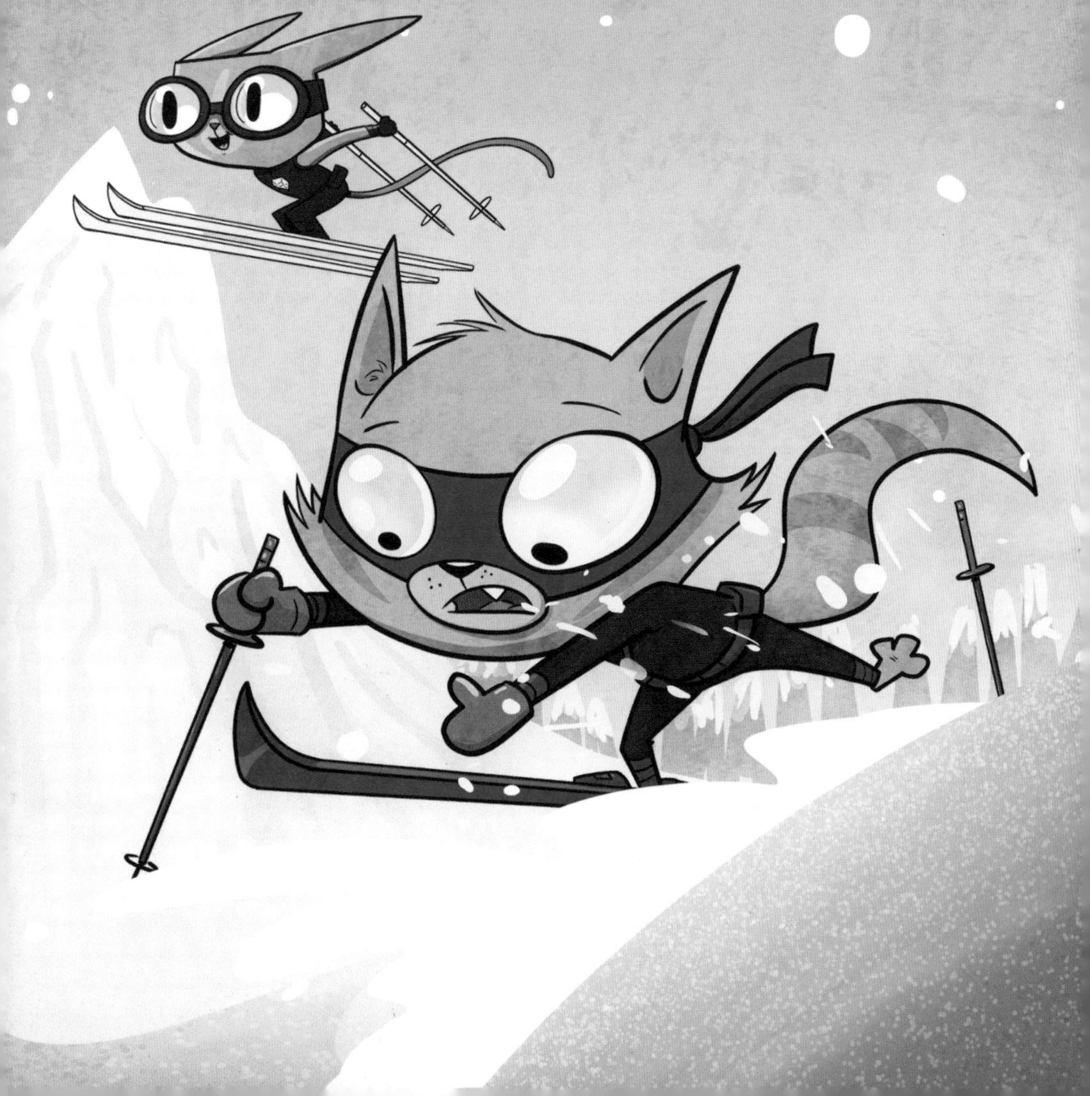

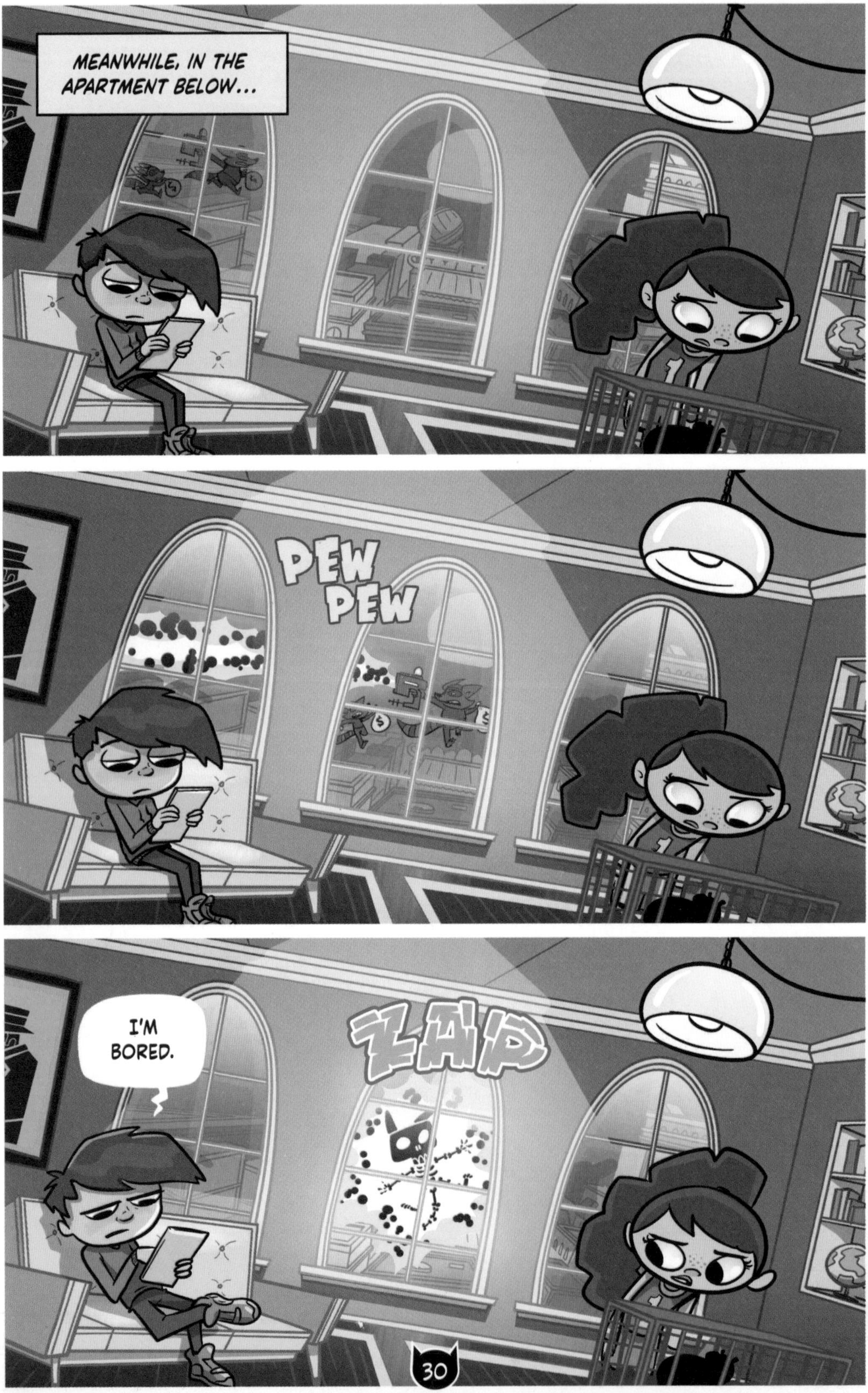
MEANWHILE, IN THE APARTMENT BELOW...
PEW PEW
ZAP
I'M BORED.

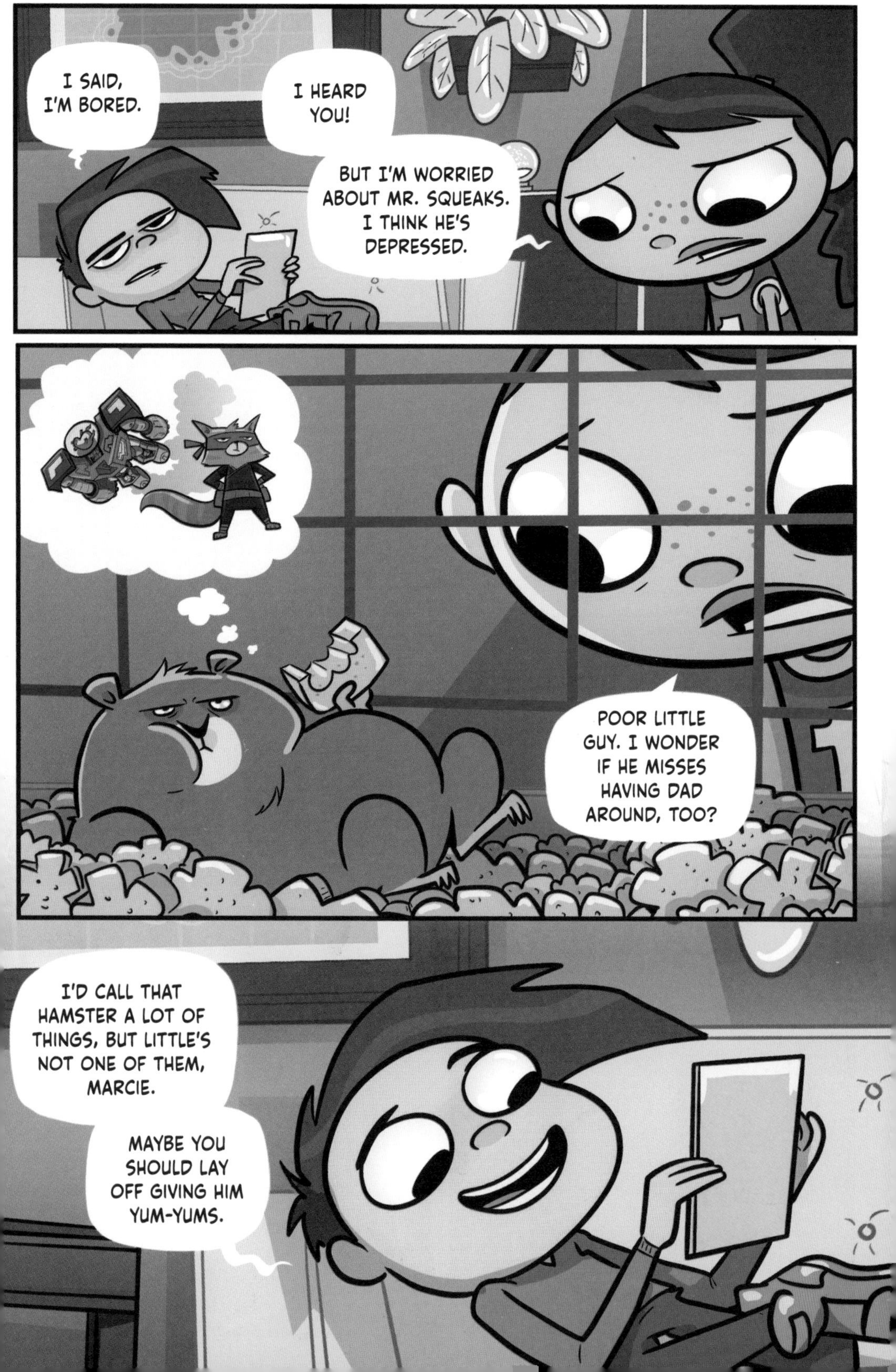
I SAID, I'M BORED.
I HEARD YOU!
BUT I'M WORRIED ABOUT MR. SQUEAKS. I THINK HE'S DEPRESSED.
POOR LITTLE GUY. I WONDER IF HE MISSES HAVING DAD AROUND, TOO?
I'D CALL THAT HAMSTER A LOT OF THINGS, BUT LITTLE'S NOT ONE OF THEM, MARCIE.
MAYBE YOU SHOULD LAY OFF GIVING HIM YUM-YUMS.

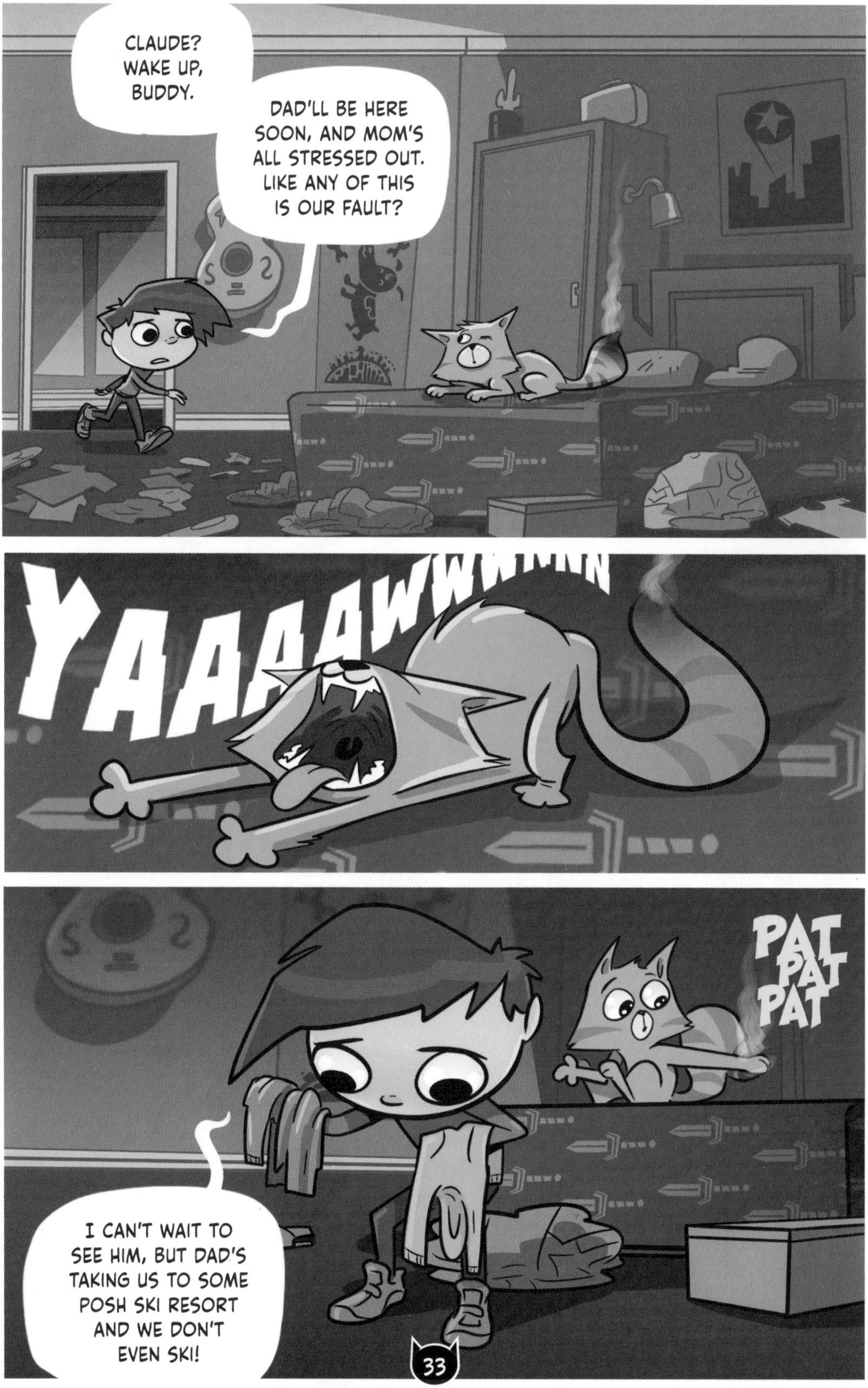
CLAUDE? WAKE UP, BUDDY.
DAD'LL BE HERE SOON, AND MOM'S ALL STRESSED OUT. LIKE ANY OF THIS IS OUR FAULT?
YAAAAWWWNNN
PAT PAT PAT
I CAN'T WAIT TO SEE HIM, BUT DAD'S TAKING US TO SOME POSH SKI RESORT AND WE DON'T EVEN SKI!

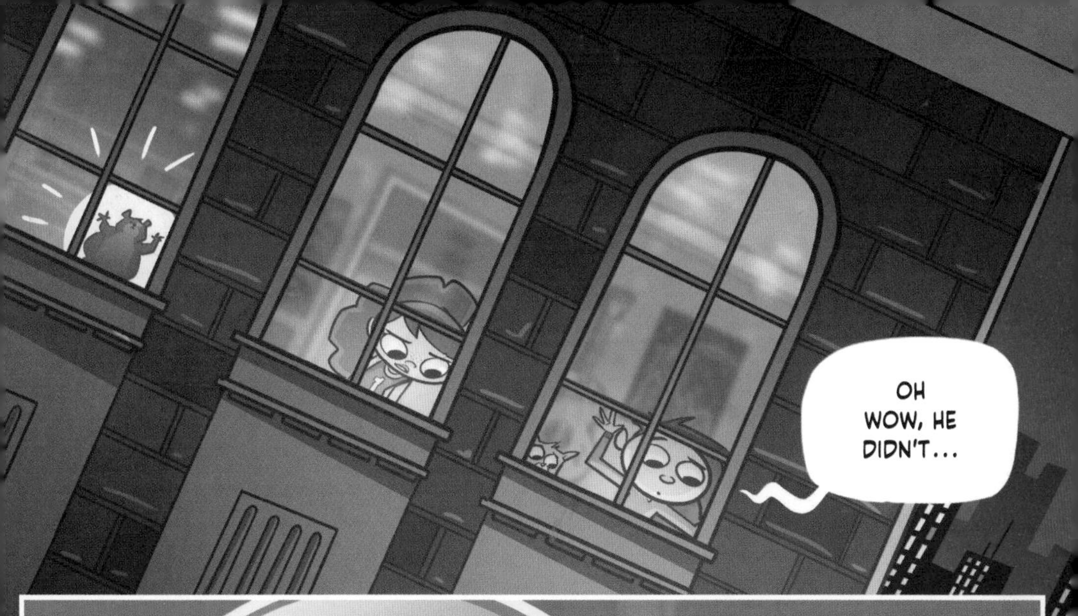
OH WOW, HE DIDN'T...

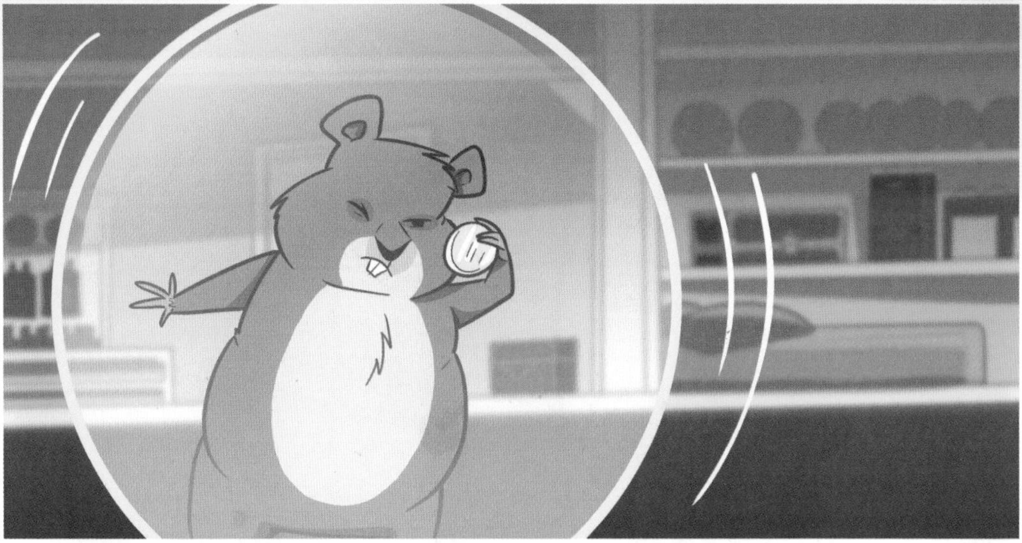

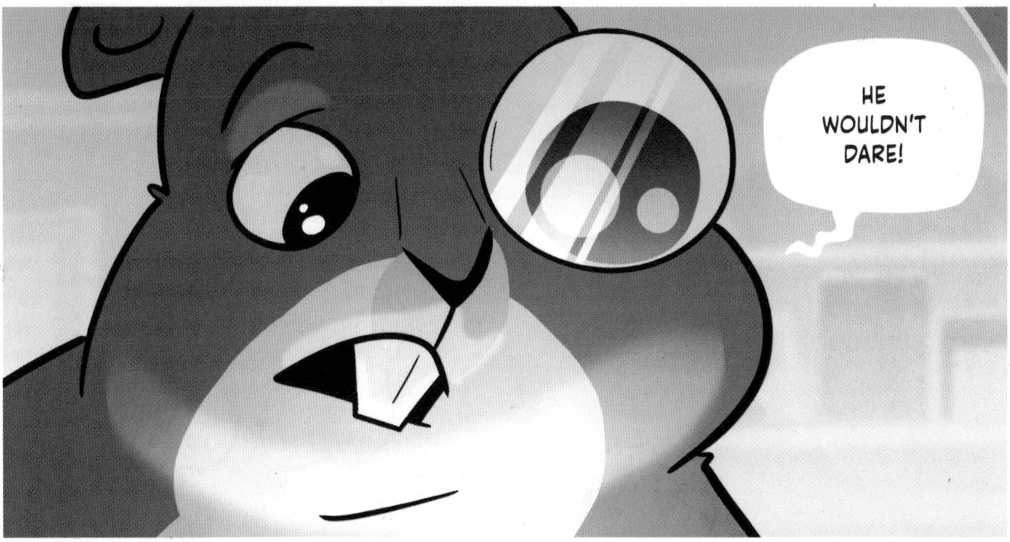
HE WOULDN'T DARE!

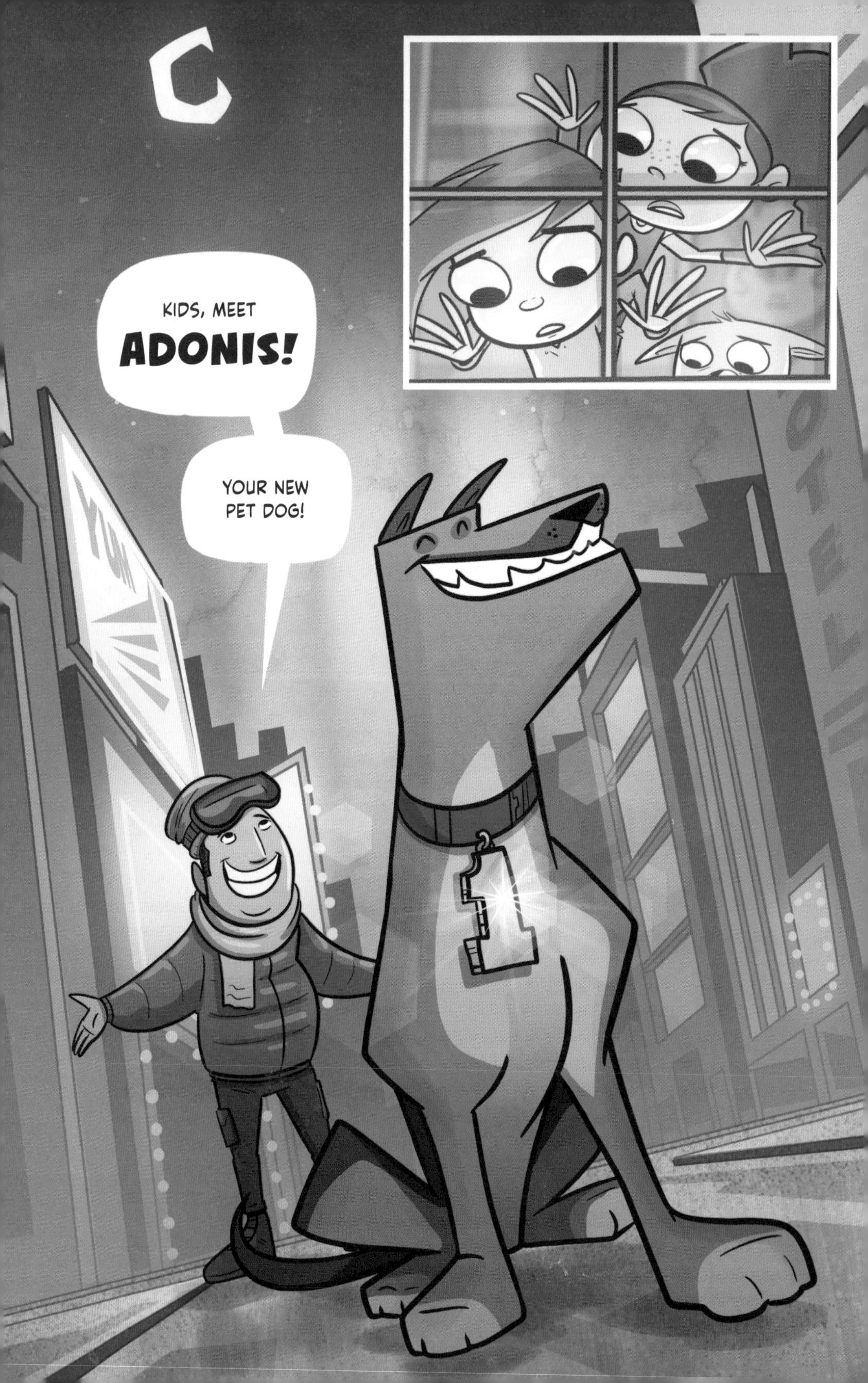

KIDS, MEET ADONIS!
YOUR NEW PET DOG!
YUM

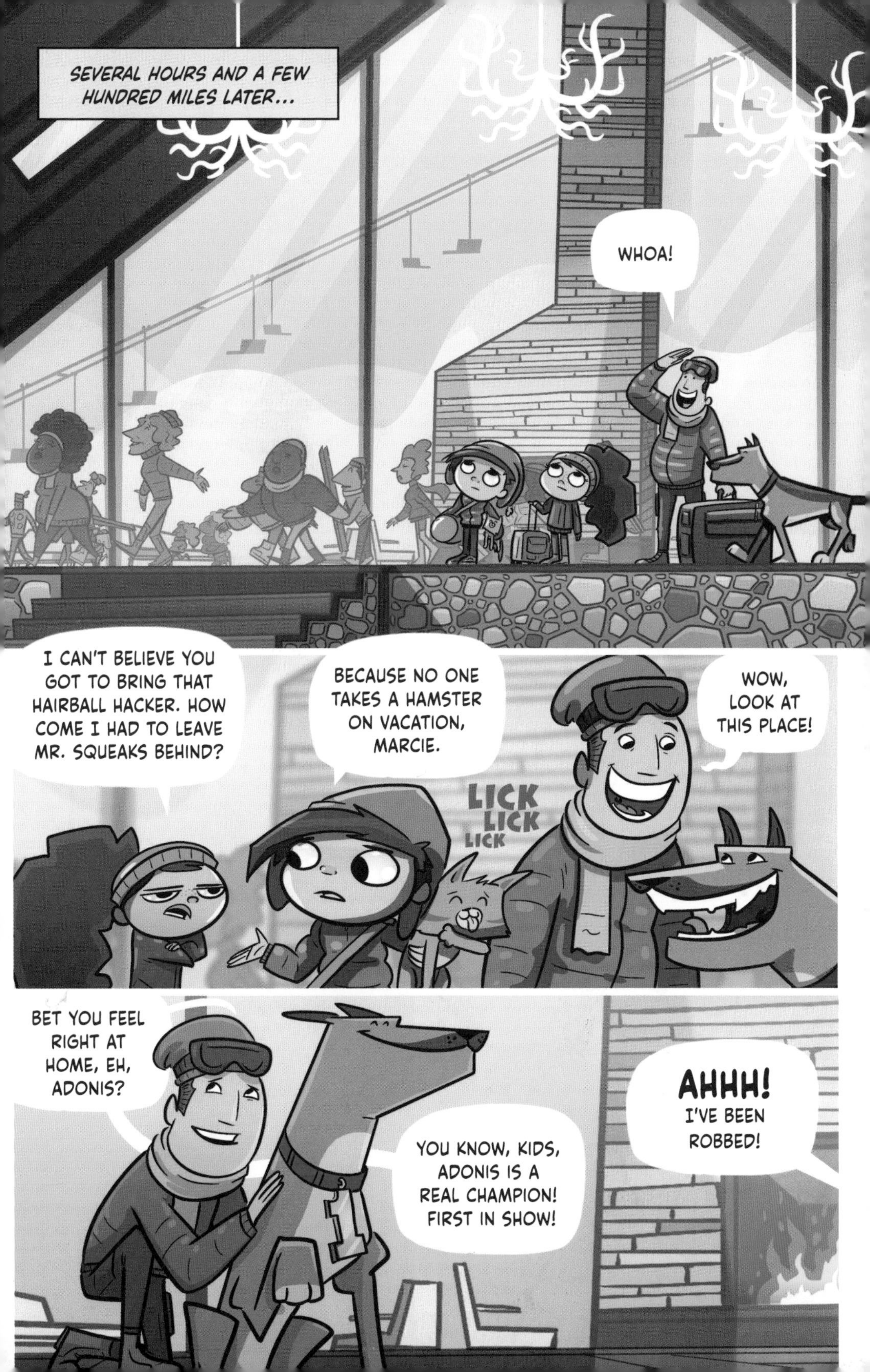
SEVERAL HOURS AND A FEW HUNDRED MILES LATER...
WHOA!
I CAN'T BELIEVE YOU GOT TO BRING THAT HAIRBALL HACKER. HOW COME I HAD TO LEAVE MR. SQUEAKS BEHIND?
BECAUSE NO ONE TAKES A HAMSTER ON VACATION, MARCIE.
WOW, LOOK AT THIS PLACE!
LICK LICK LICK
BET YOU FEEL RIGHT AT HOME, EH, ADONIS?
YOU KNOW, KIDS, ADONIS IS A REAL CHAMPION! FIRST IN SHOW!
AHHH! I'VE BEEN ROBBED!

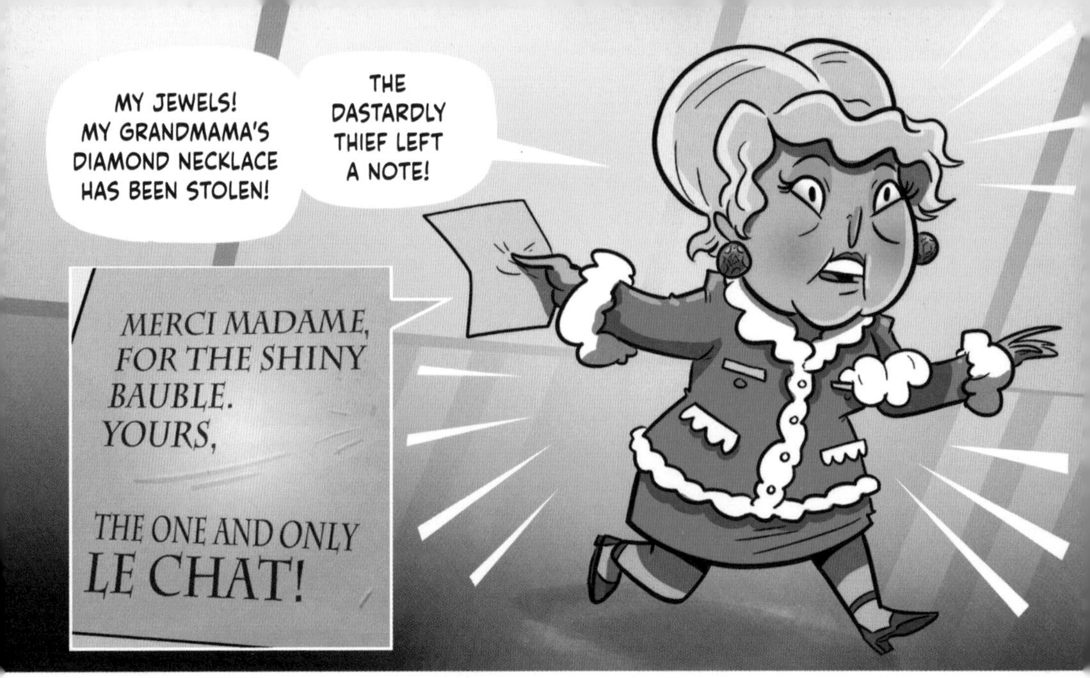
MY JEWELS! MY GRANDMAMA'S DIAMOND NECKLACE HAS BEEN STOLEN!
THE DASTARDLY THIEF LEFT A NOTE!
MERCI MADAME, FOR THE SHINY BAUBLE. YOURS,
THE ONE AND ONLY LE CHAT!

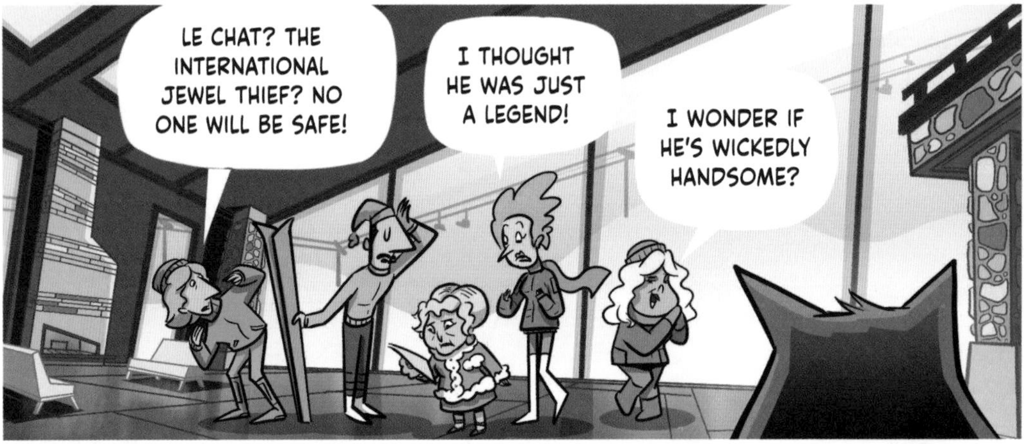
LE CHAT? THE INTERNATIONAL JEWEL THIEF? NO ONE WILL BE SAFE!
I THOUGHT HE WAS JUST A LEGEND!
I WONDER IF HE'S WICKEDLY HANDSOME?

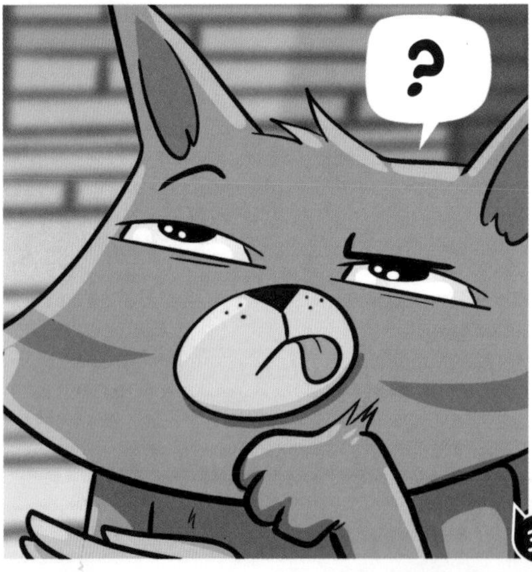
?

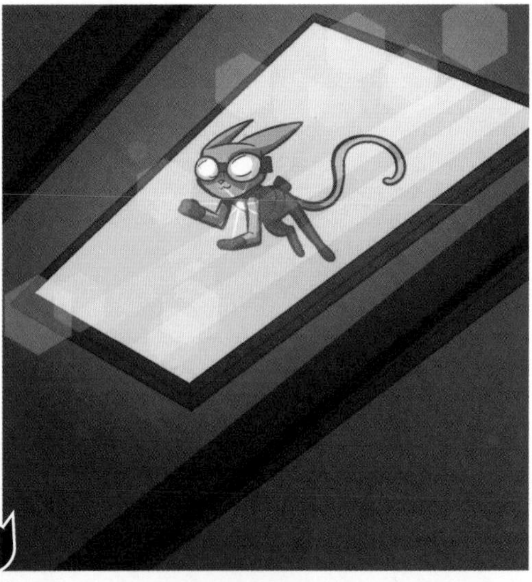

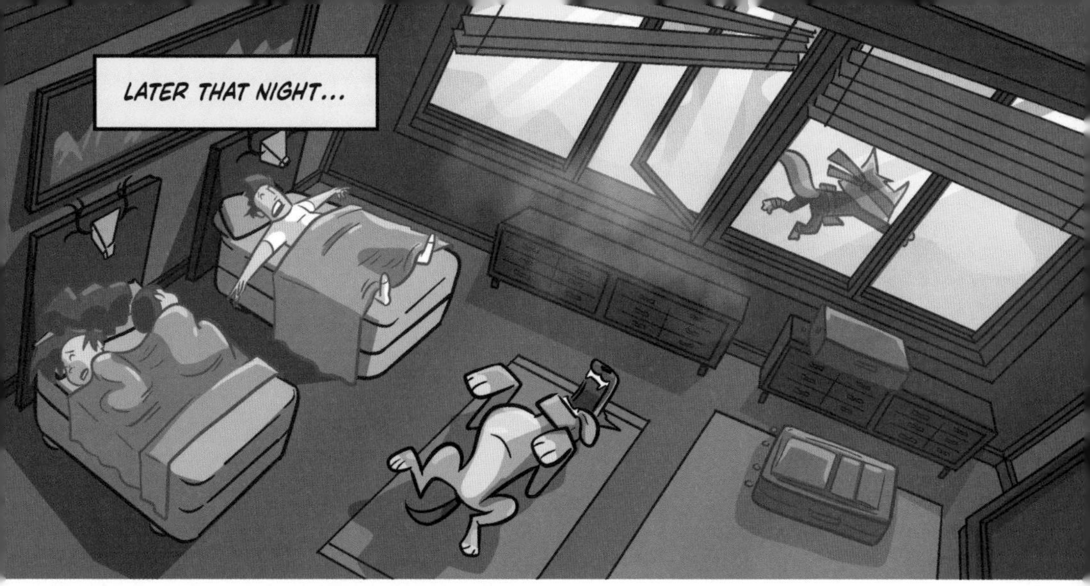
LATER THAT NIGHT...

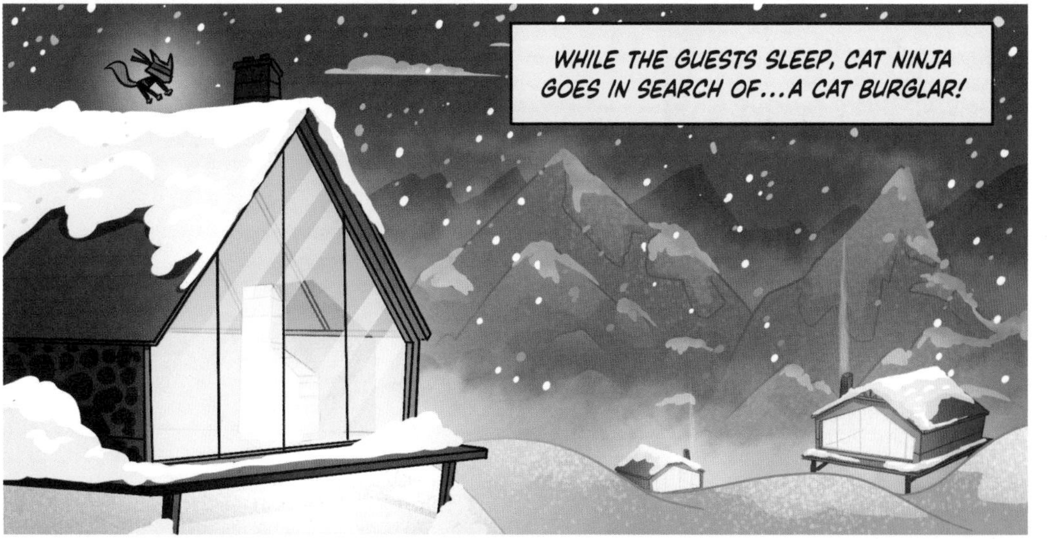
WHILE THE GUESTS SLEEP, CAT NINJA GOES IN SEARCH OF...A CAT BURGLAR!

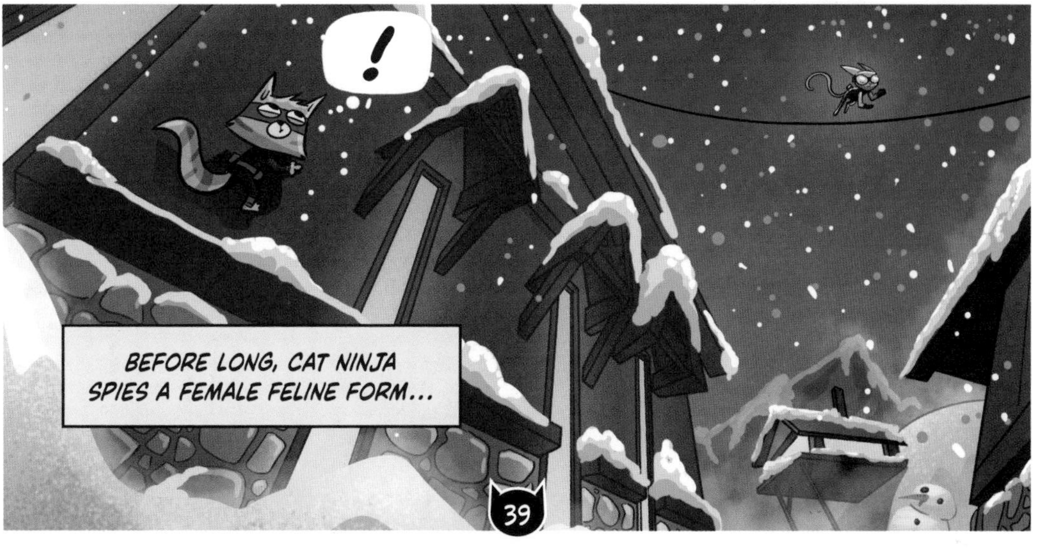
!
BEFORE LONG, CAT NINJA SPIES A FEMALE FELINE FORM...

BONJOUR, MONSIEUR NINJA! THIS IS AN UNEXPECTED PLEASURE.
TELL ME, WHAT BRINGS METRO CITY'S FAMOUS CRIME-FIGHTER TO THIS SLEEPY LITTLE GETAWAY?

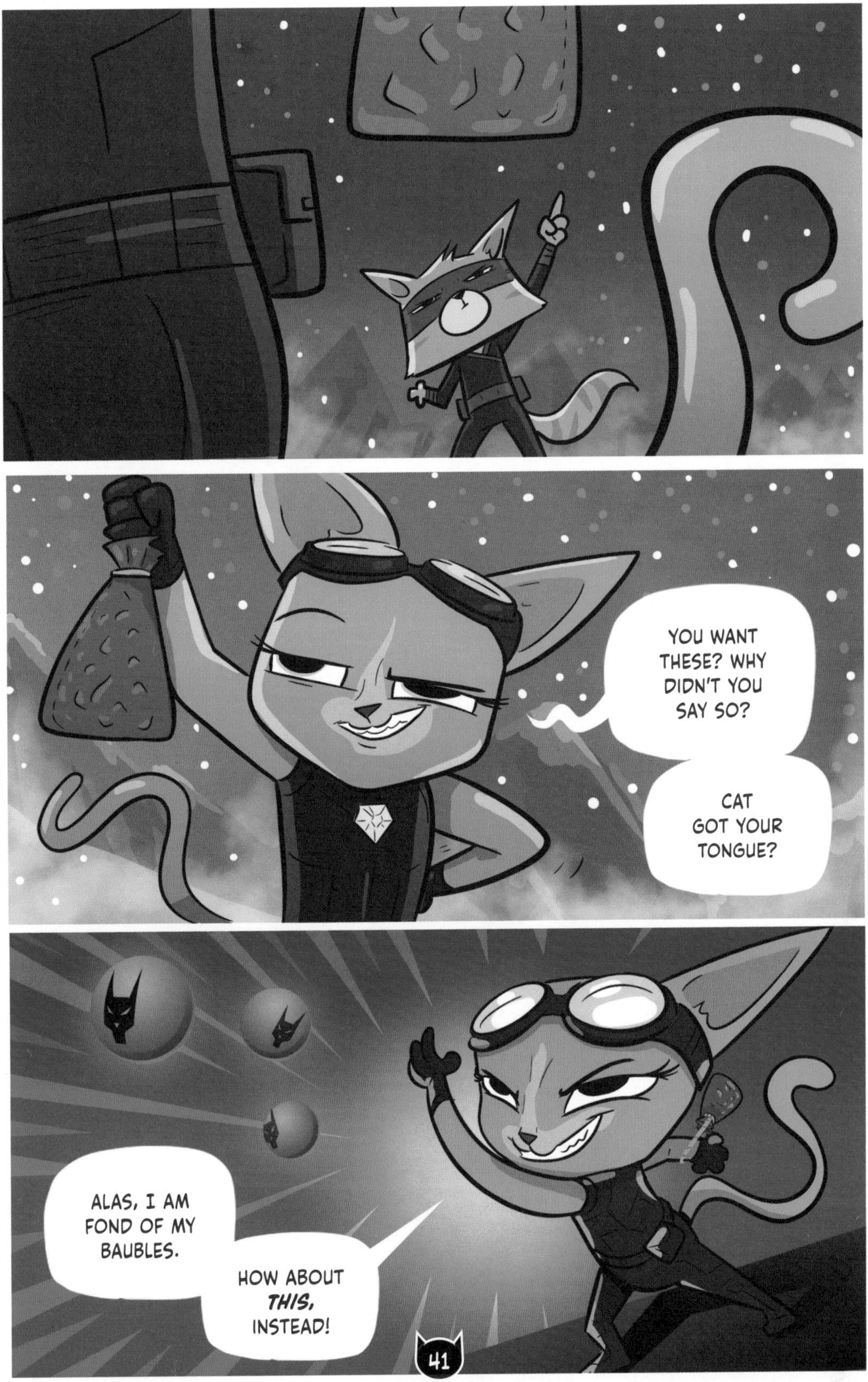
YOU WANT THESE? WHY DIDN'T YOU SAY SO?
CAT GOT YOUR TONGUE?
ALAS, I AM FOND OF MY BAUBLES.
HOW ABOUT *THIS,* INSTEAD!

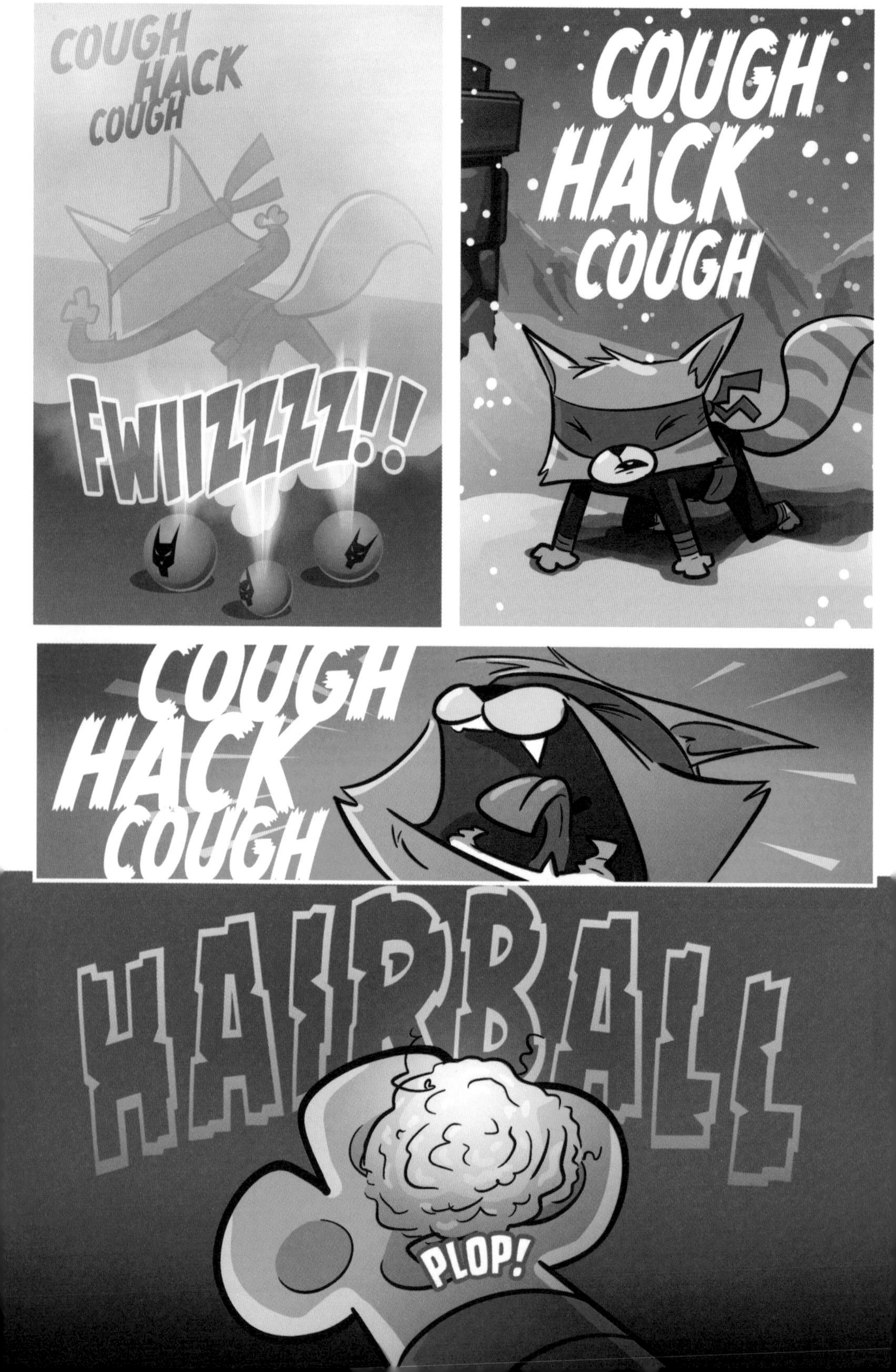
COUGH
HACK
COUGH
FWIIZZZZ!!
COUGH
HACK
COUGH
COUGH
HACK
COUGH
HAIRBALL
PLOP!

WASN'T ICE SKATING GREAT? SURE, THERE WERE A FEW BUMPS AND BRUISES, BUT STILL. AND HOW ABOUT THAT EARLY MORNING NATURE HIKE, HUH?

YEAH, GREAT. BUT CAN WE REST, PLEASE?

WE CAN REST ON THE SKI LIFT! I'VE BOOKED US LESSONS AT THREE O'CLOCK.

IT'S JUST... WE'VE BEEN GOING NONSTOP.

WOW! EVERYONE IN THE HOTEL IS ON THE SKI LIFT!

!

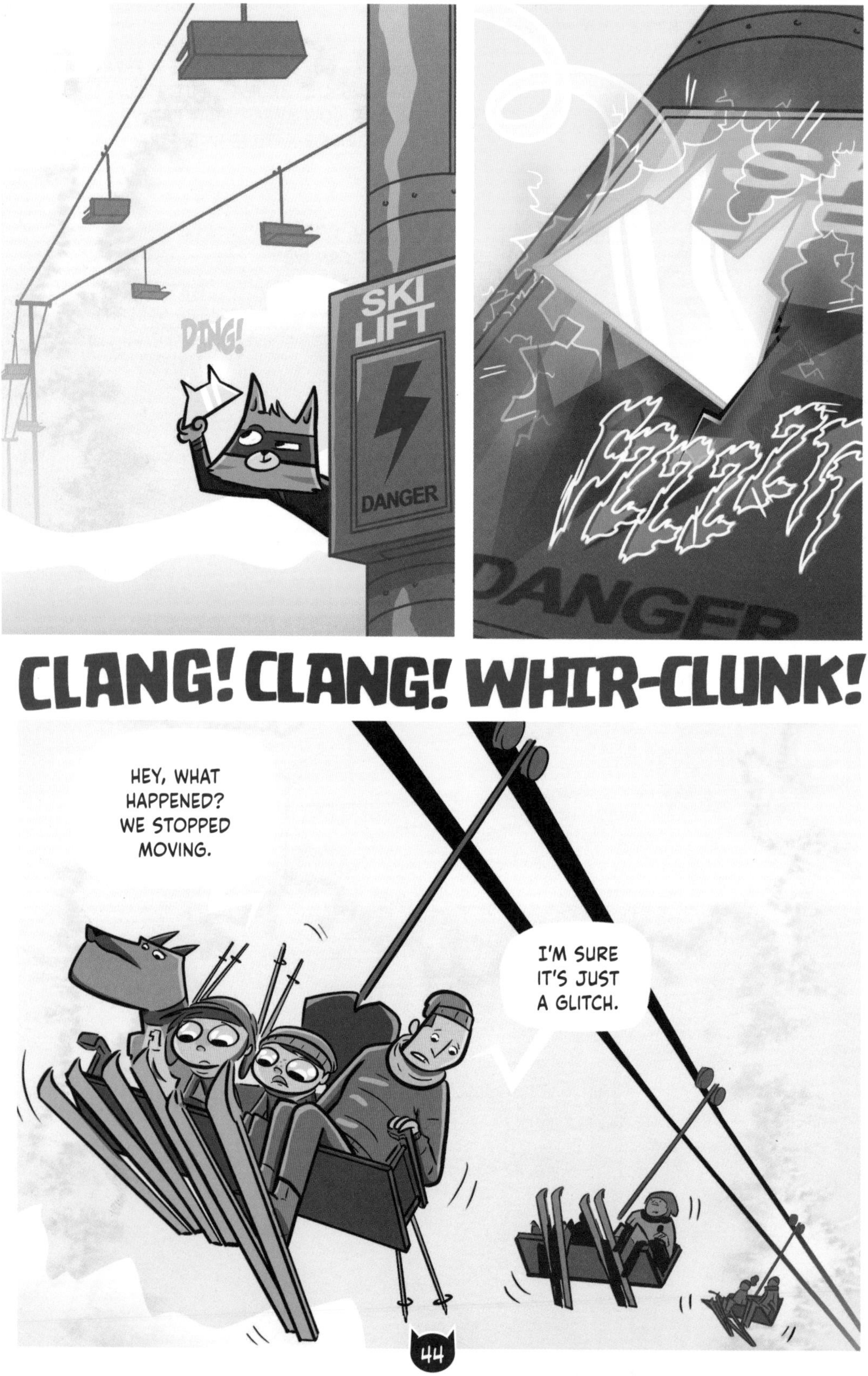
DING!
SKI LIFT
DANGER
DANGER
CLANG! CLANG! WHIR-CLUNK!
HEY, WHAT HAPPENED? WE STOPPED MOVING.
I'M SURE IT'S JUST A GLITCH.

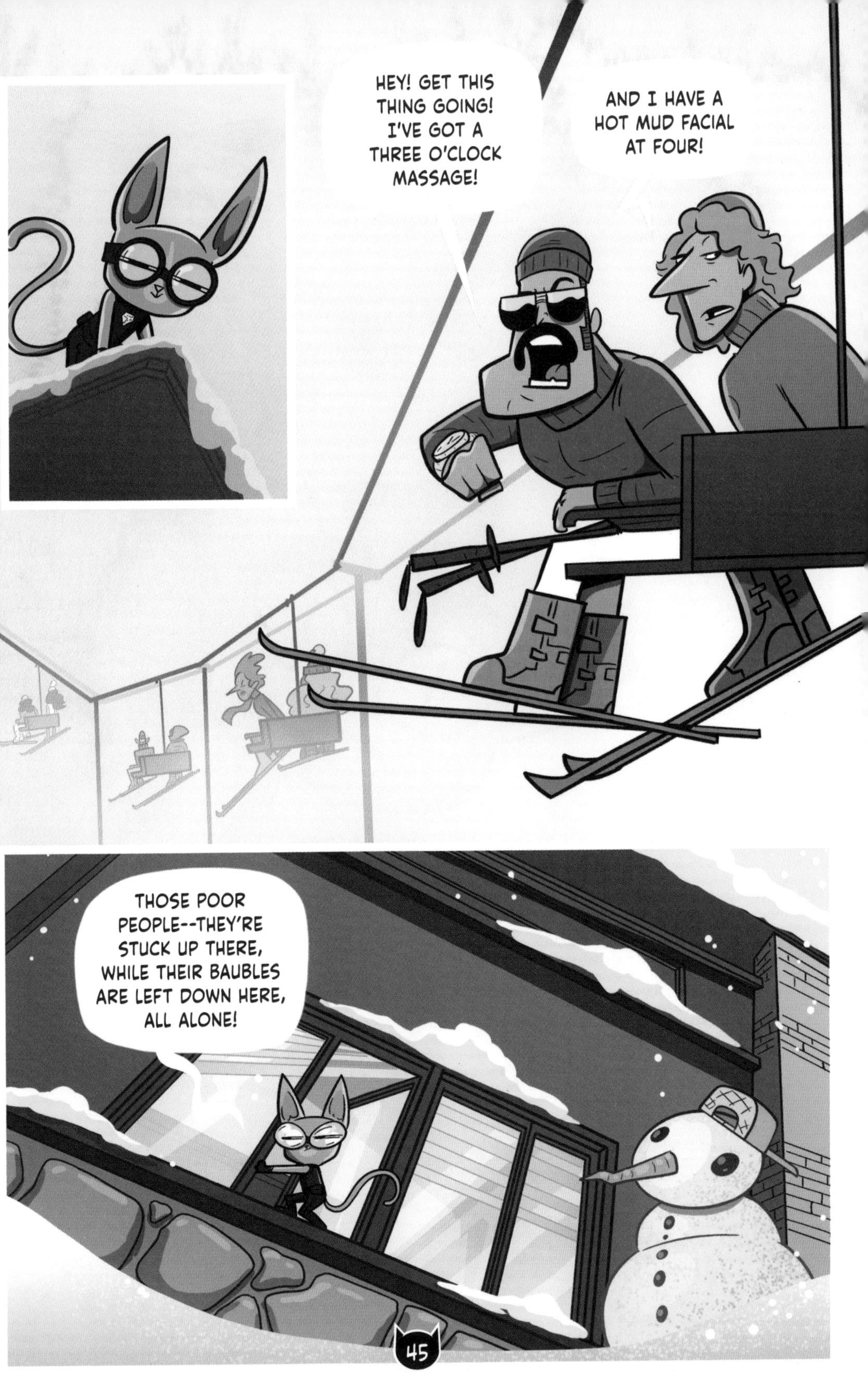
HEY! GET THIS THING GOING! I'VE GOT A THREE O'CLOCK MASSAGE!
AND I HAVE A HOT MUD FACIAL AT FOUR!
THOSE POOR PEOPLE--THEY'RE STUCK UP THERE, WHILE THEIR BAUBLES ARE LEFT DOWN HERE, ALL ALONE!

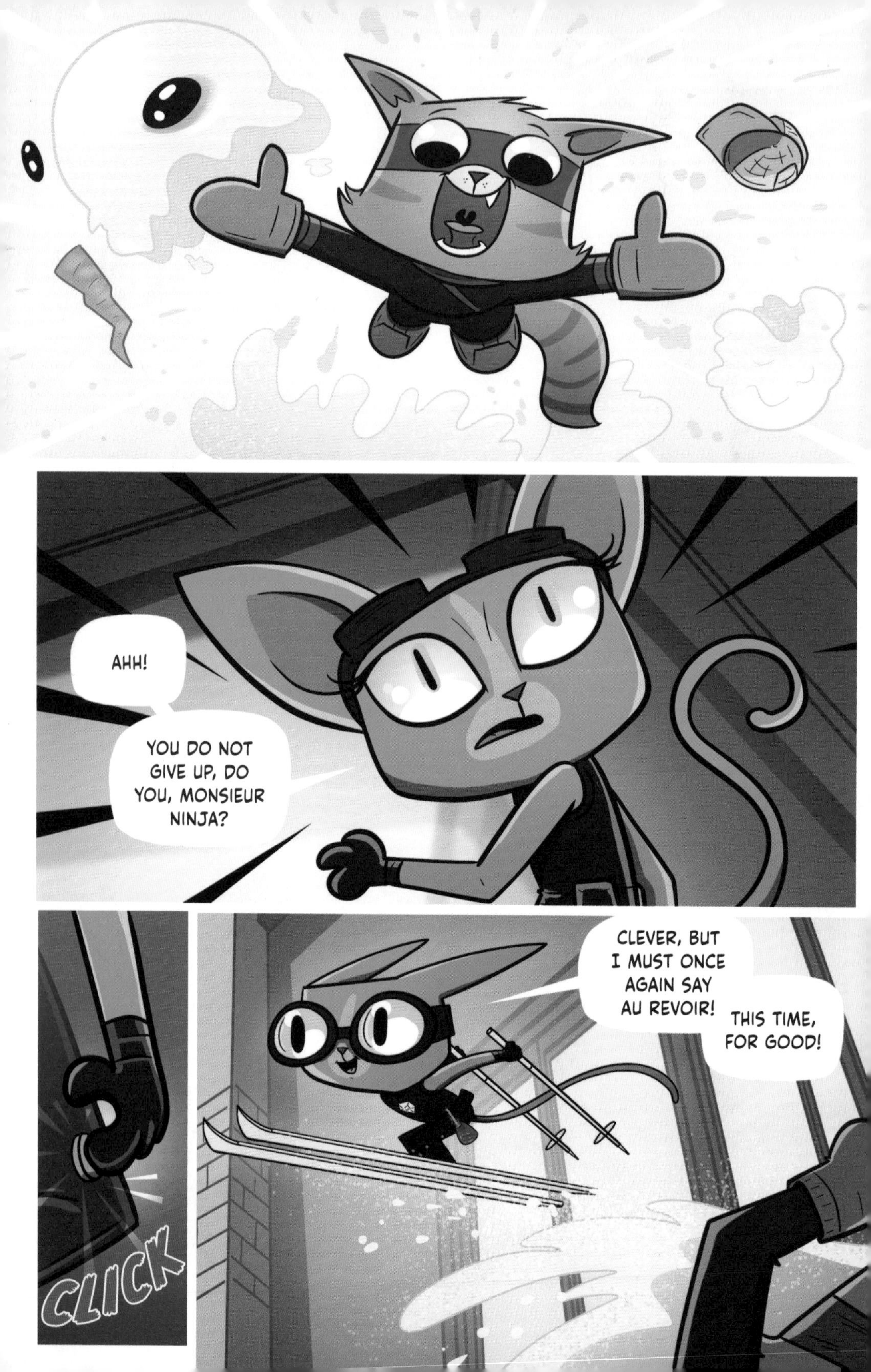
AHH!
YOU DO NOT GIVE UP, DO YOU, MONSIEUR NINJA?
CLICK
CLEVER, BUT I MUST ONCE AGAIN SAY AU REVOIR!
THIS TIME, FOR GOOD!

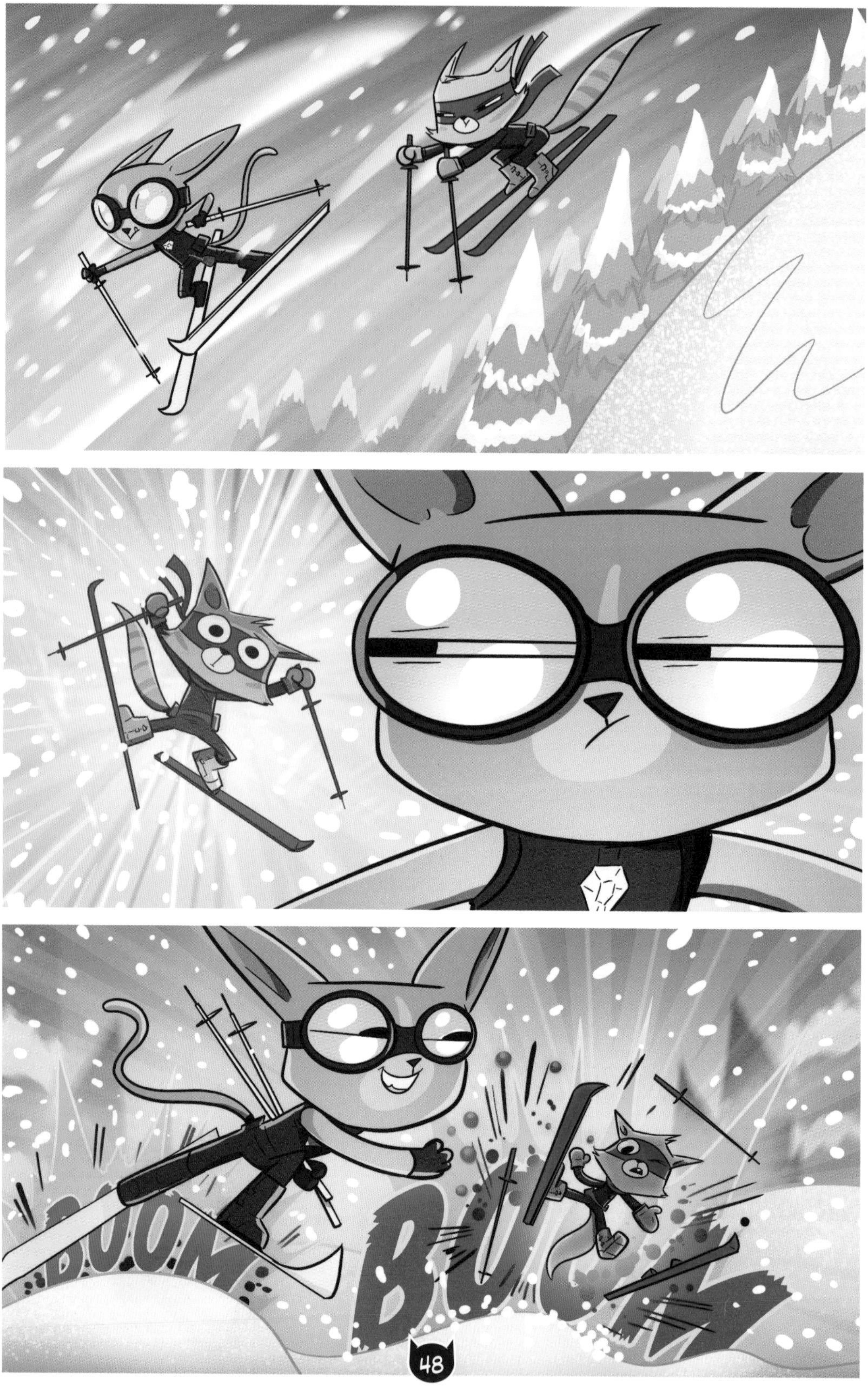
BOOM

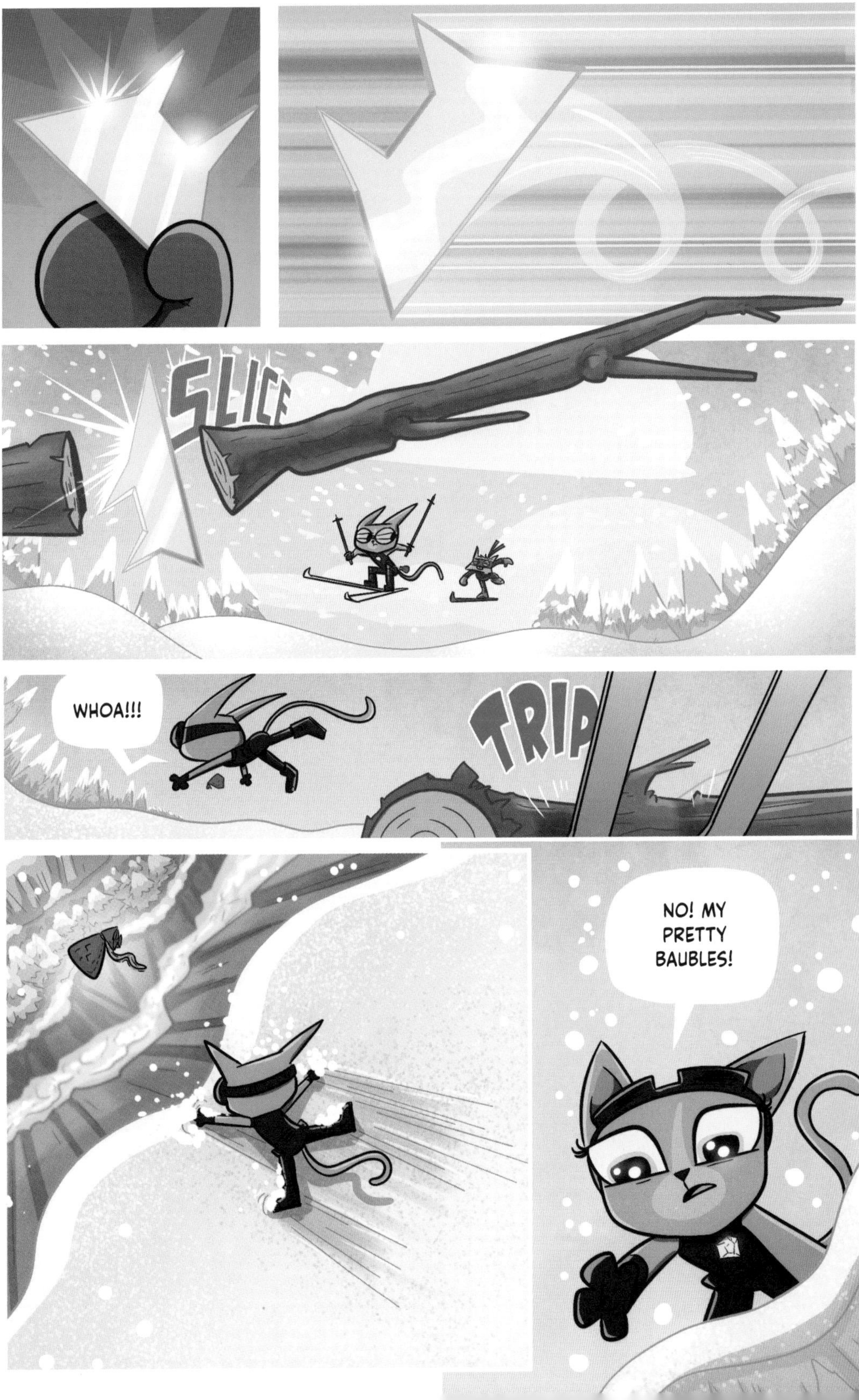
SLICE
WHOA!!!
TRIP
NO! MY PRETTY BAUBLES!

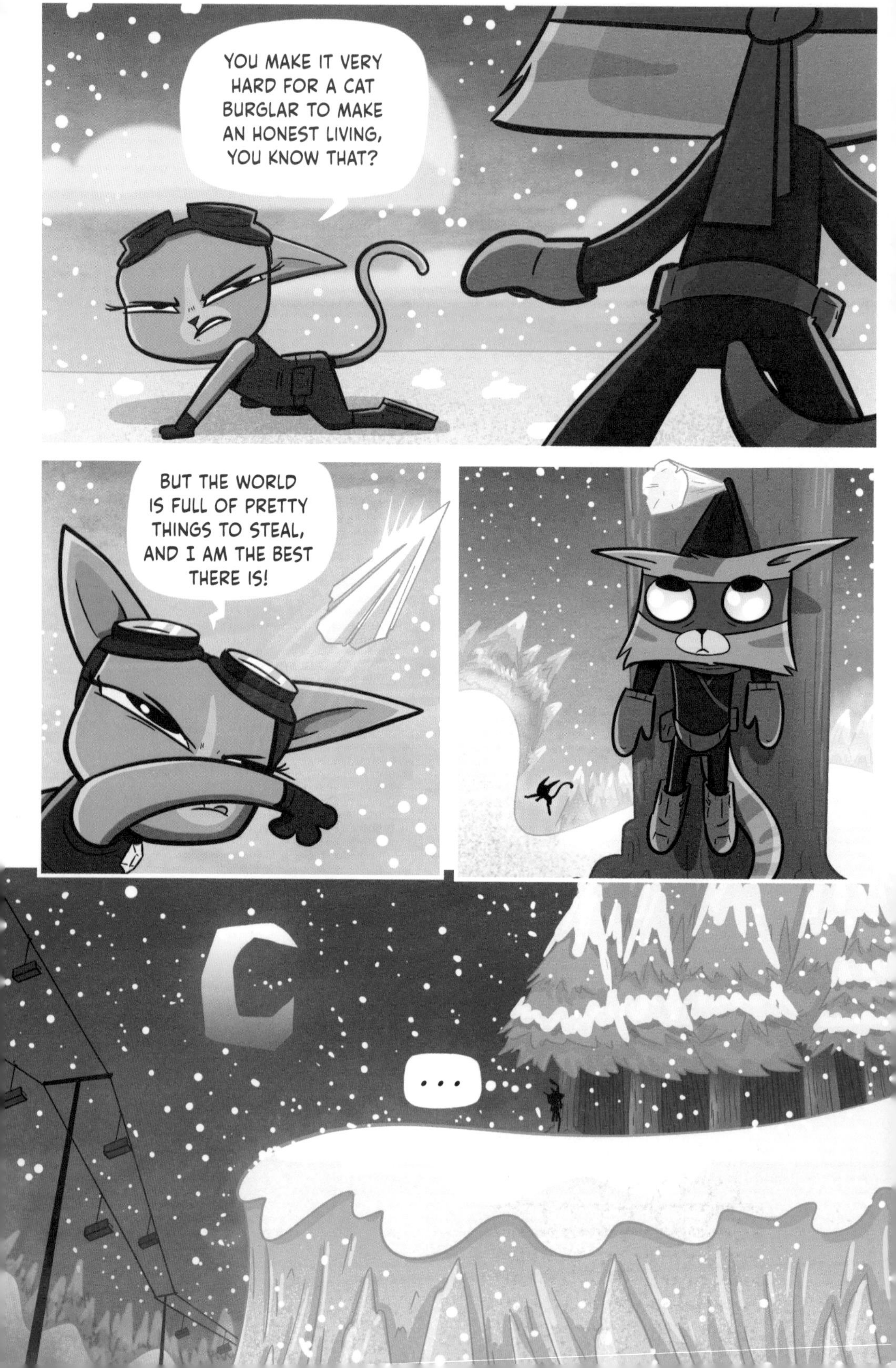
YOU MAKE IT VERY HARD FOR A CAT BURGLAR TO MAKE AN HONEST LIVING, YOU KNOW THAT?
BUT THE WORLD IS FULL OF PRETTY THINGS TO STEAL, AND I AM THE BEST THERE IS!
...

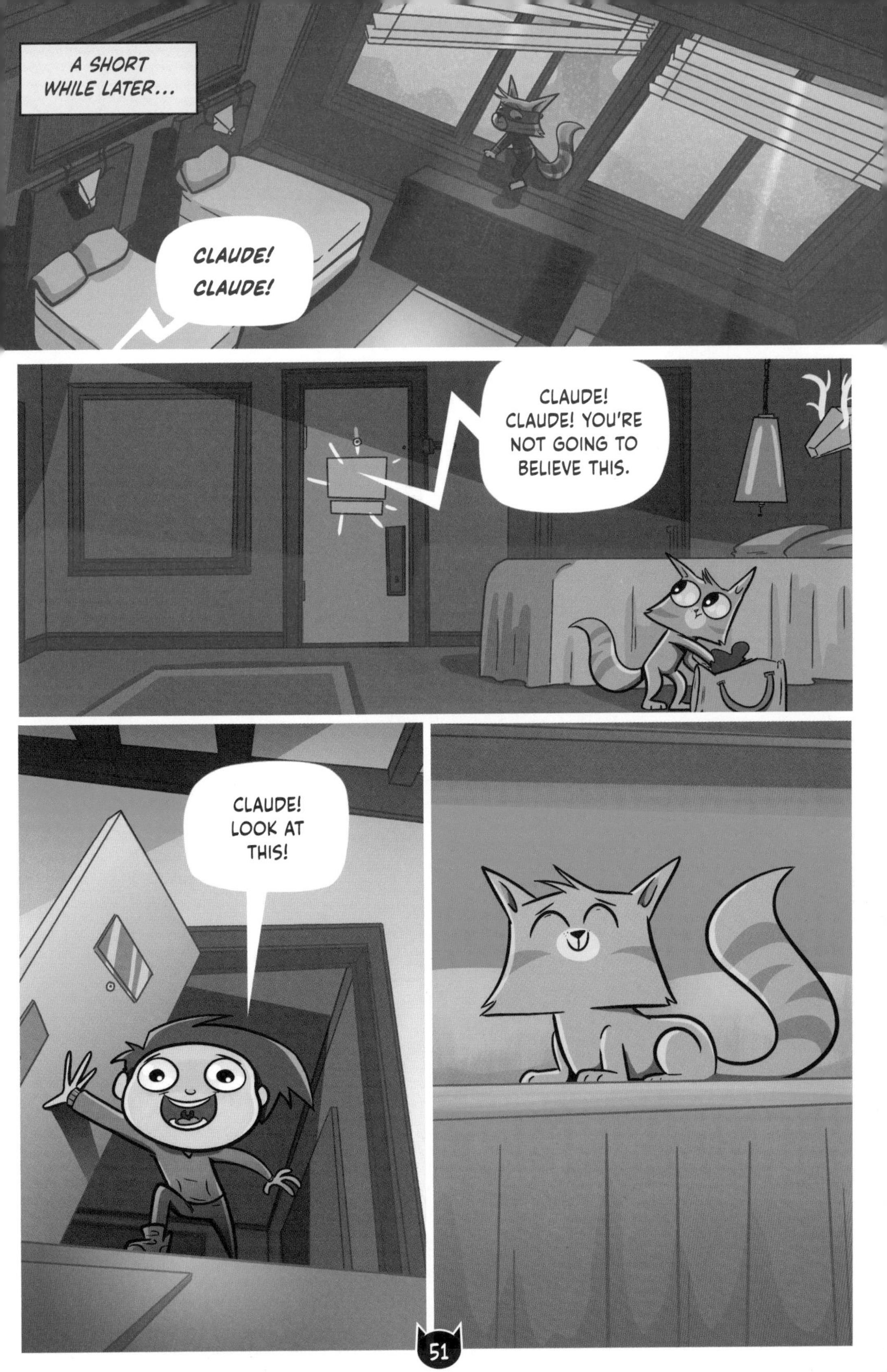
A SHORT WHILE LATER...
CLAUDE! CLAUDE!
CLAUDE! CLAUDE! YOU'RE NOT GOING TO BELIEVE THIS.
CLAUDE! LOOK AT THIS!

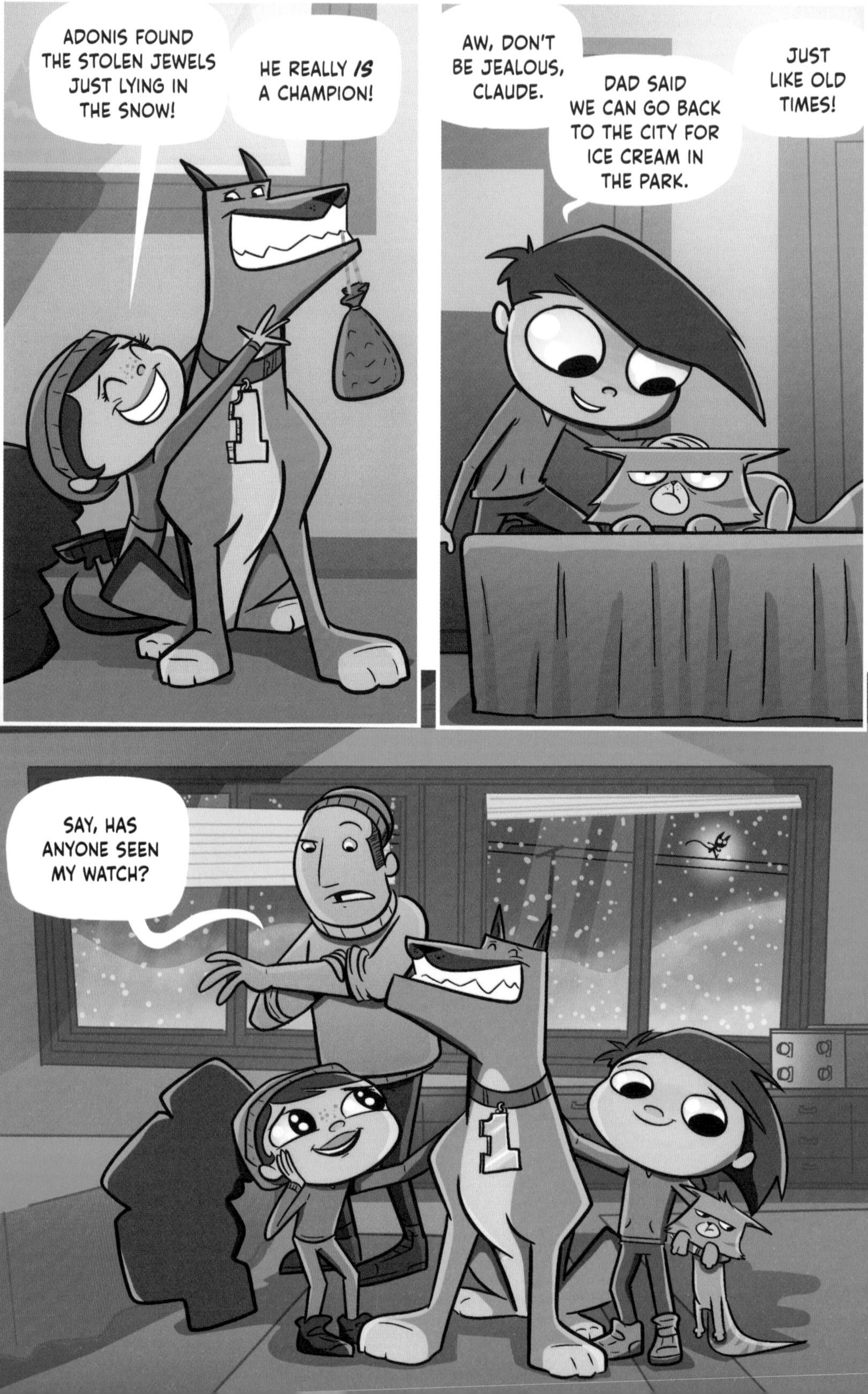
ADONIS FOUND THE STOLEN JEWELS JUST LYING IN THE SNOW!
HE REALLY *IS* A CHAMPION!
AW, DON'T BE JEALOUS, CLAUDE.
DAD SAID WE CAN GO BACK TO THE CITY FOR ICE CREAM IN THE PARK.
JUST LIKE OLD TIMES!
SAY, HAS ANYONE SEEN MY WATCH?

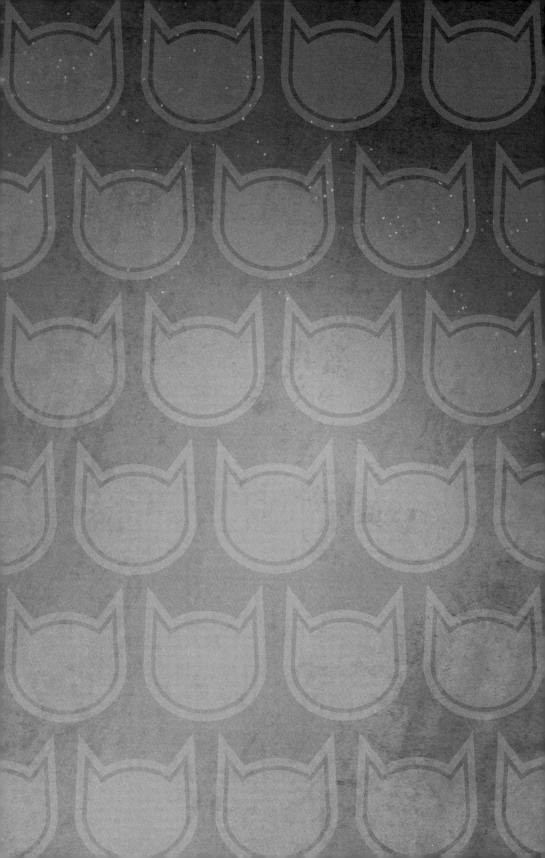

Chapter 3: You Only Live 9 Times

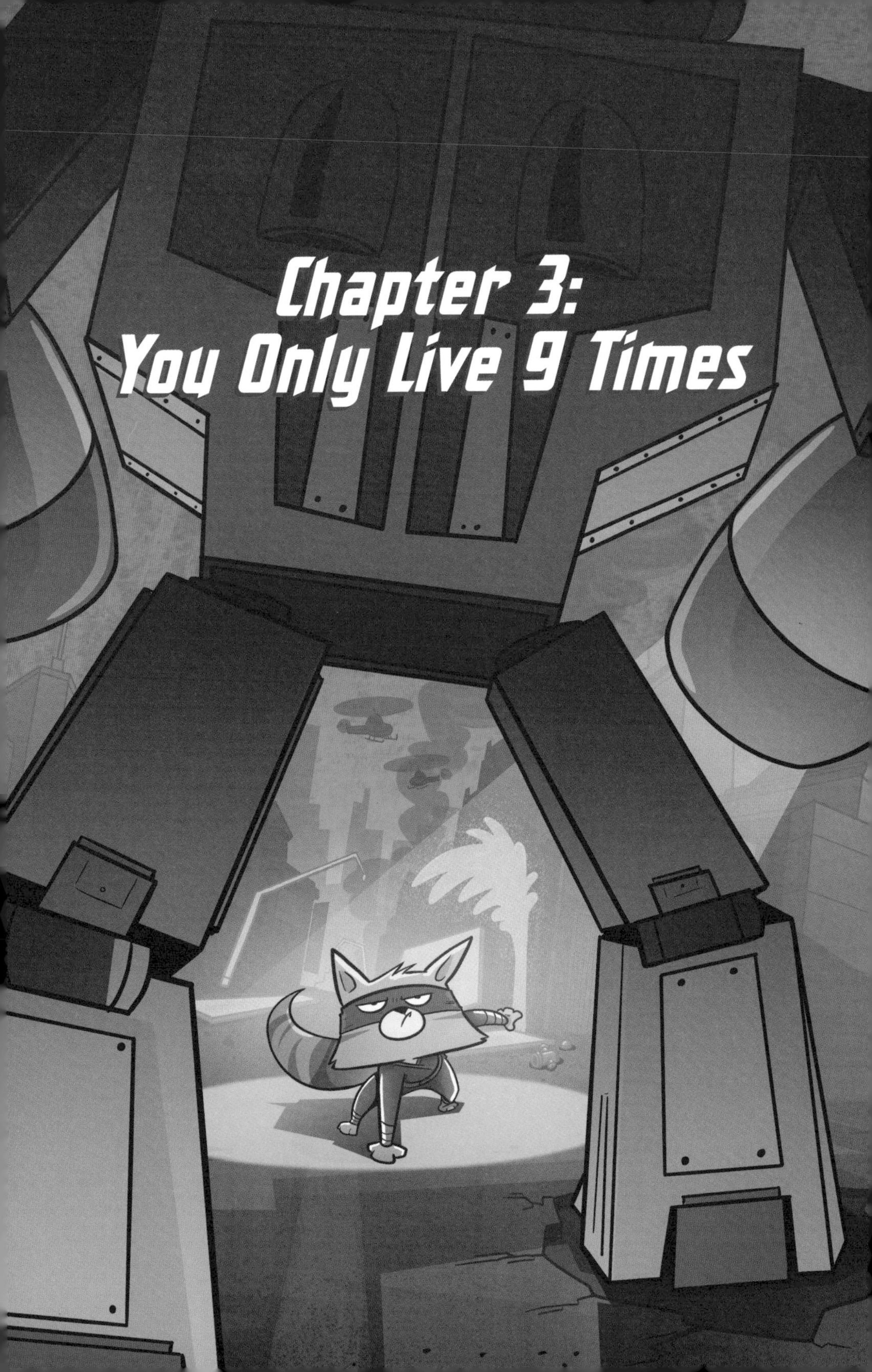

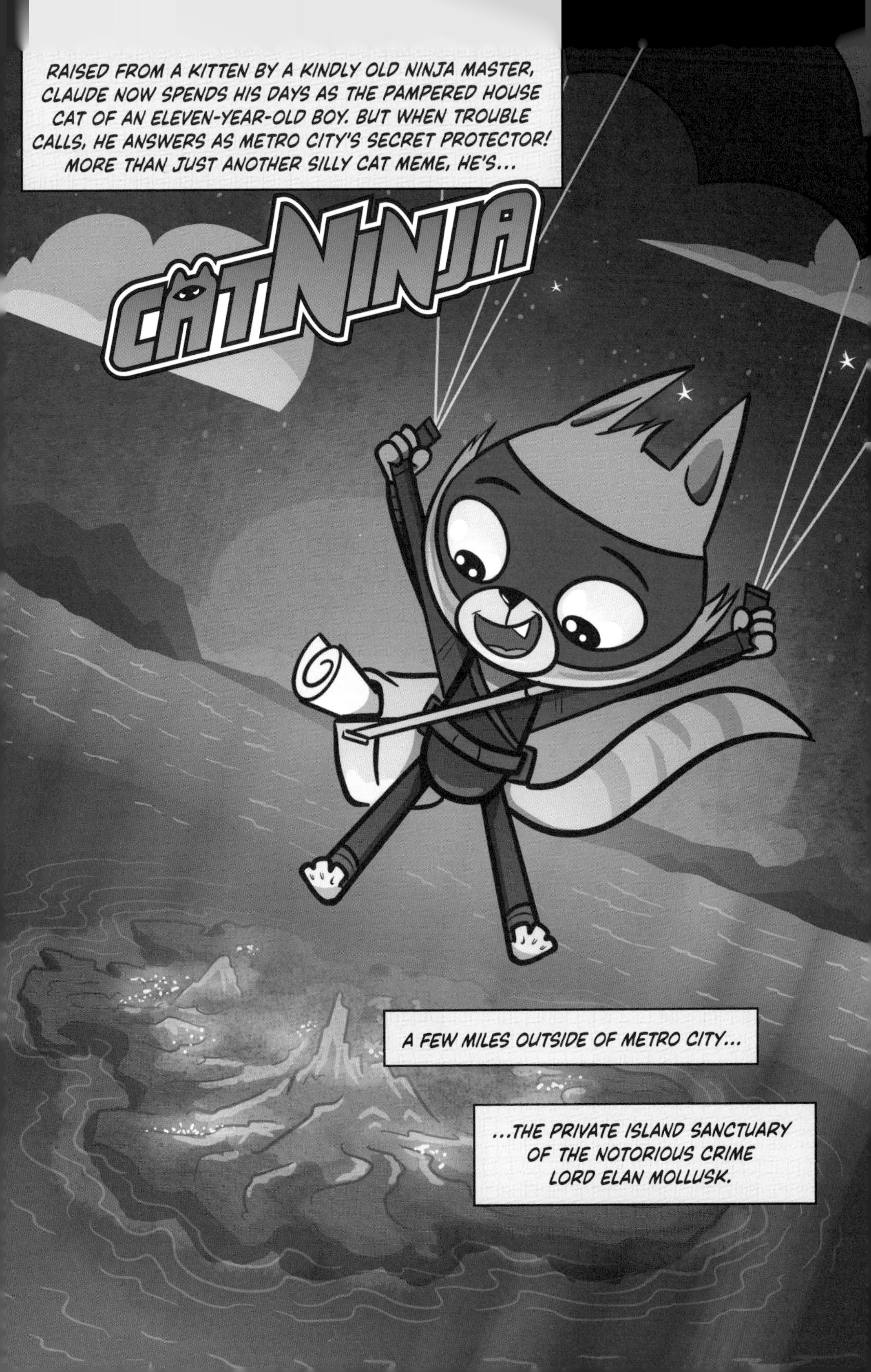
RAISED FROM A KITTEN BY A KINDLY OLD NINJA MASTER, CLAUDE NOW SPENDS HIS DAYS AS THE PAMPERED HOUSE CAT OF AN ELEVEN-YEAR-OLD BOY. BUT WHEN TROUBLE CALLS, HE ANSWERS AS METRO CITY'S SECRET PROTECTOR! MORE THAN JUST ANOTHER SILLY CAT MEME, HE'S...
CATNINJA
A FEW MILES OUTSIDE OF METRO CITY...
...THE PRIVATE ISLAND SANCTUARY OF THE NOTORIOUS CRIME LORD ELAN MOLLUSK.

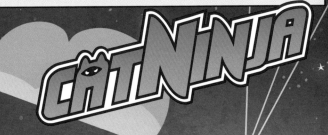

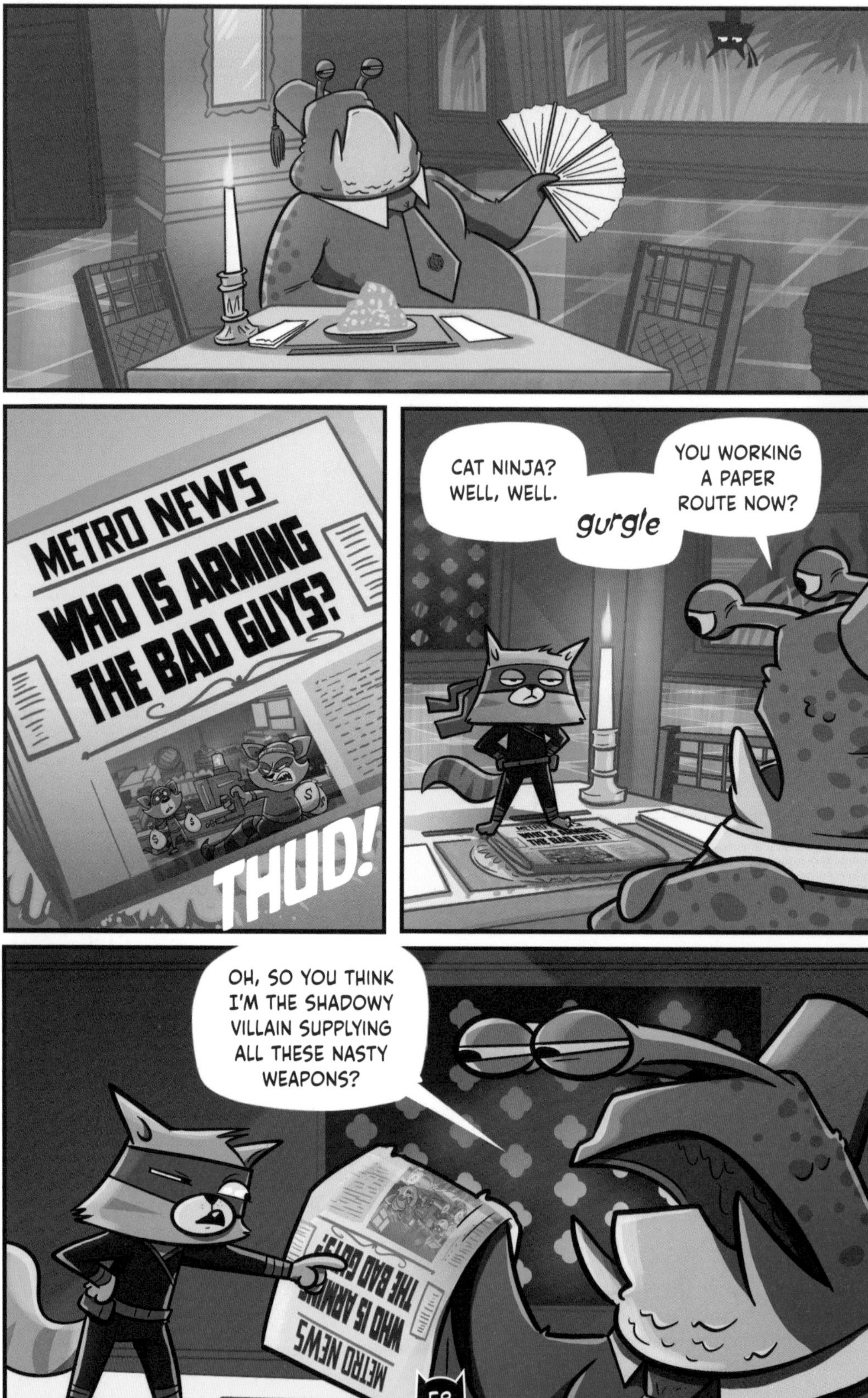
METRO NEWS
WHO IS ARMING THE BAD GUYS?
THUD!
CAT NINJA? WELL, WELL.
gurgle
YOU WORKING A PAPER ROUTE NOW?
OH, SO YOU THINK I'M THE SHADOWY VILLAIN SUPPLYING ALL THESE NASTY WEAPONS?
METRO NEWS
WHO IS ARMING THE BAD GUYS?

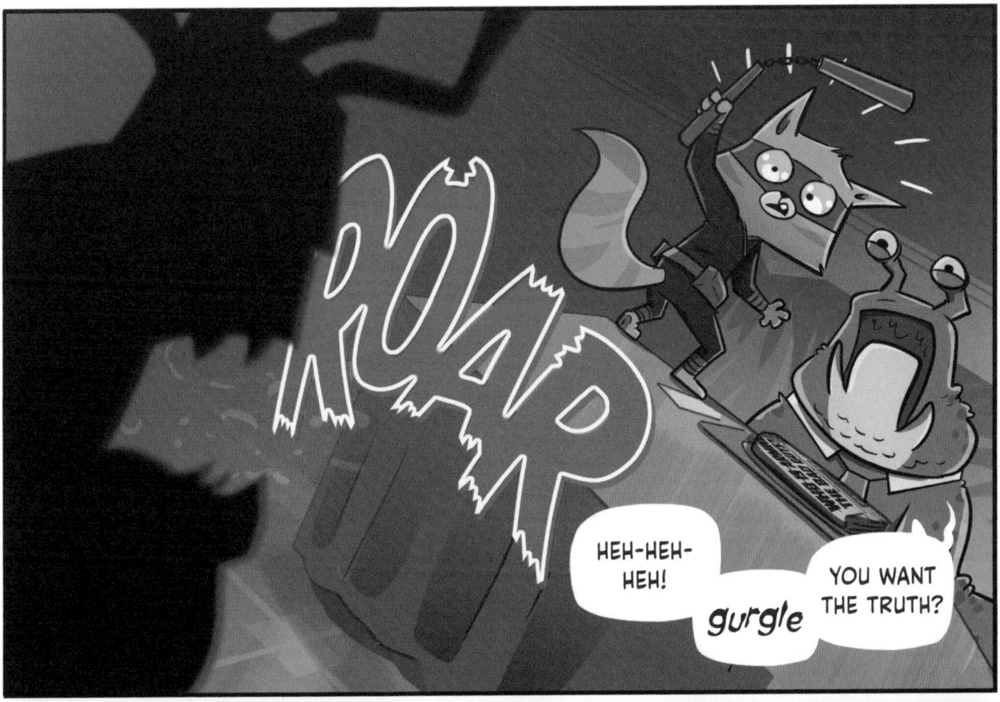
ROAR
HEH-HEH-HEH!
gurgle
YOU WANT THE TRUTH?

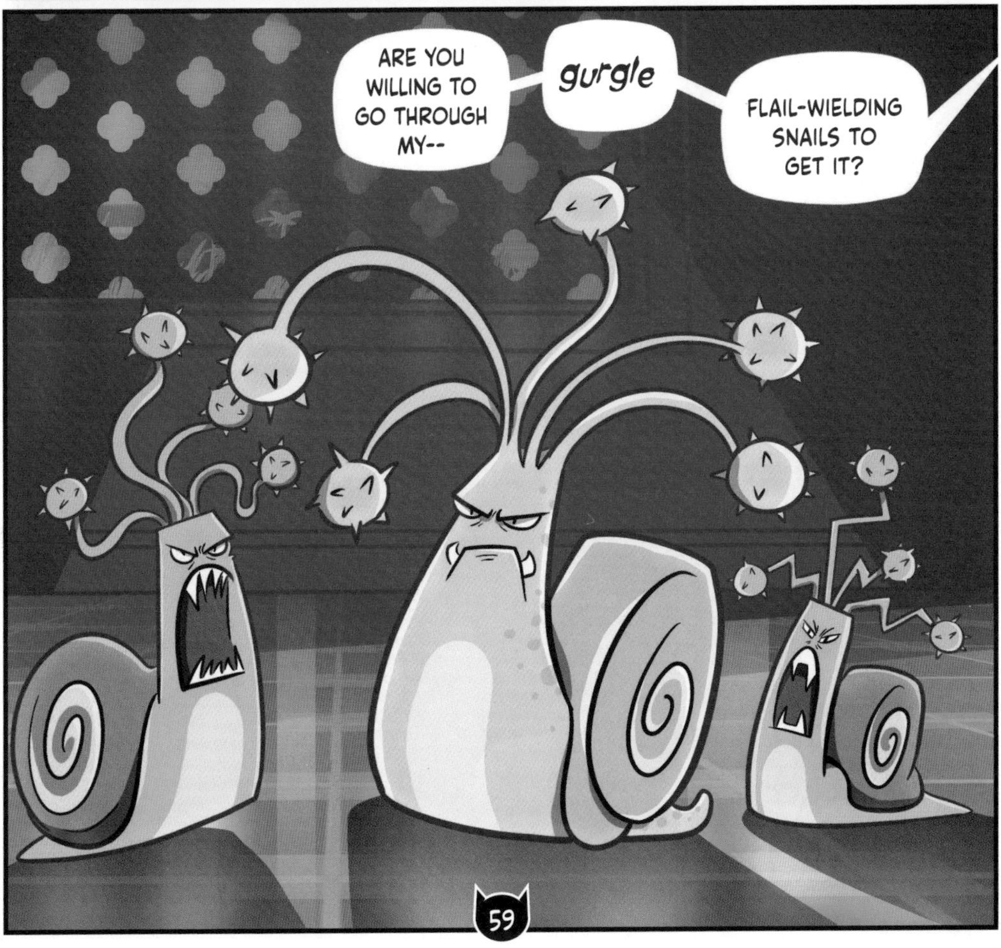
ARE YOU WILLING TO GO THROUGH MY--
gurgle
FLAIL-WIELDING SNAILS TO GET IT?

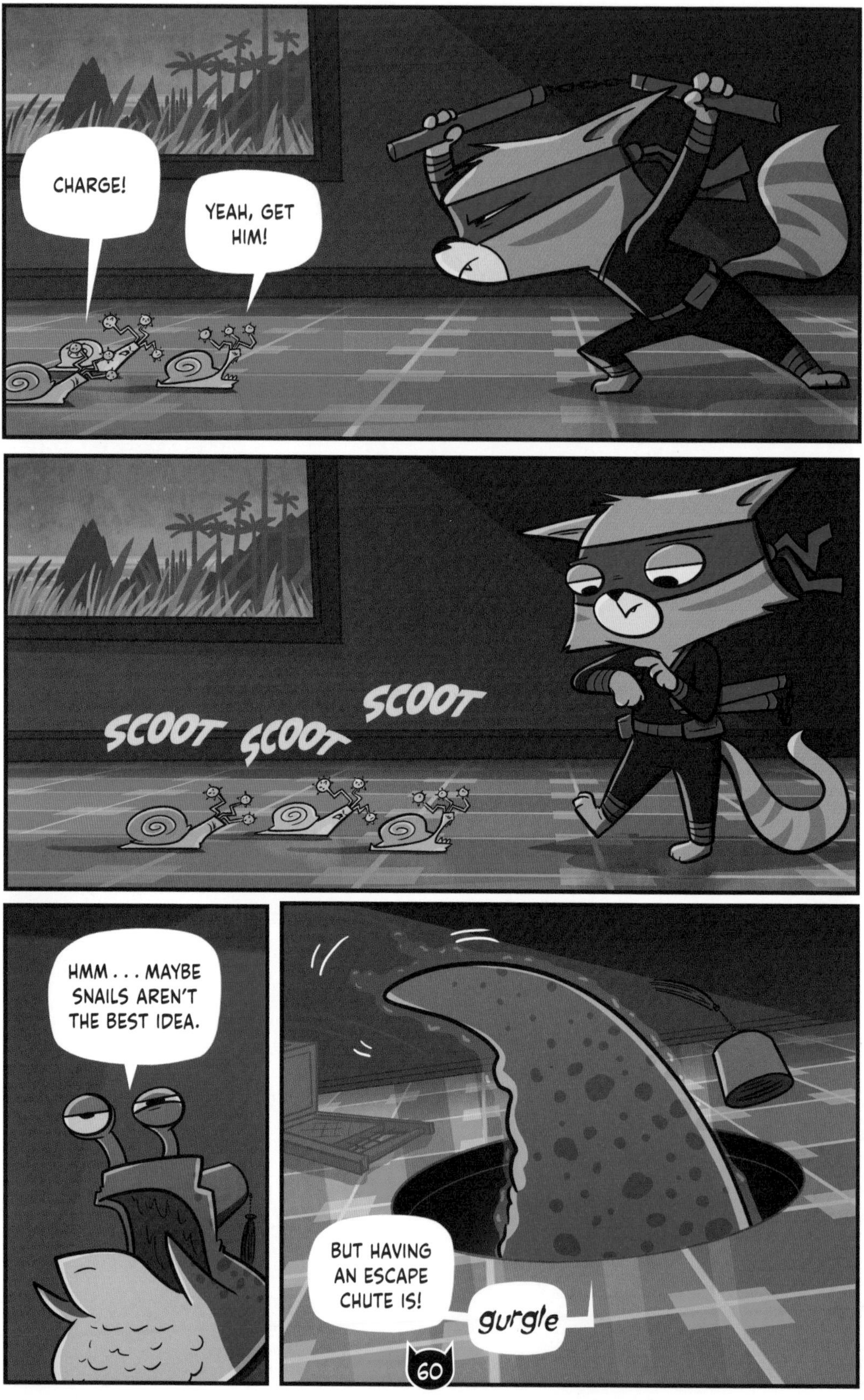
CHARGE!
YEAH, GET HIM!
SCOOT
SCOOT
SCOOT
HMM . . . MAYBE SNAILS AREN'T THE BEST IDEA.
BUT HAVING AN ESCAPE CHUTE IS!
gurgle

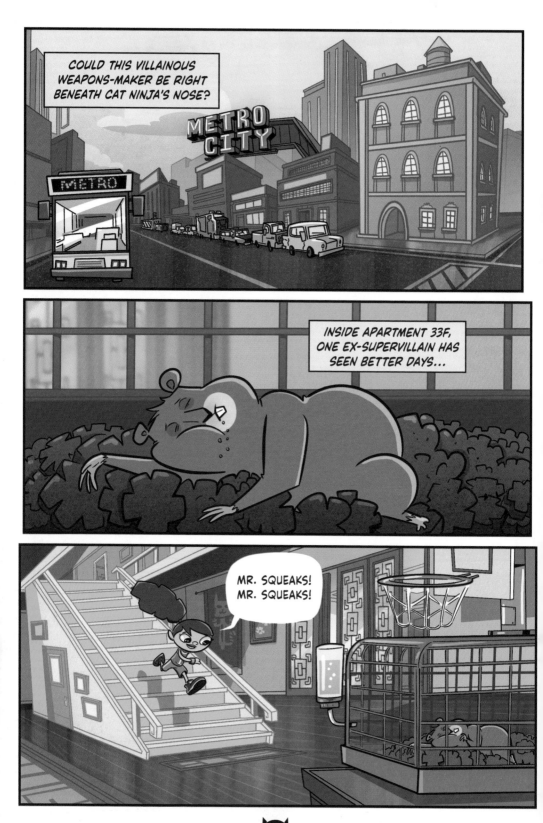

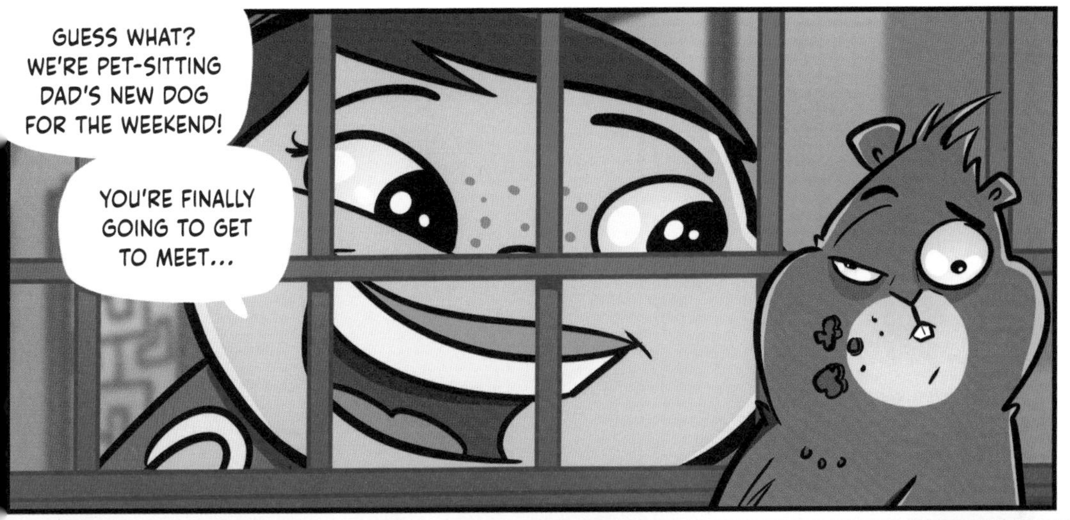
GUESS WHAT? WE'RE PET-SITTING DAD'S NEW DOG FOR THE WEEKEND!
YOU'RE FINALLY GOING TO GET TO MEET...

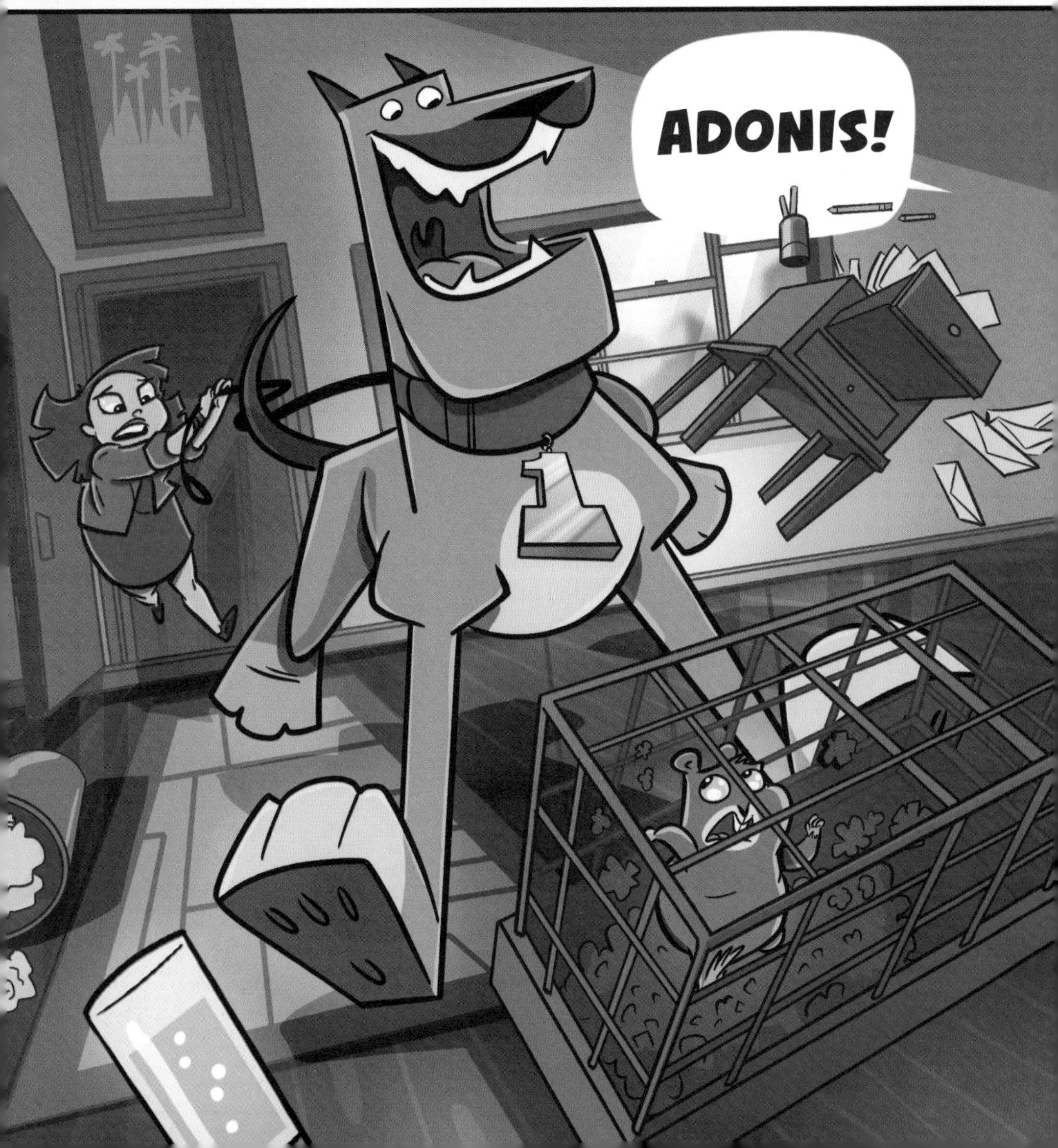
ADONIS!

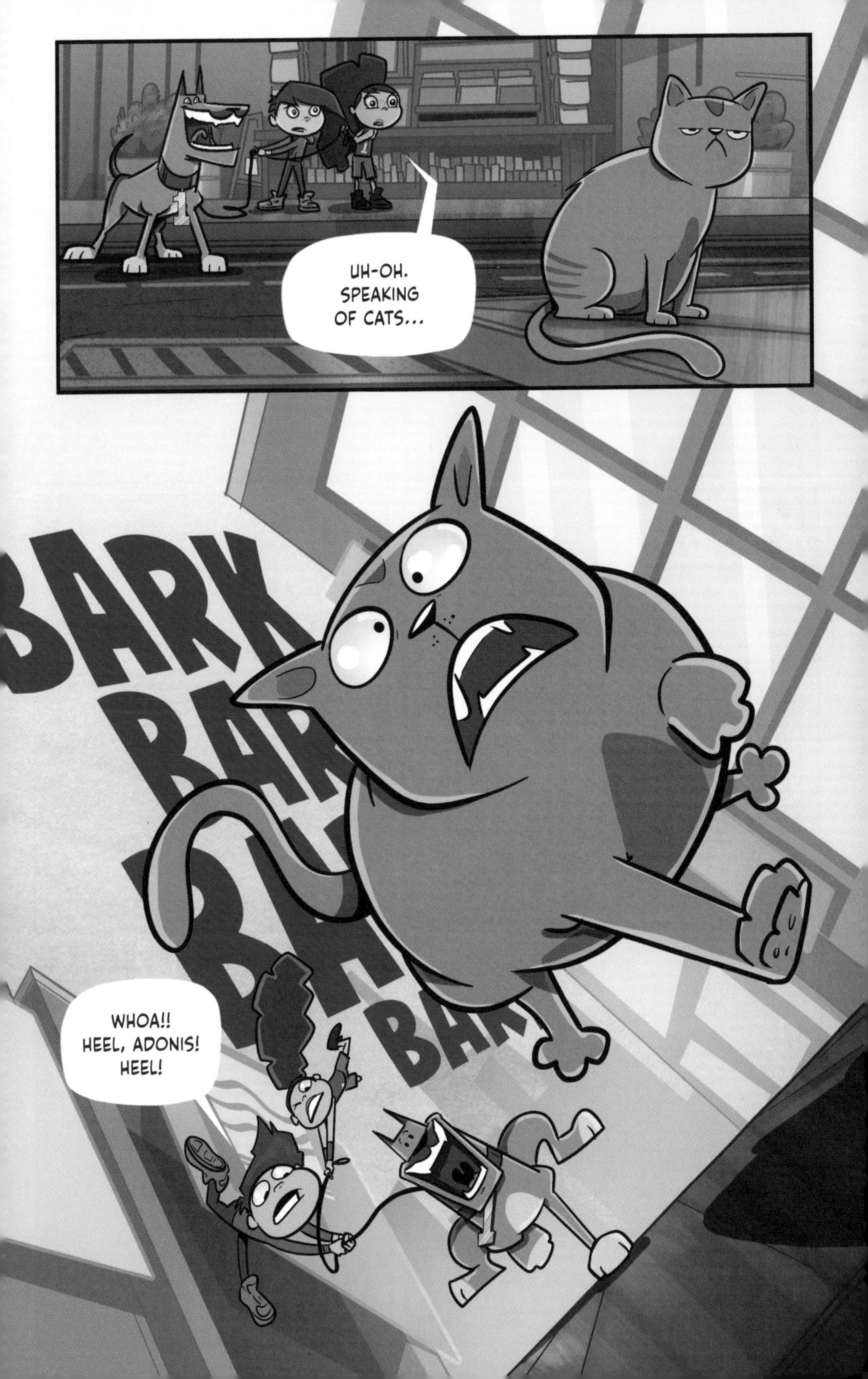
UH-OH. SPEAKING OF CATS...
BARK
BARK
BARK
BARK
BARK
WHOA!! HEEL, ADONIS! HEEL!

WHOA! UH, GOOD BOY?

WOW, I THINK HE WALKED US.

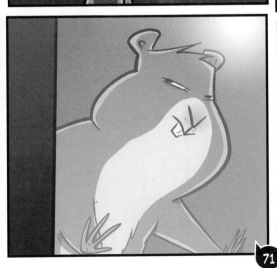

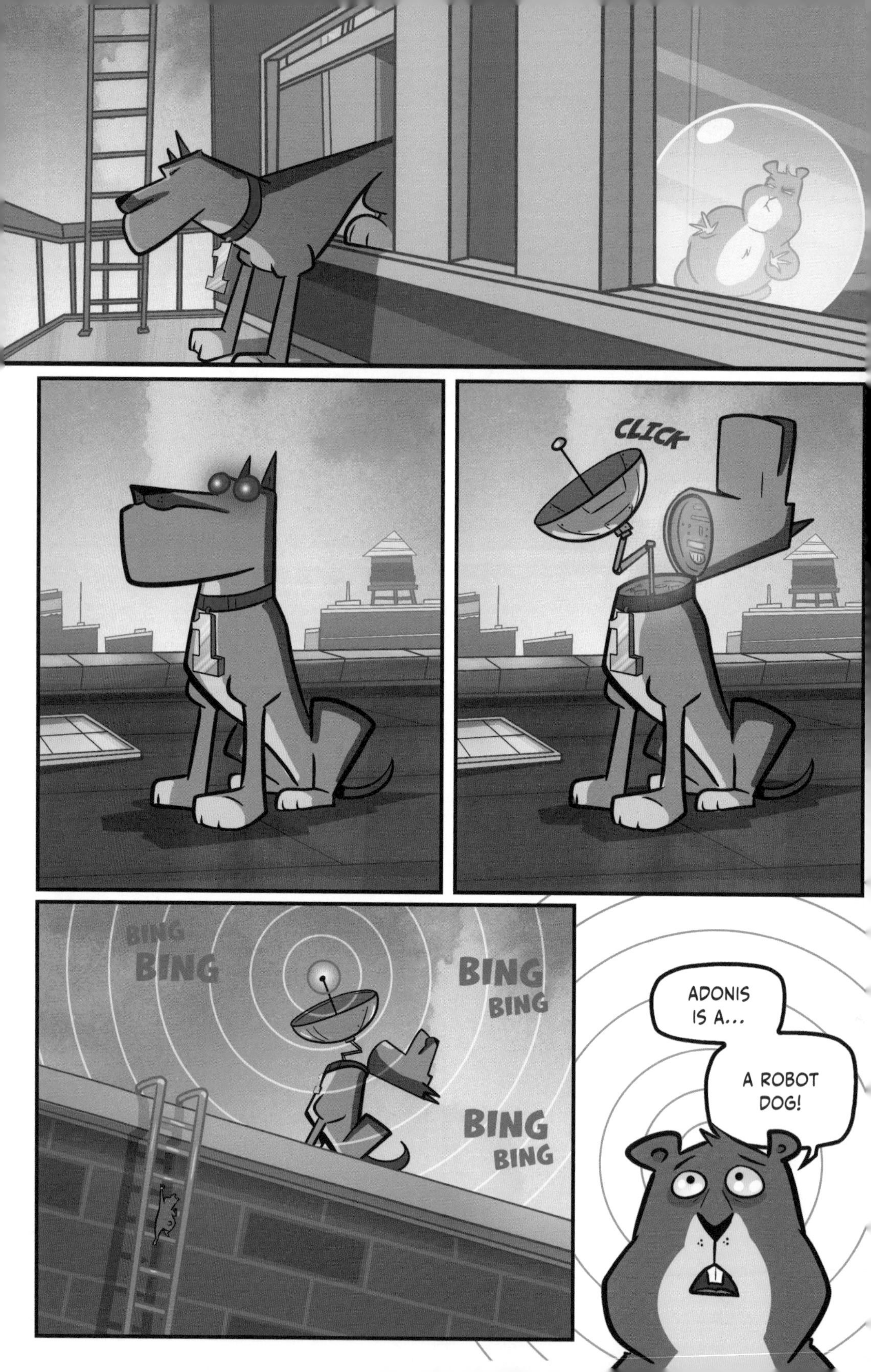
CLICK
BING
BING
BING
BING
BING
BING
ADONIS IS A...
A ROBOT DOG!

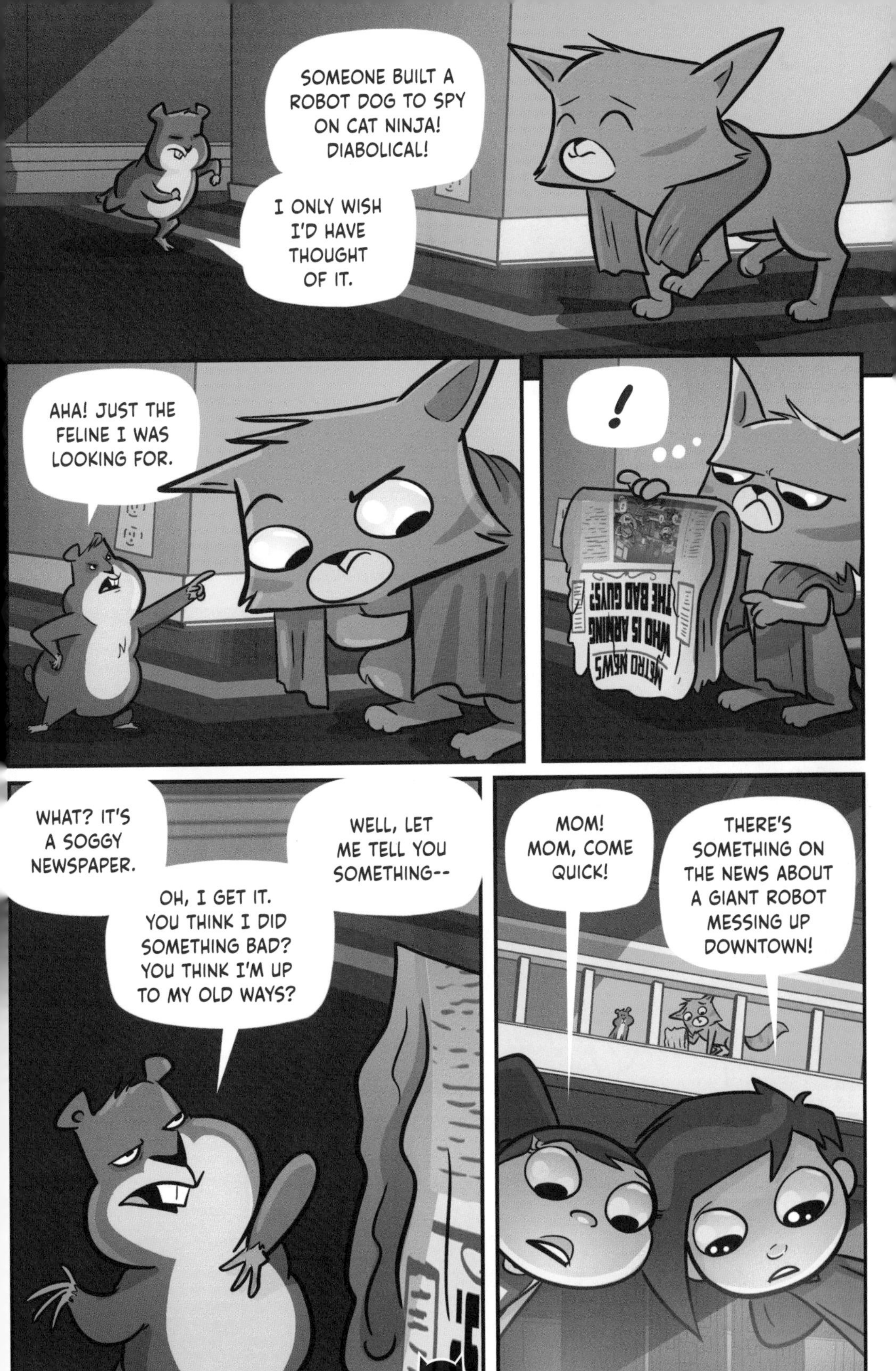
SOMEONE BUILT A ROBOT DOG TO SPY ON CAT NINJA! DIABOLICAL!
I ONLY WISH I'D HAVE THOUGHT OF IT.
AHA! JUST THE FELINE I WAS LOOKING FOR.
!
METRO NEWS
WHO IS ARMING THE BAD GUYS?
WHAT? IT'S A SOGGY NEWSPAPER.
WELL, LET ME TELL YOU SOMETHING--
OH, I GET IT. YOU THINK I DID SOMETHING BAD? YOU THINK I'M UP TO MY OLD WAYS?
MOM! MOM, COME QUICK!
THERE'S SOMETHING ON THE NEWS ABOUT A GIANT ROBOT MESSING UP DOWNTOWN!

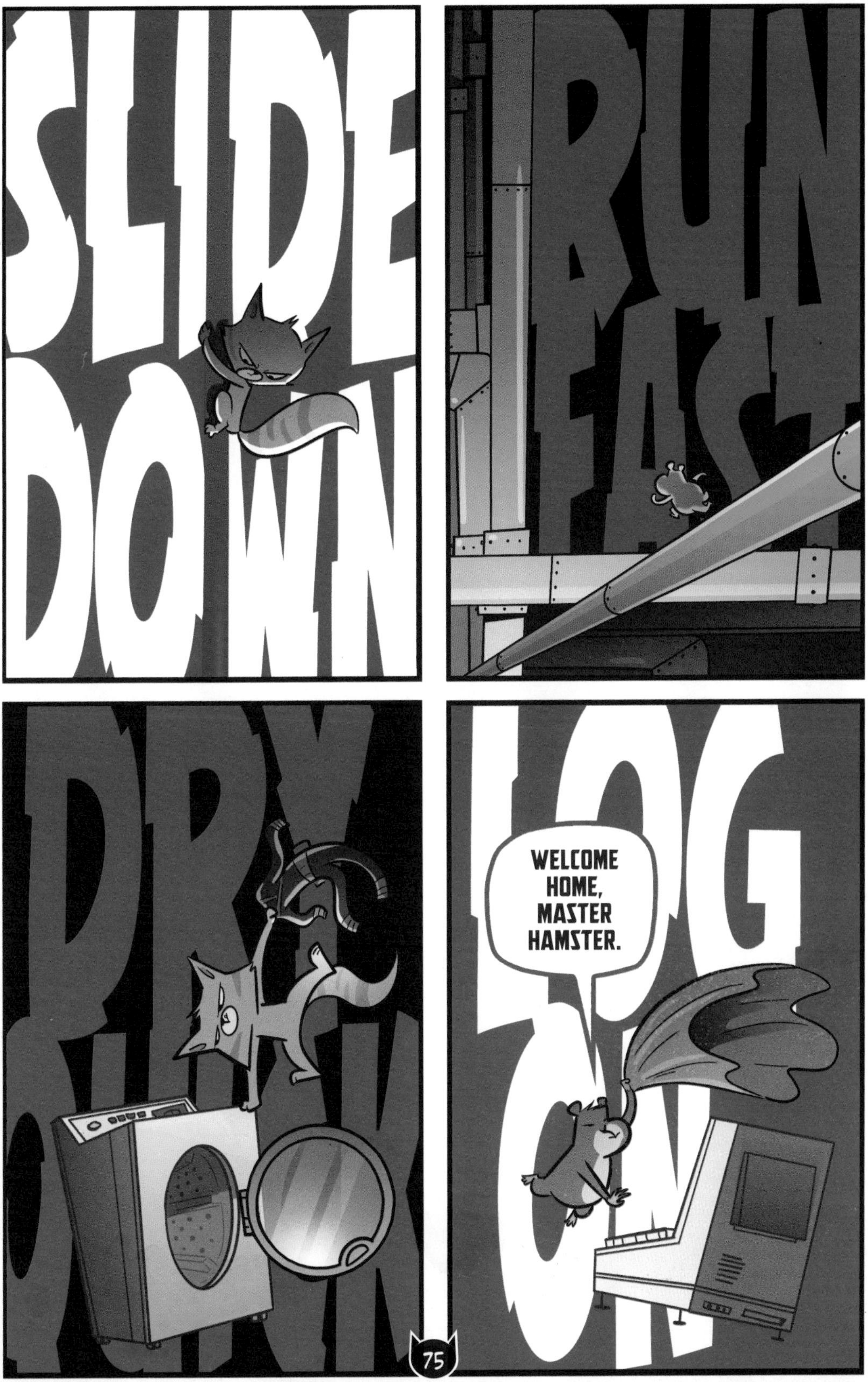
SLIDE DOWN
RUN FAST
DRY
LOG ON
WELCOME HOME, MASTER HAMSTER.

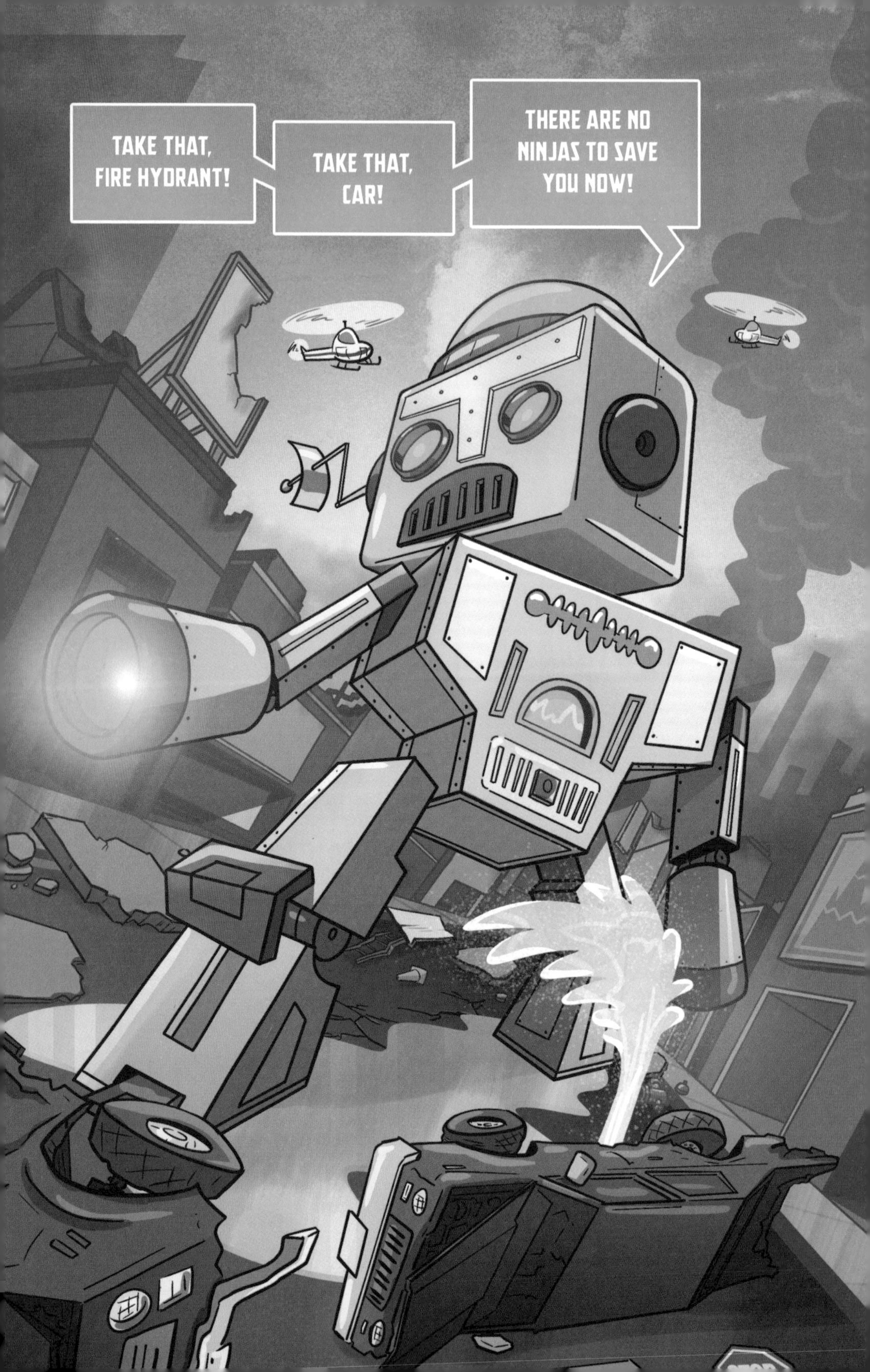
TAKE THAT, FIRE HYDRANT!
TAKE THAT, CAR!
THERE ARE NO NINJAS TO SAVE YOU NOW!

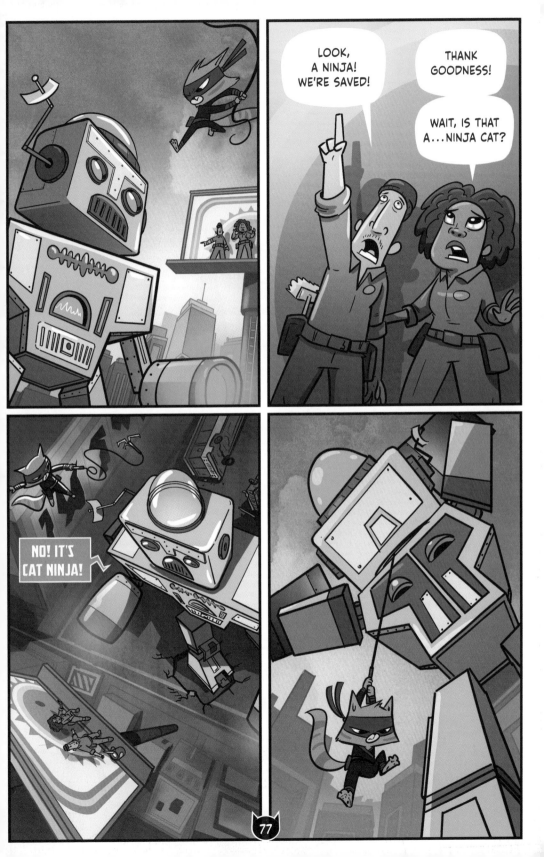

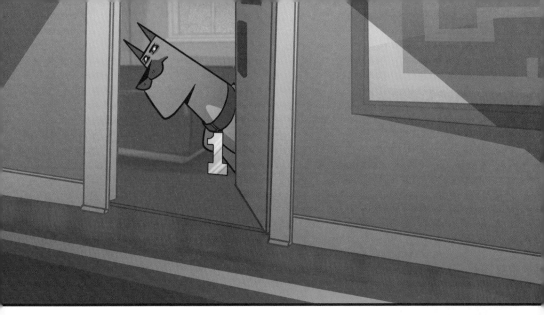

AND I HAVE CONFIRMED THE SUBJECTS' SECRET IDENTITIES. YOUR SUSPICIONS WERE CORRECT, DR. VON MALICE.
GOOD. THE WEAPONS ARE NEARLY COMPLETE. EVERY TWO-BIT THUG IN METRO CITY WILL HAVE ENOUGH FIREPOWER TO LEVEL A BUILDING.
AND NO CAT NINJA WILL BE ABLE TO STOP US!

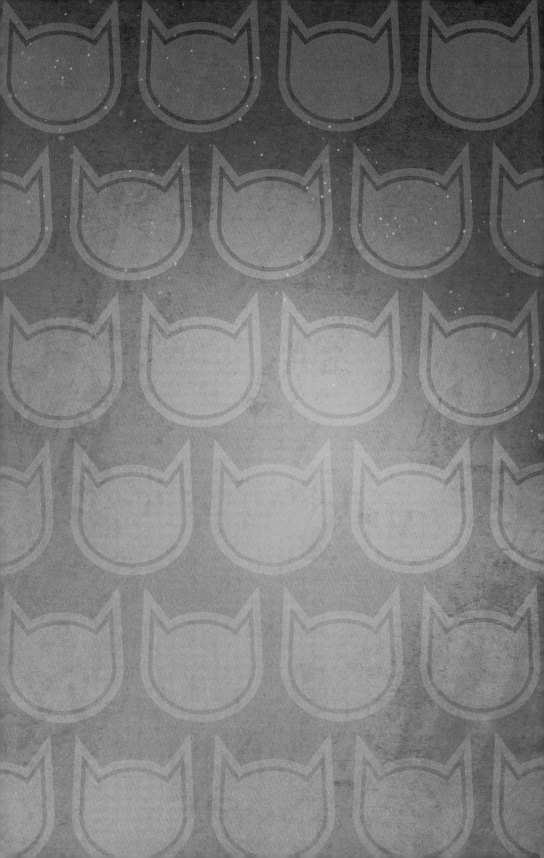

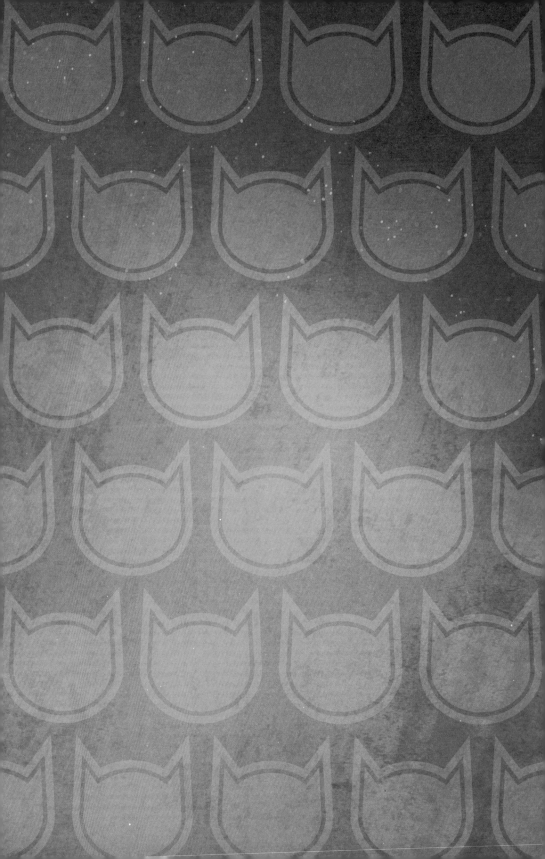

Chapter 4: The Life and Times of the Fury Roach

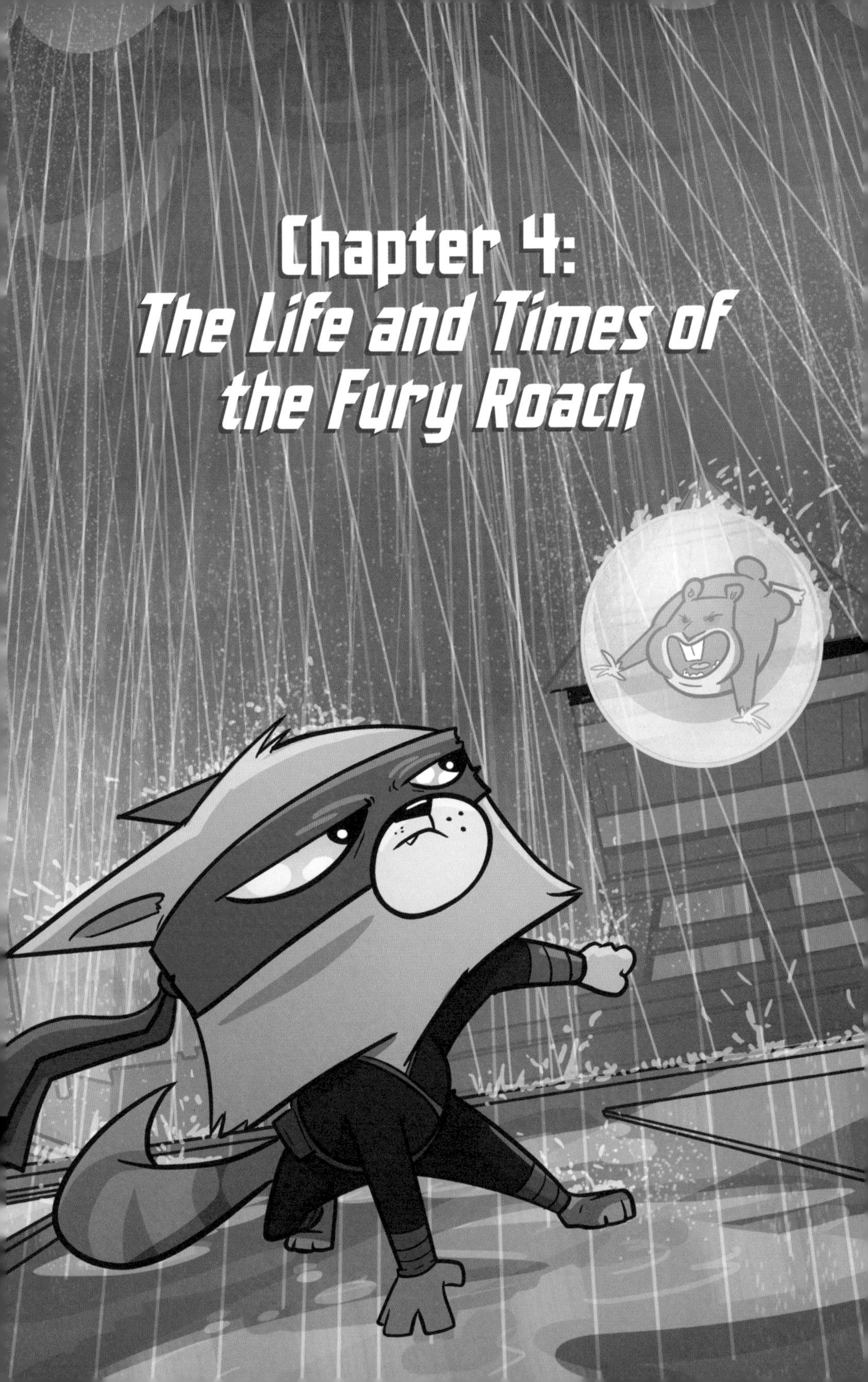

PREPARE TO MEET THE RACCOON BROS-- *EXTREME!*
BOX
THIS AIN'T GONNA END WELL.
!

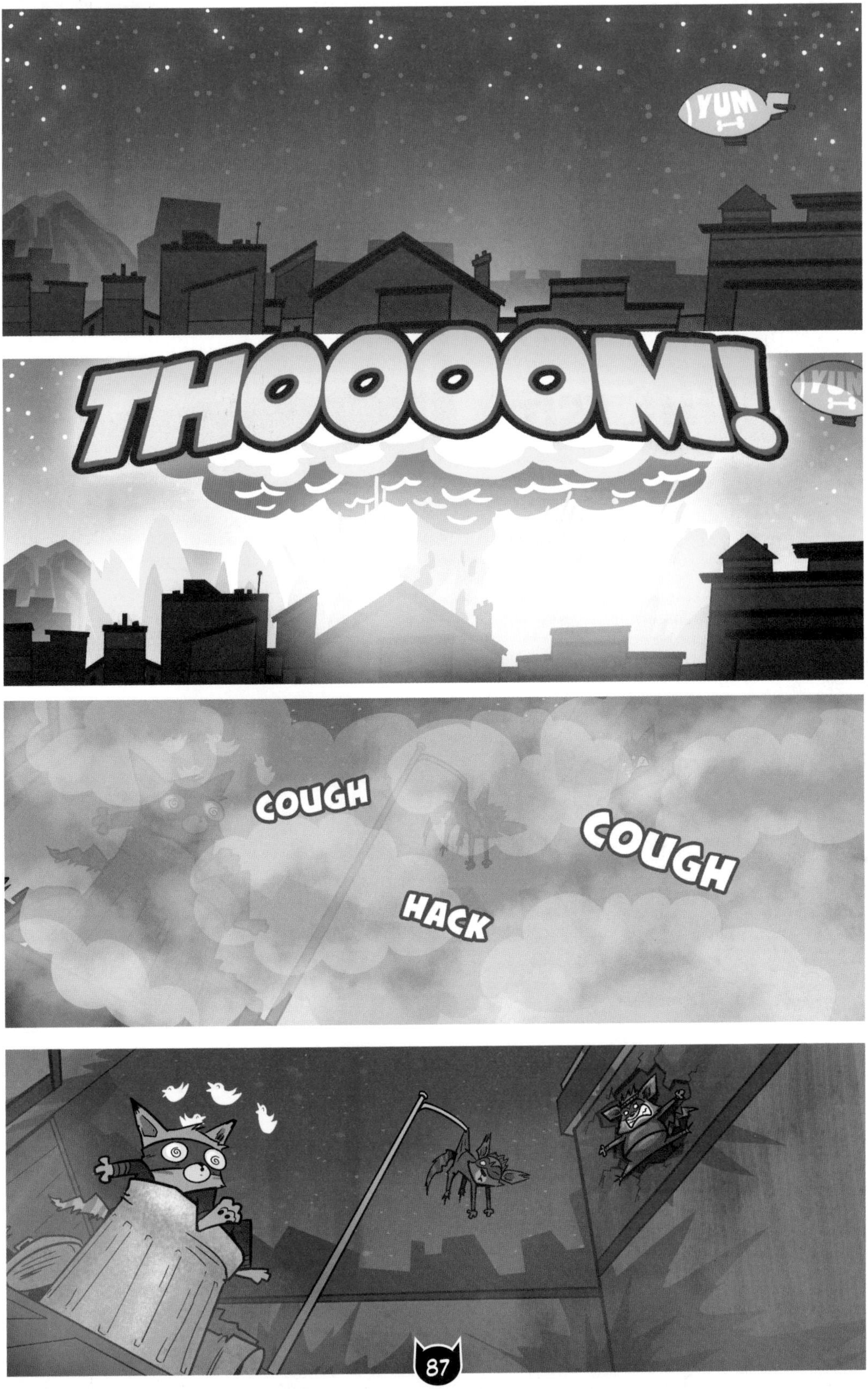
YUM
THOOOOM!
COUGH
COUGH
HACK

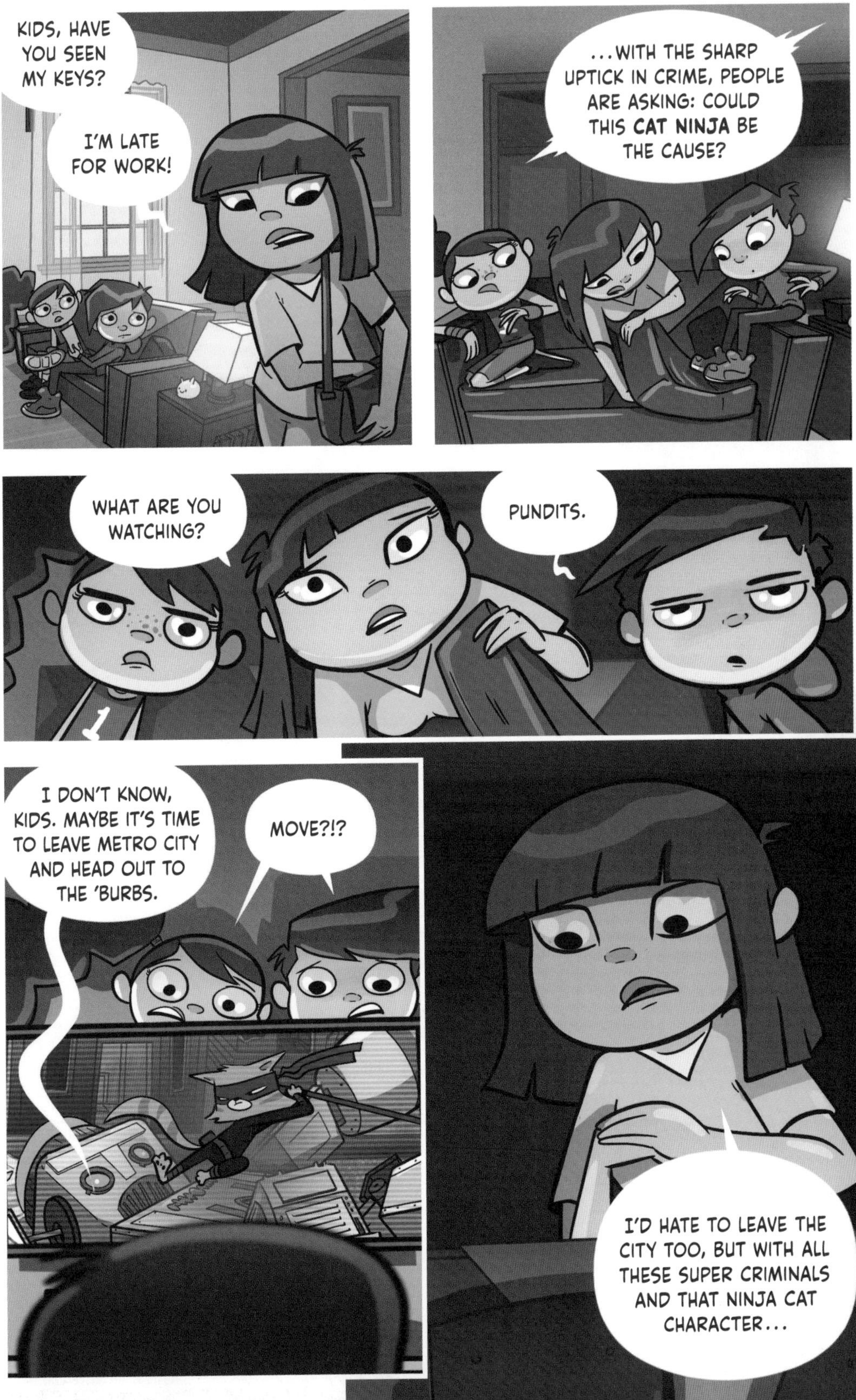
KIDS, HAVE YOU SEEN MY KEYS?
I'M LATE FOR WORK!
...WITH THE SHARP UPTICK IN CRIME, PEOPLE ARE ASKING: COULD THIS **CAT NINJA** BE THE CAUSE?
WHAT ARE YOU WATCHING?
PUNDITS.
I DON'T KNOW, KIDS. MAYBE IT'S TIME TO LEAVE METRO CITY AND HEAD OUT TO THE 'BURBS.
MOVE?!?
I'D HATE TO LEAVE THE CITY TOO, BUT WITH ALL THESE SUPER CRIMINALS AND THAT NINJA CAT CHARACTER...

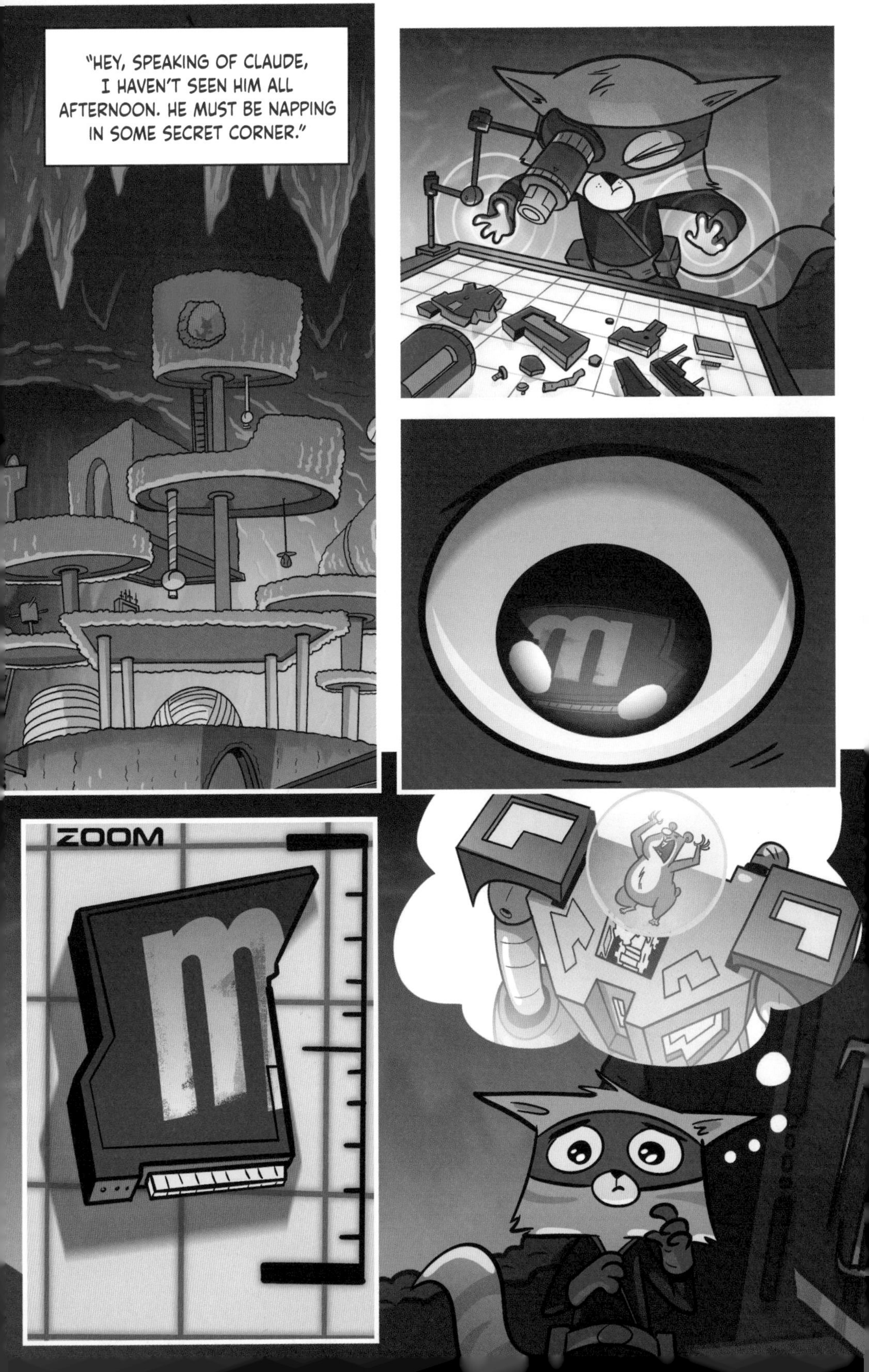
"HEY, SPEAKING OF CLAUDE, I HAVEN'T SEEN HIM ALL AFTERNOON. HE MUST BE NAPPING IN SOME SECRET CORNER."
ZOOM

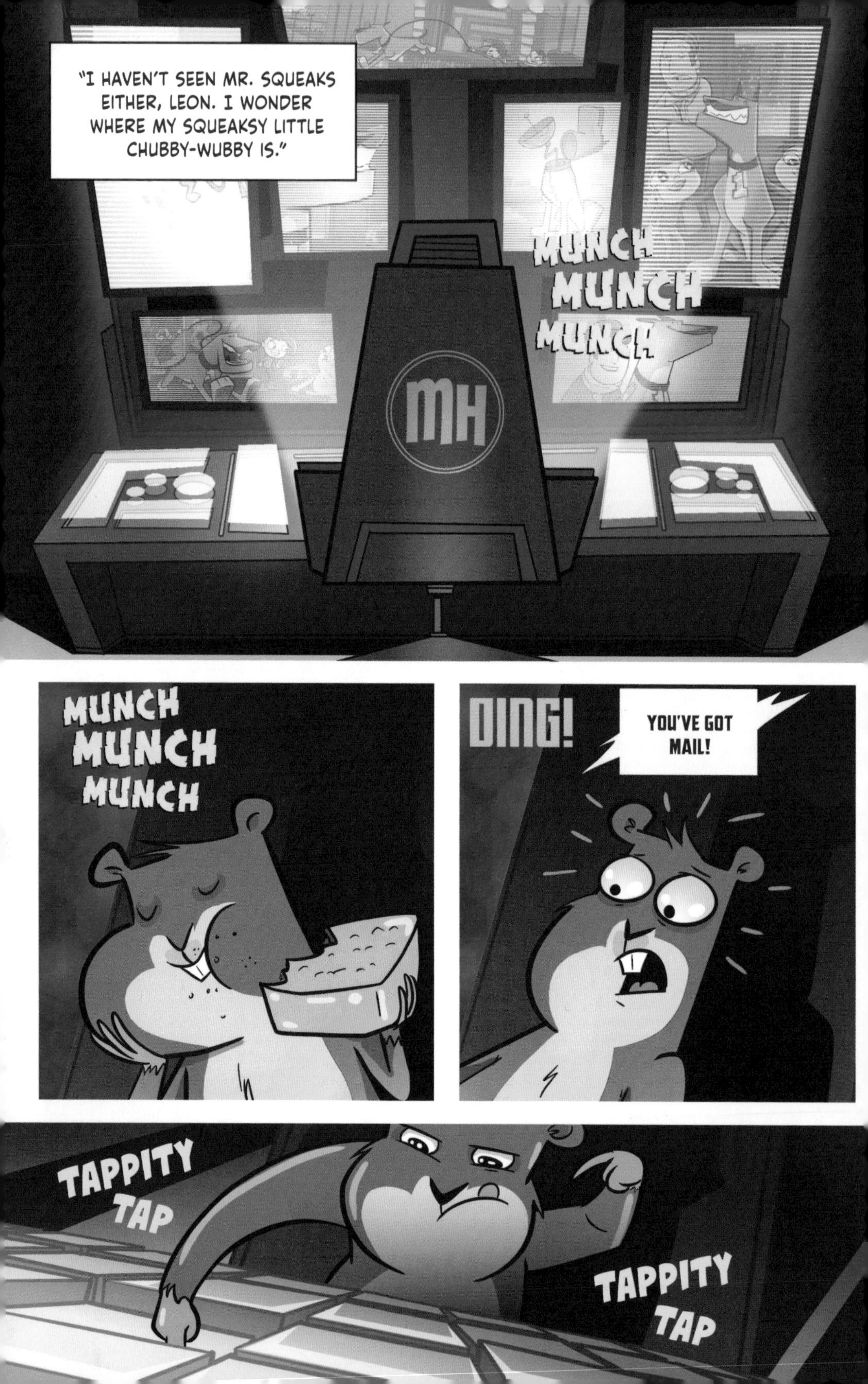
"I HAVEN'T SEEN MR. SQUEAKS EITHER, LEON. I WONDER WHERE MY SQUEAKSY LITTLE CHUBBY-WUBBY IS."
MUNCH
MUNCH
MUNCH
MH
MUNCH
MUNCH
MUNCH
DING!
YOU'VE GOT MAIL!
TAPPITY
TAP
TAPPITY
TAP

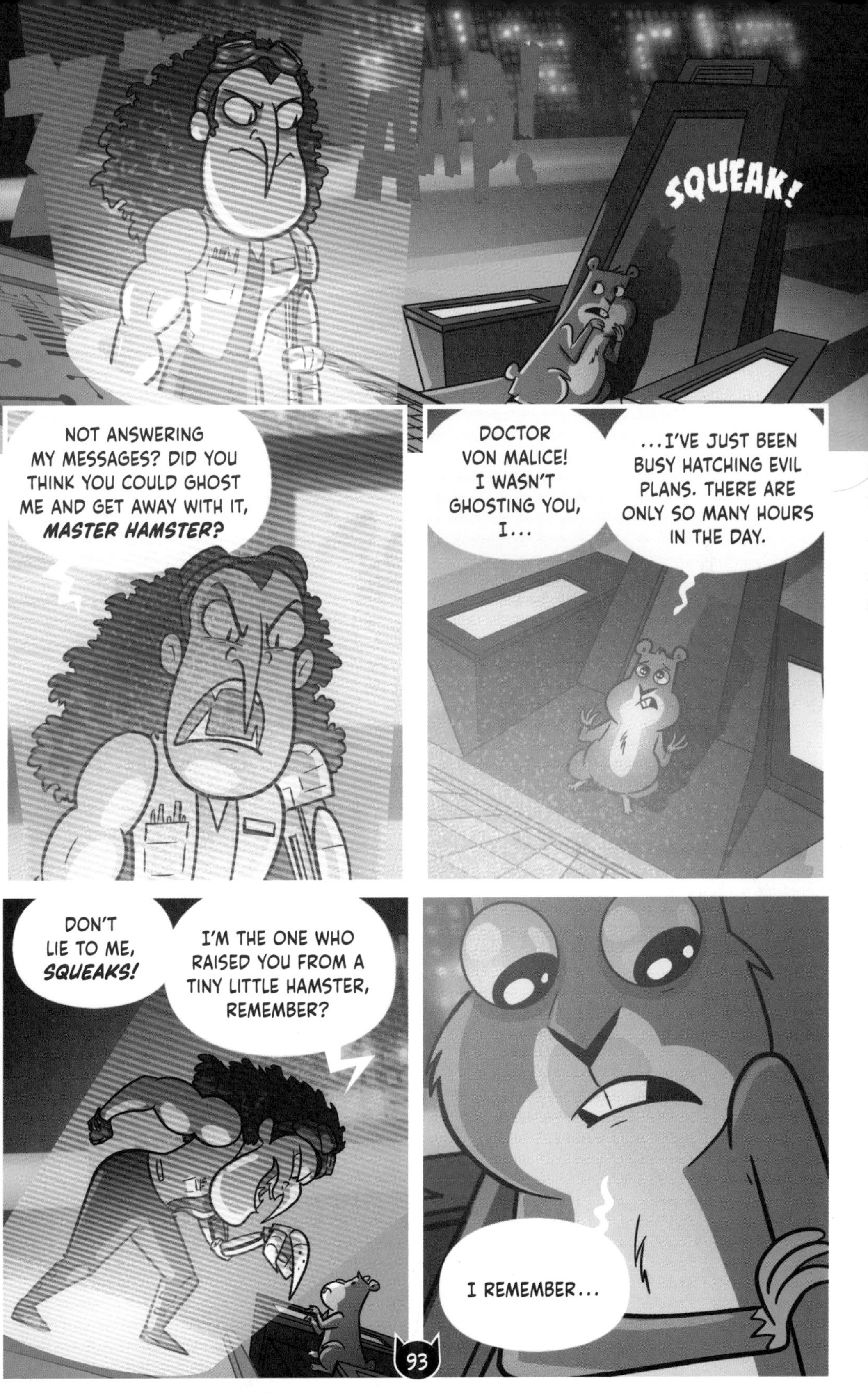
SQUEAK!
NOT ANSWERING MY MESSAGES? DID YOU THINK YOU COULD GHOST ME AND GET AWAY WITH IT, MASTER HAMSTER?
DOCTOR VON MALICE! I WASN'T GHOSTING YOU, I...
...I'VE JUST BEEN BUSY HATCHING EVIL PLANS. THERE ARE ONLY SO MANY HOURS IN THE DAY.
DON'T LIE TO ME, SQUEAKS!
I'M THE ONE WHO RAISED YOU FROM A TINY LITTLE HAMSTER, REMEMBER?
I REMEMBER...

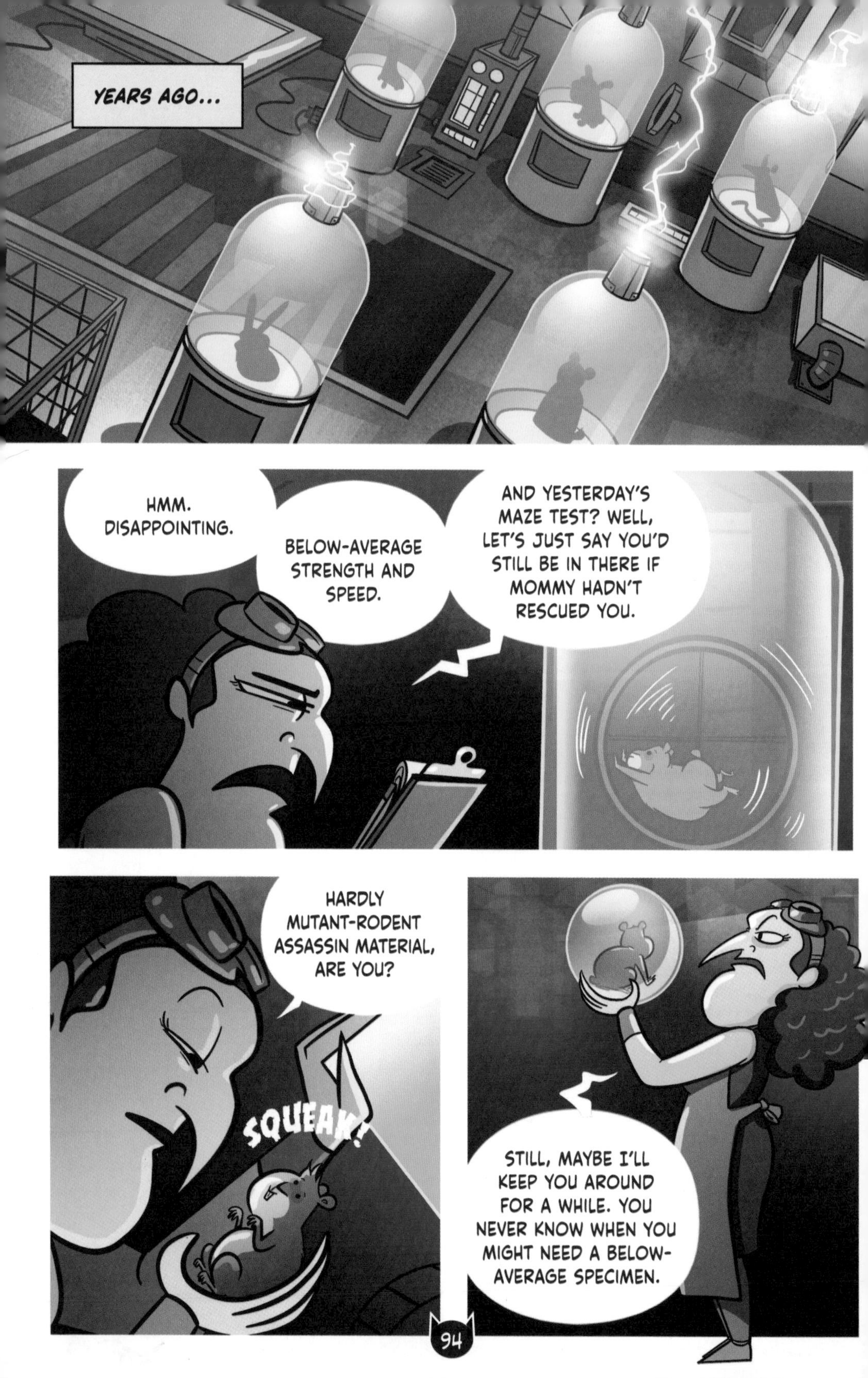
YEARS AGO...
HMM. DISAPPOINTING.
BELOW-AVERAGE STRENGTH AND SPEED.
AND YESTERDAY'S MAZE TEST? WELL, LET'S JUST SAY YOU'D STILL BE IN THERE IF MOMMY HADN'T RESCUED YOU.
HARDLY MUTANT-RODENT ASSASSIN MATERIAL, ARE YOU?
SQUEAK!
STILL, MAYBE I'LL KEEP YOU AROUND FOR A WHILE. YOU NEVER KNOW WHEN YOU MIGHT NEED A BELOW-AVERAGE SPECIMEN.

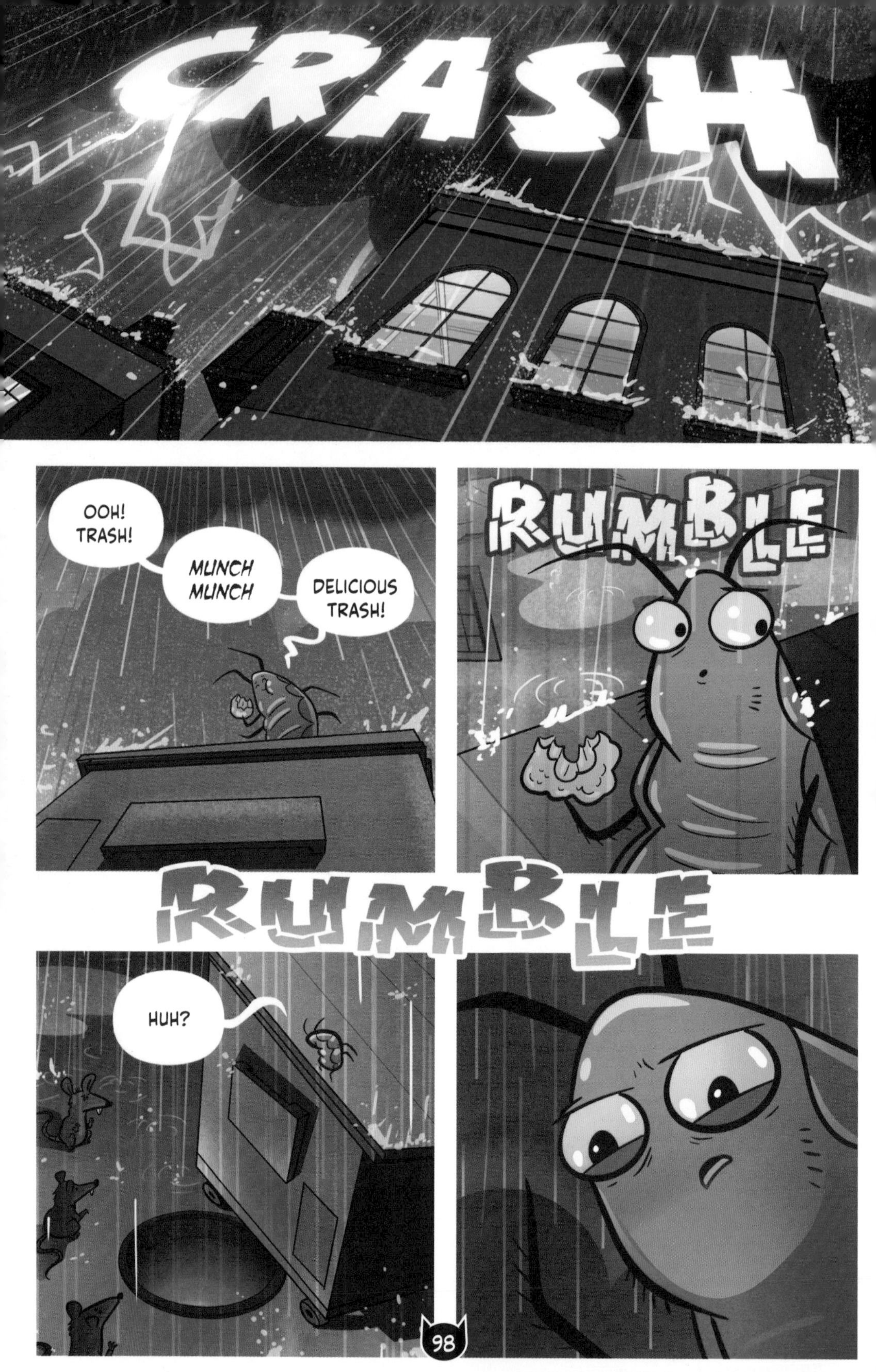
CRASH
OOH! TRASH!
MUNCH MUNCH
DELICIOUS TRASH!
RUMBLE
RUMBLE
HUH?

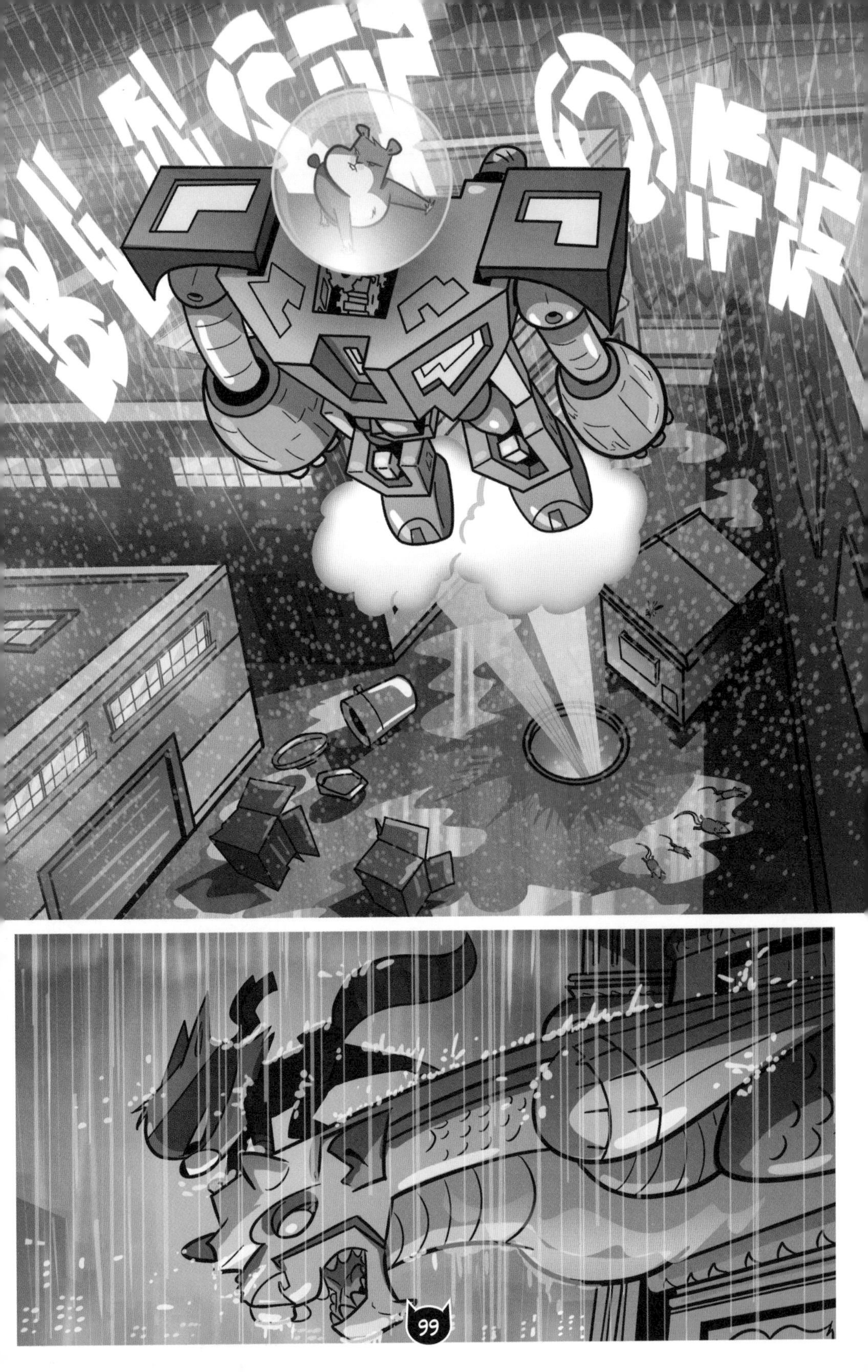
BLAST OFF

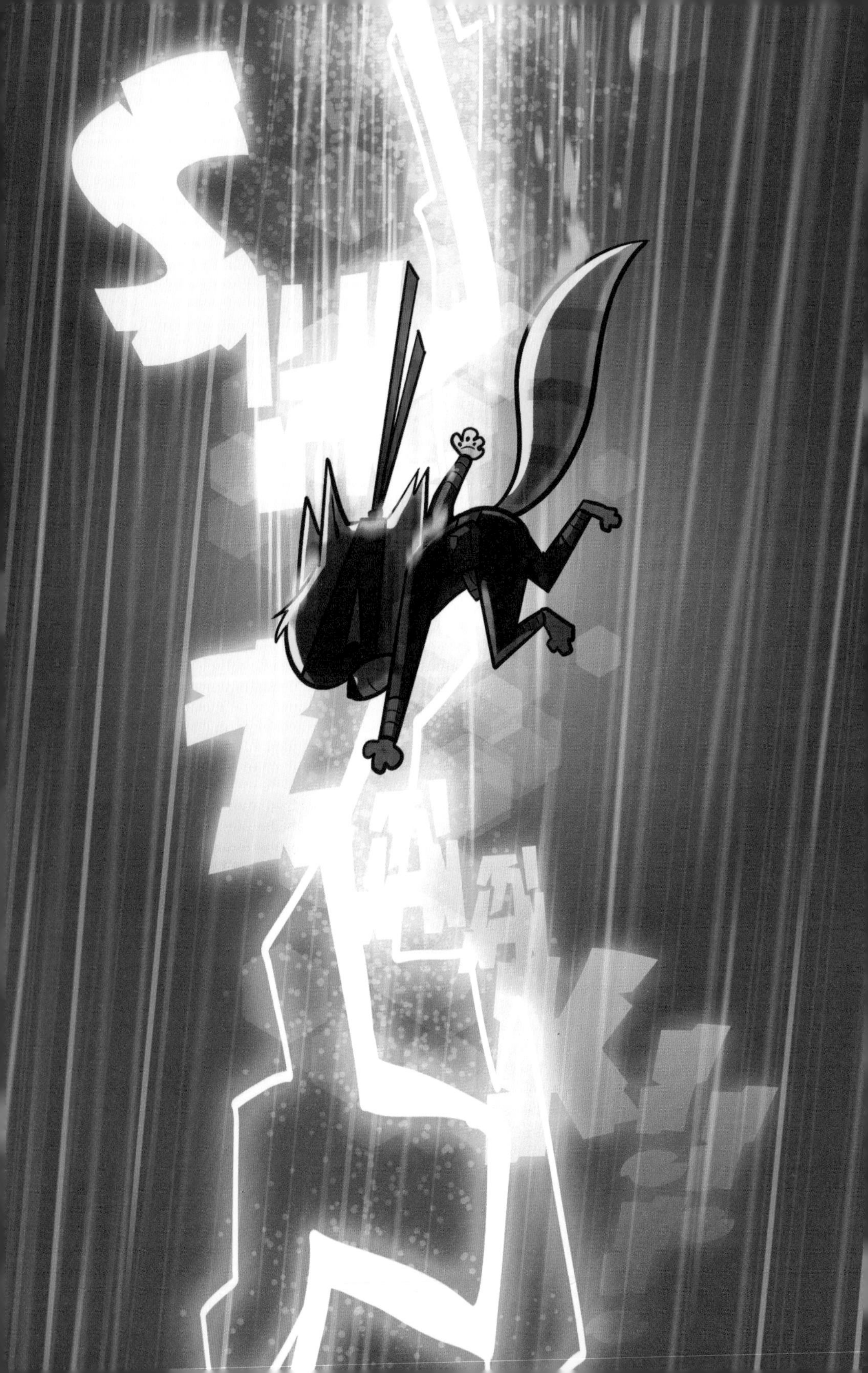

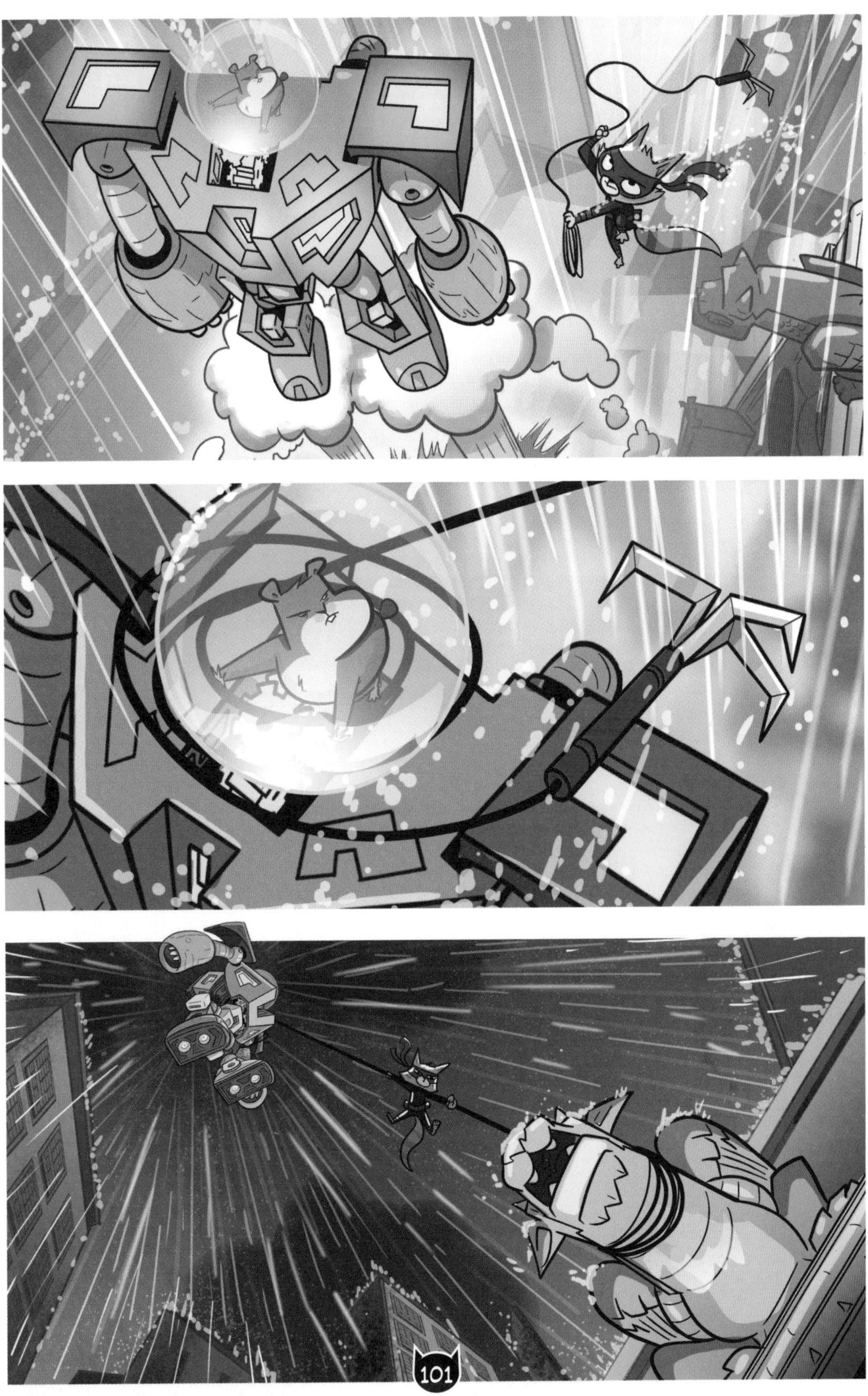

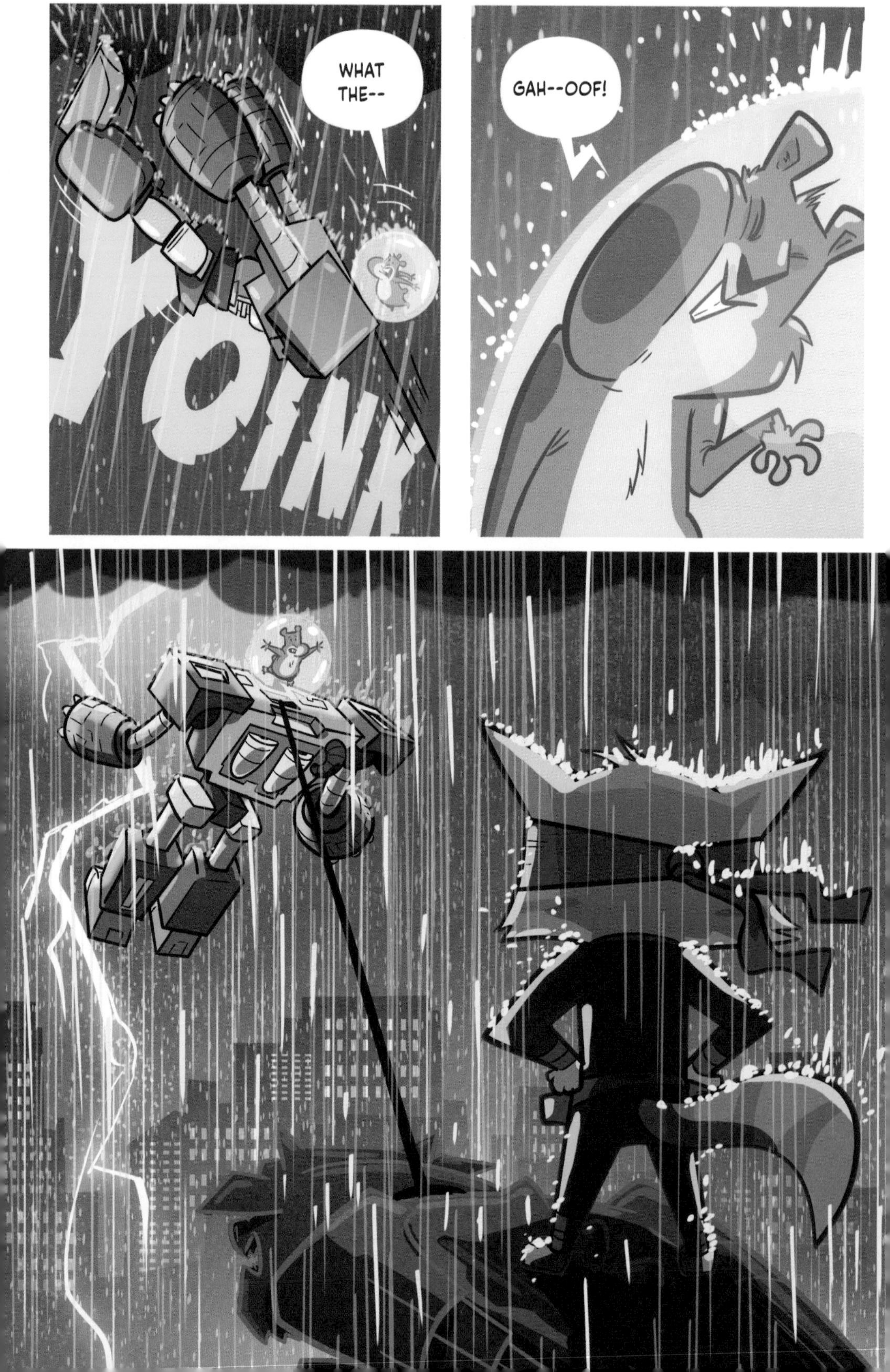
WHAT THE--
YOINK
GAH--OOF!

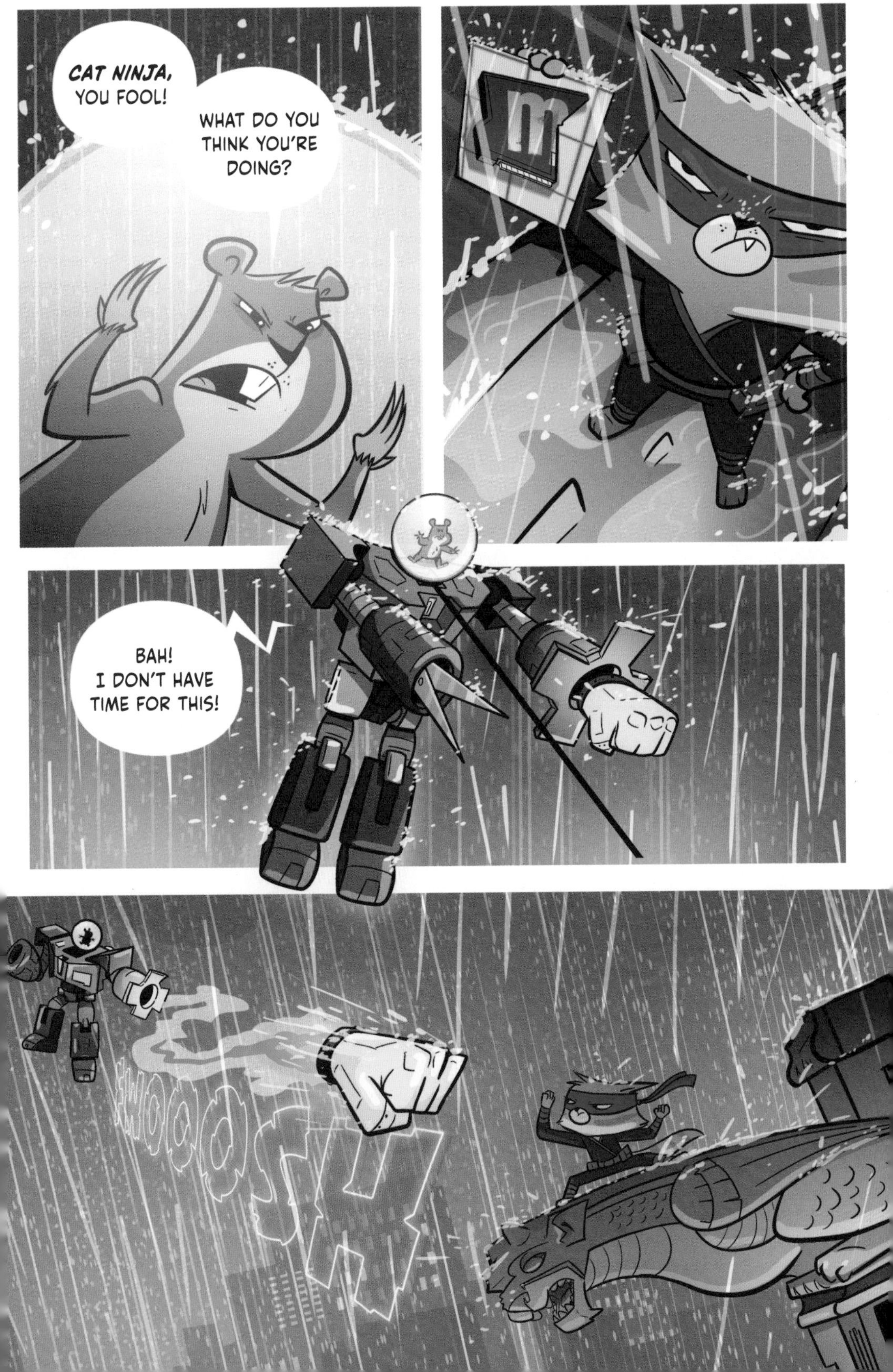
CAT NINJA, YOU FOOL!
WHAT DO YOU THINK YOU'RE DOING?
BAH! I DON'T HAVE TIME FOR THIS!

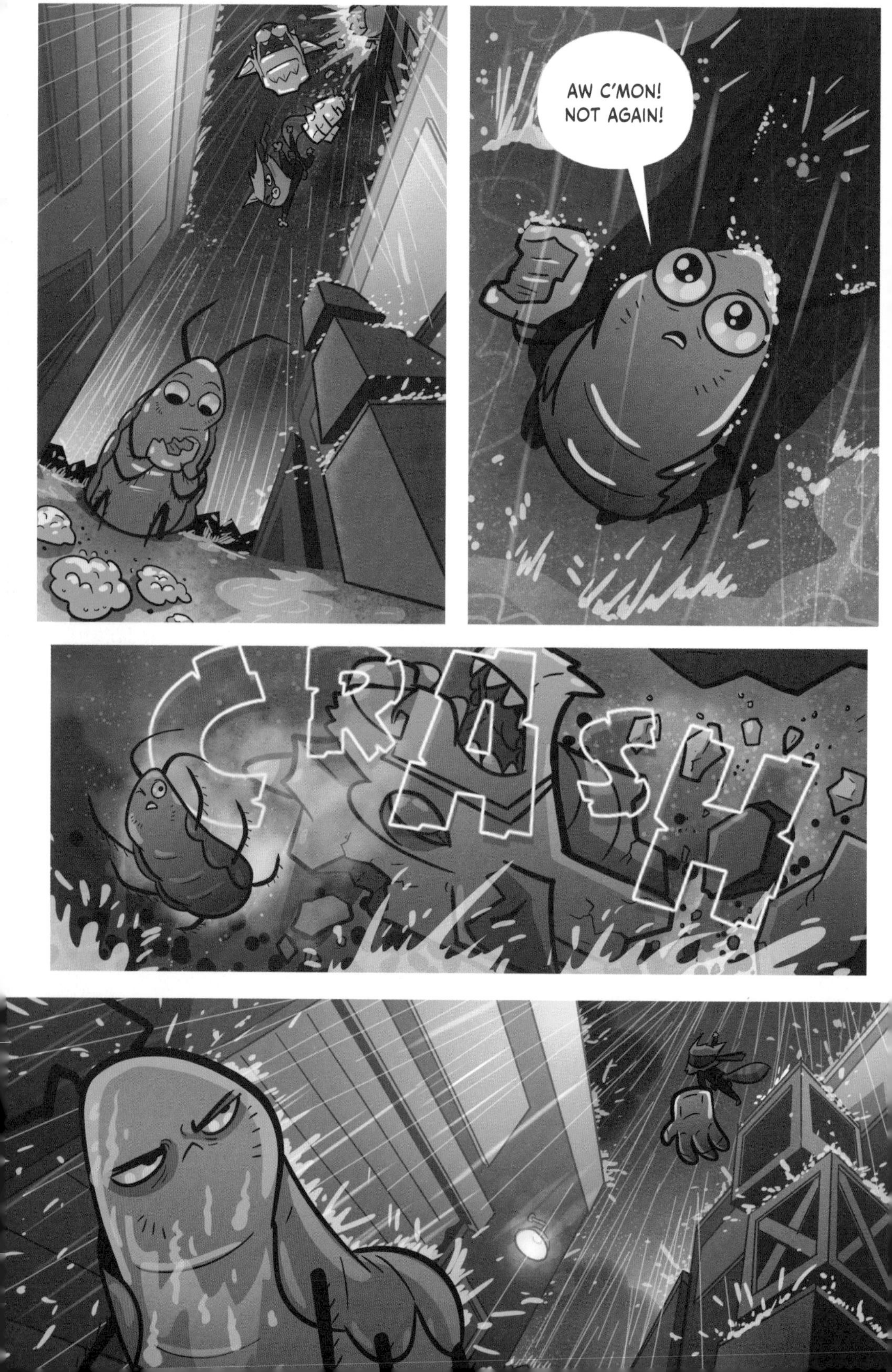
AW C'MON!
NOT AGAIN!
CRASH

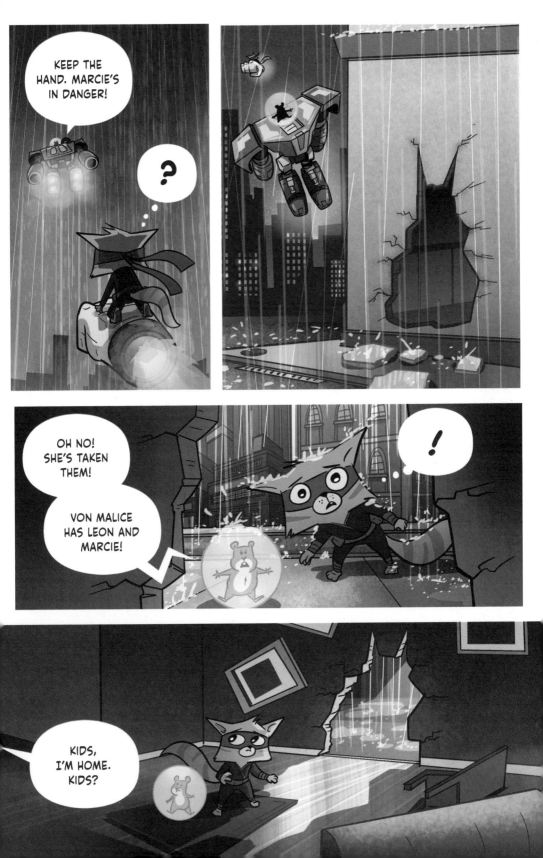

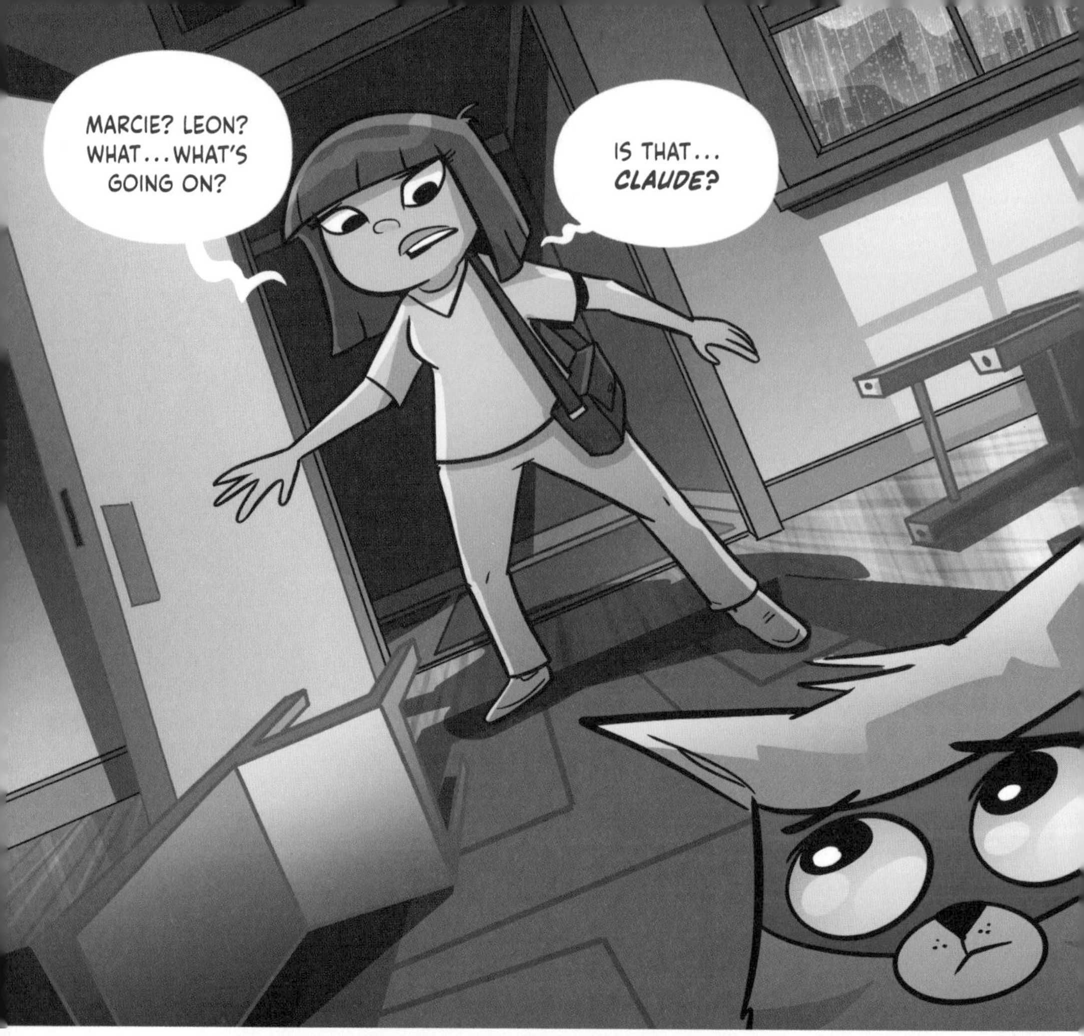
MARCIE? LEON? WHAT...WHAT'S GOING ON?
IS THAT... *CLAUDE?*

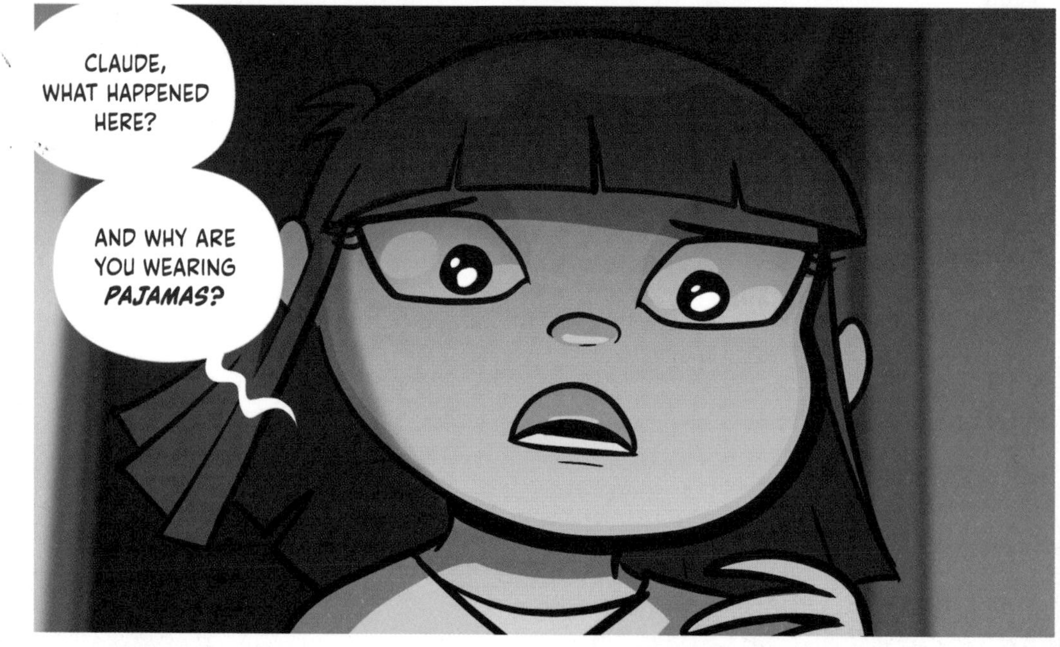
CLAUDE, WHAT HAPPENED HERE?
AND WHY ARE YOU WEARING *PAJAMAS?*

Chapter 5: *Family Squabbles*

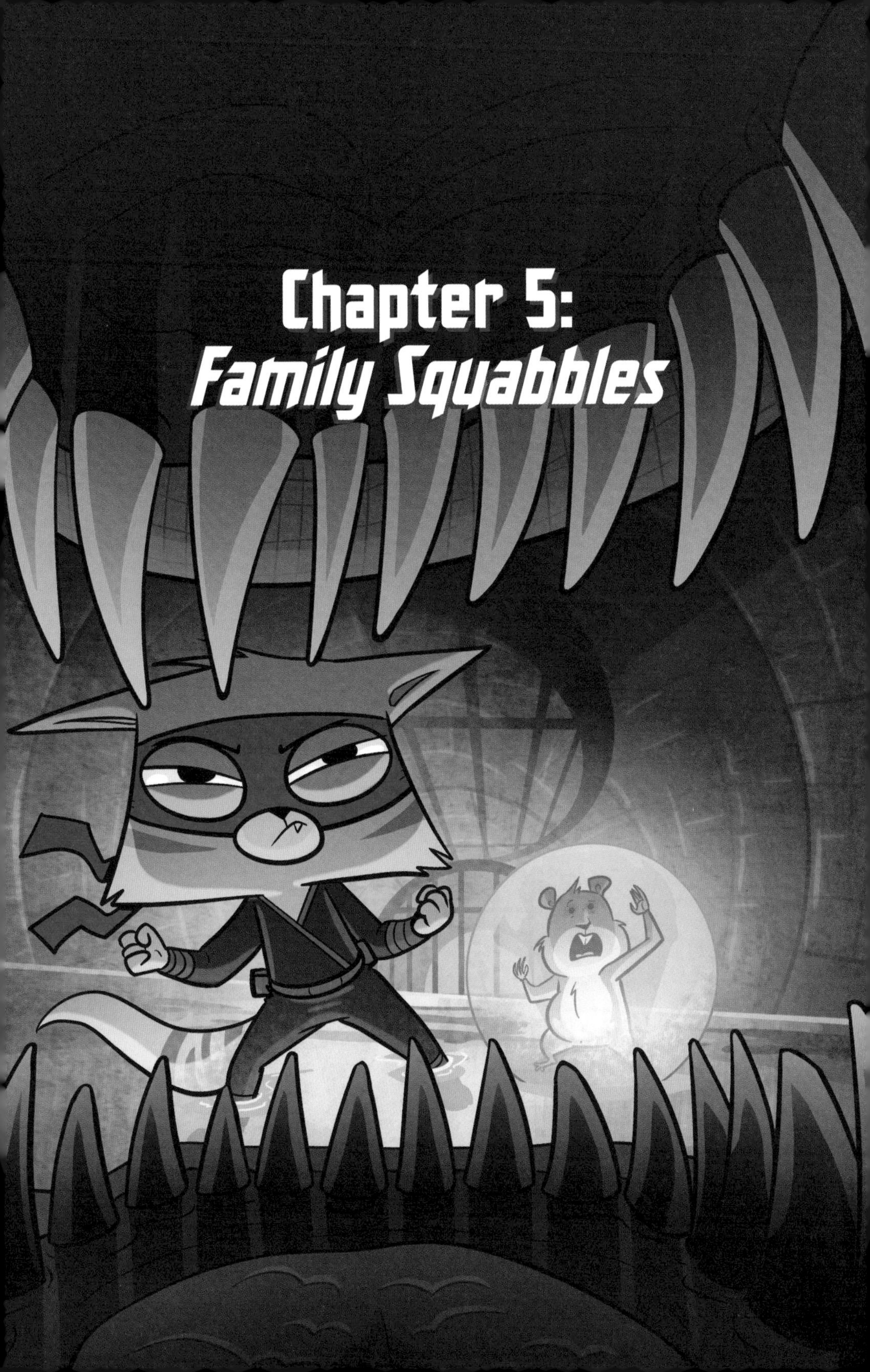

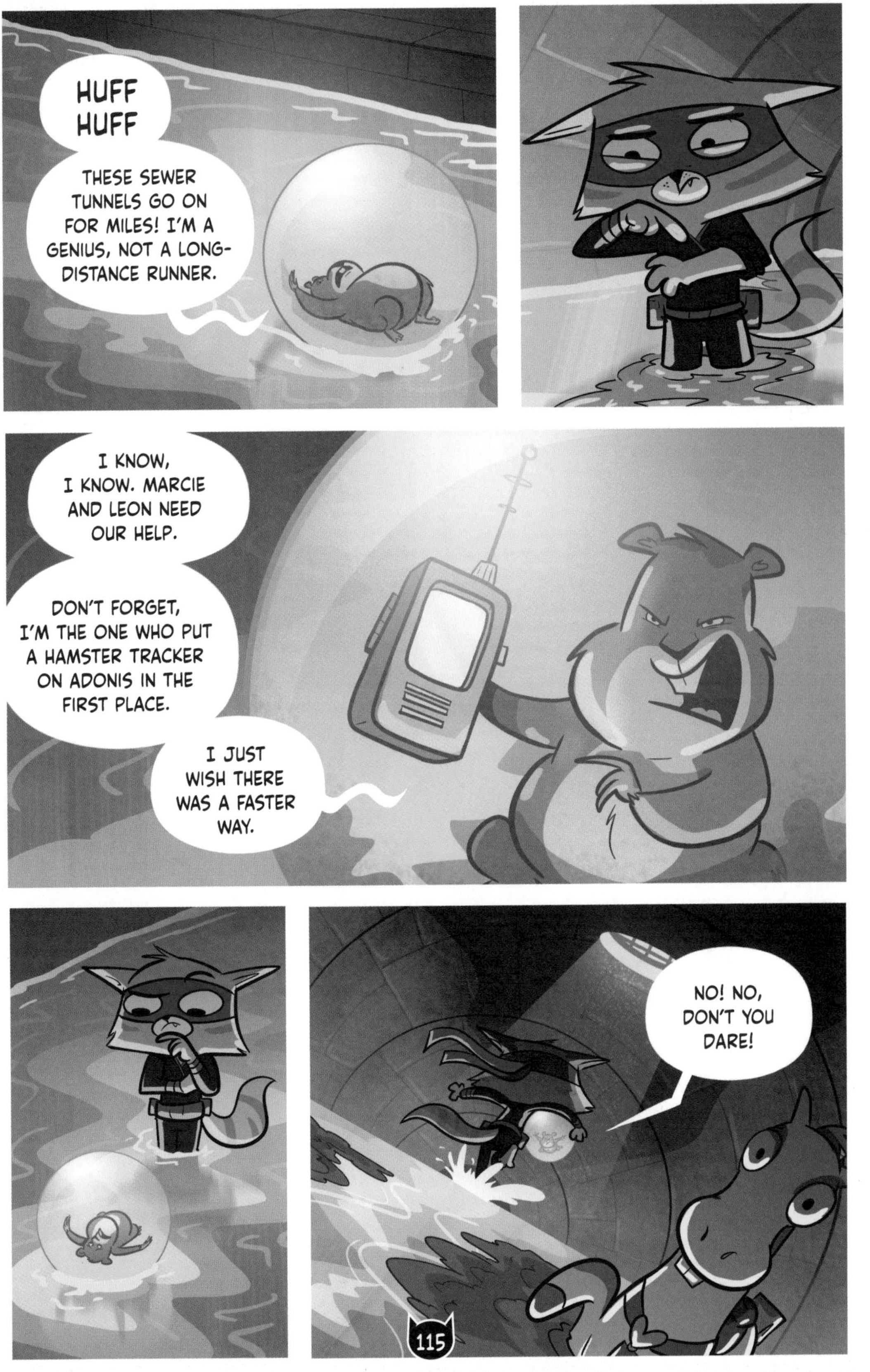
HUFF HUFF
THESE SEWER TUNNELS GO ON FOR MILES! I'M A GENIUS, NOT A LONG-DISTANCE RUNNER.
I KNOW, I KNOW. MARCIE AND LEON NEED OUR HELP.
DON'T FORGET, I'M THE ONE WHO PUT A HAMSTER TRACKER ON ADONIS IN THE FIRST PLACE.
I JUST WISH THERE WAS A FASTER WAY.
NO! NO, DON'T YOU DARE!

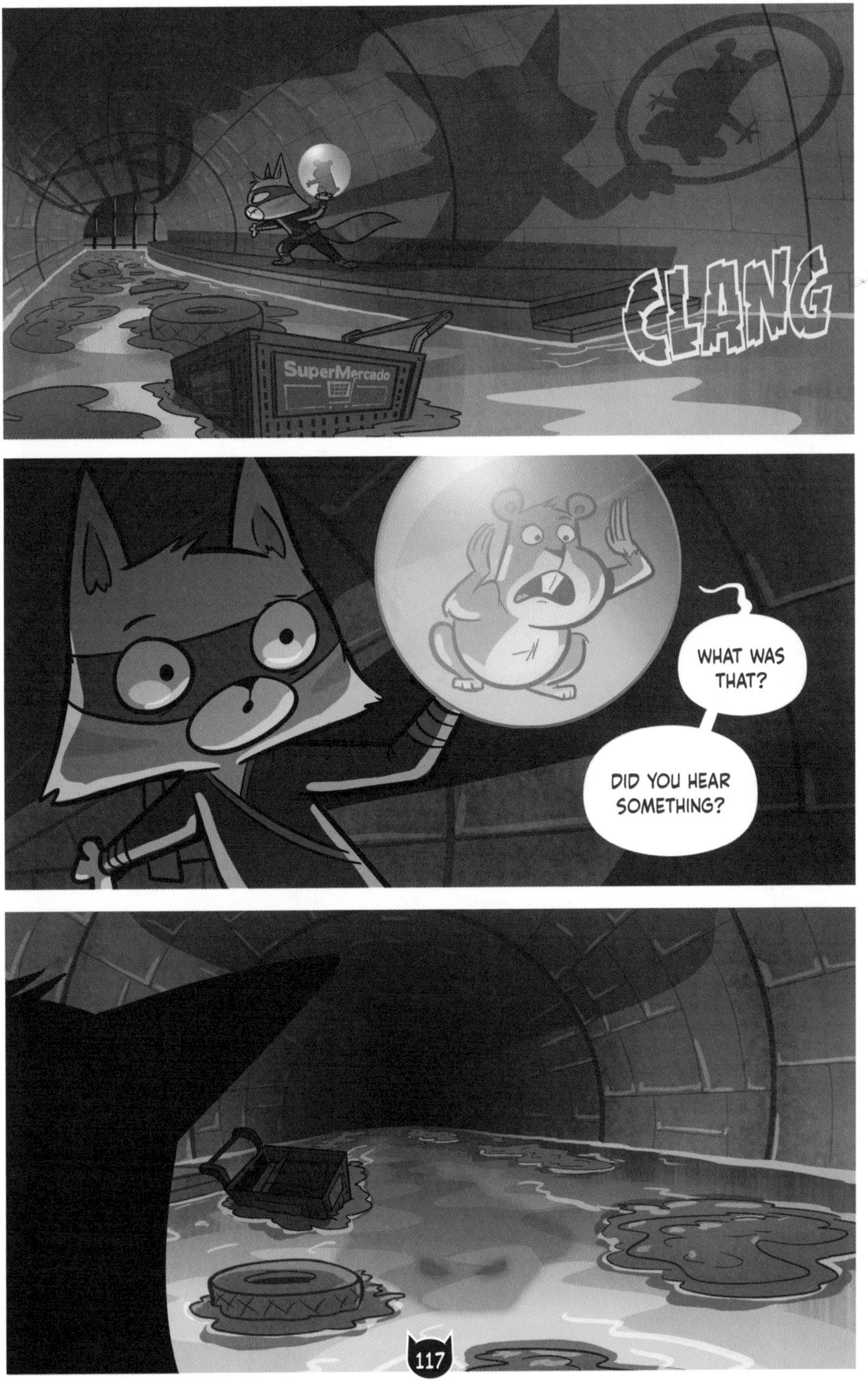
CLANG
WHAT WAS THAT?
DID YOU HEAR SOMETHING?

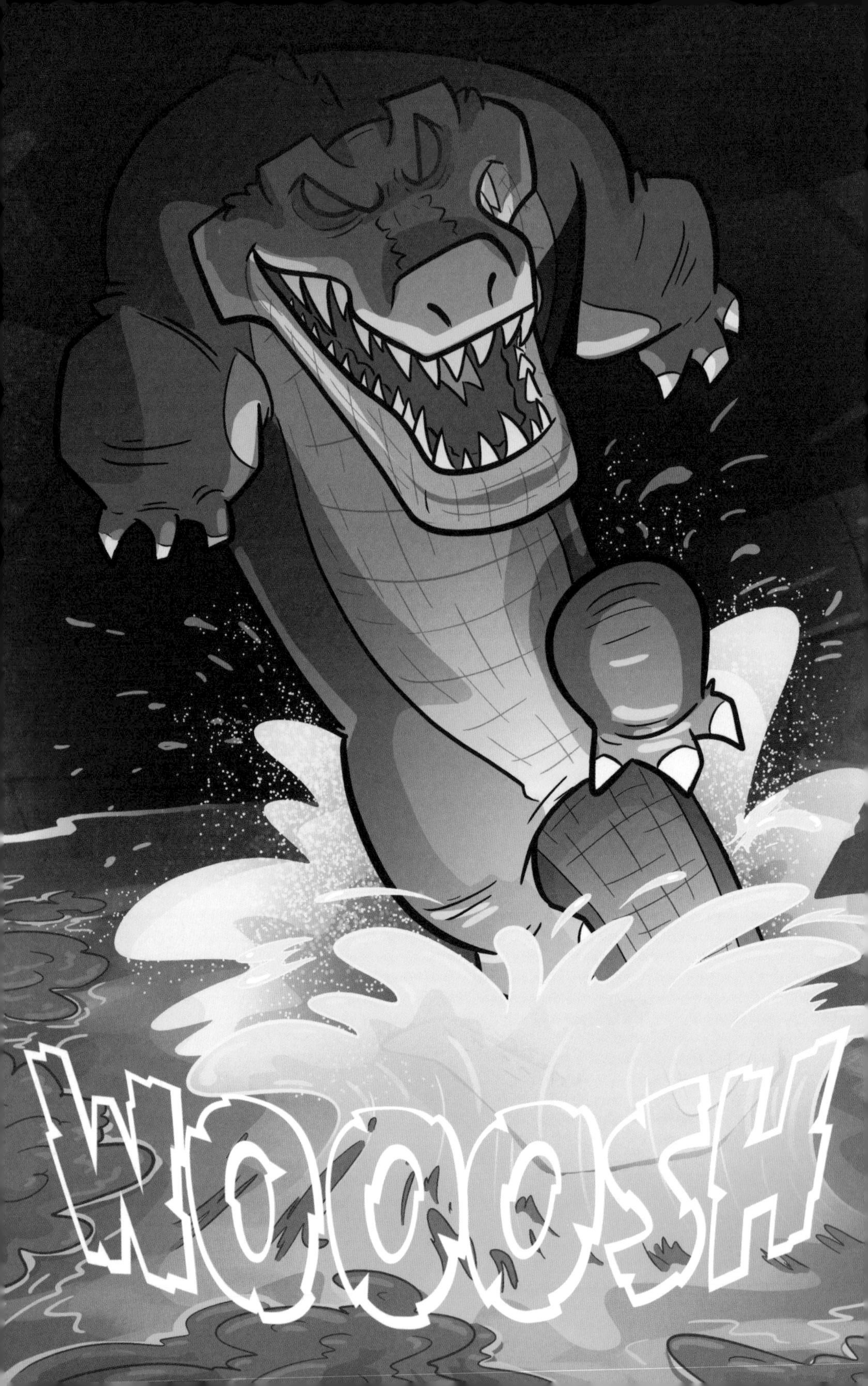
WOOOSH

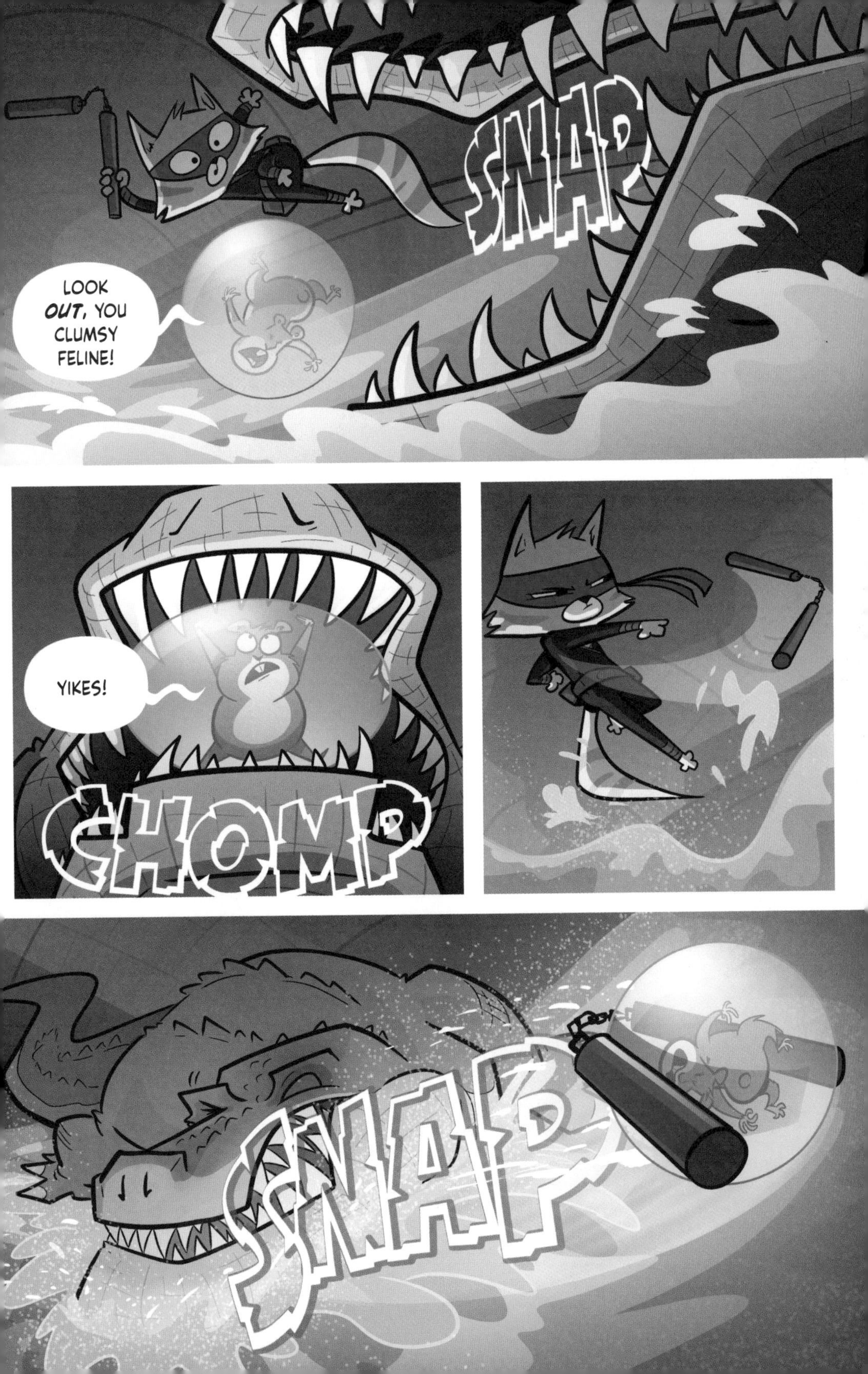

SNAP
LOOK OUT, YOU CLUMSY FELINE!
YIKES!
CHOMP
SNAP

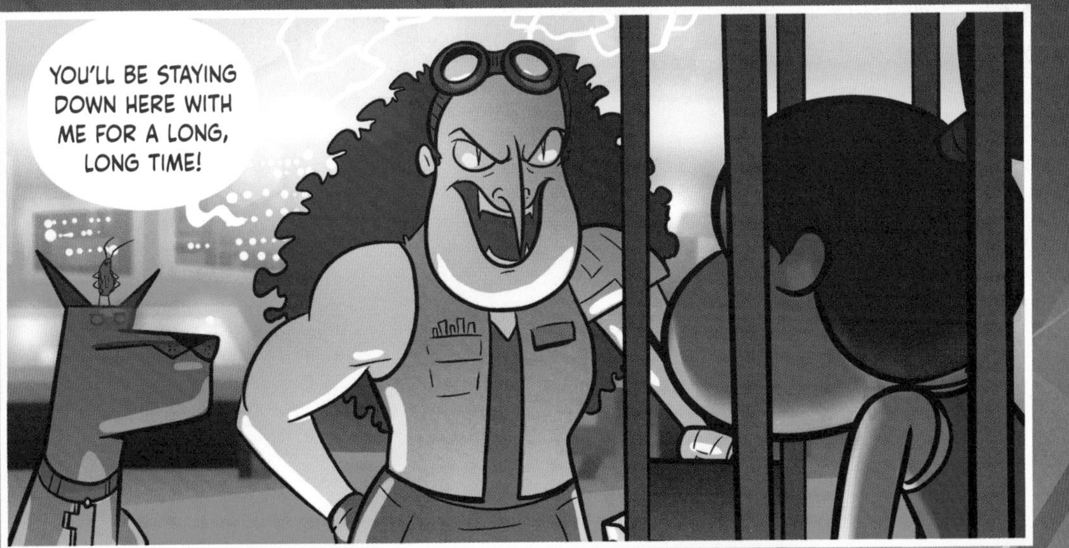

YOU'LL BE STAYING DOWN HERE WITH ME FOR A LONG, LONG TIME!

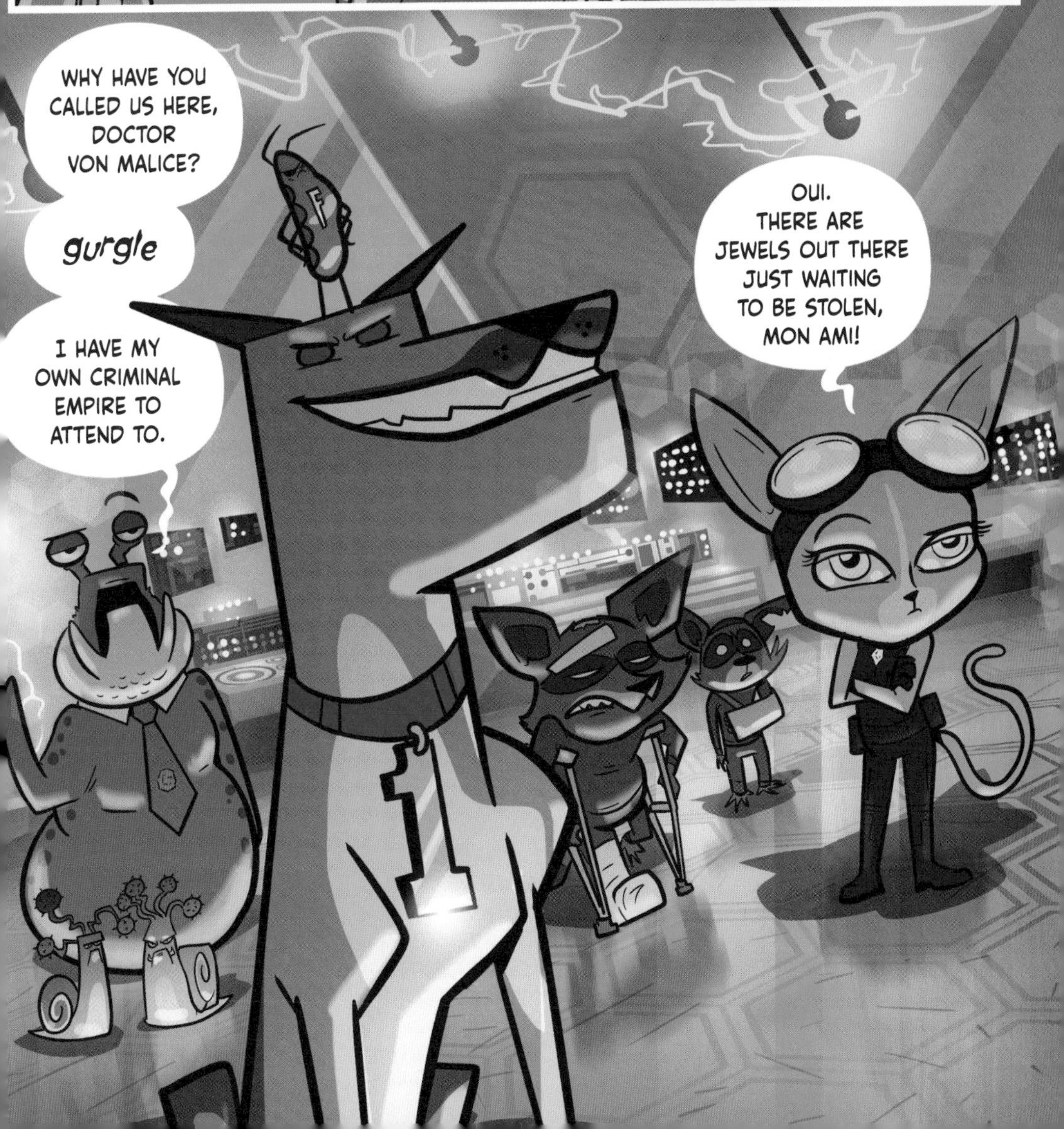

WHY HAVE YOU CALLED US HERE, DOCTOR VON MALICE?
gurgle
I HAVE MY OWN CRIMINAL EMPIRE TO ATTEND TO.
OUI. THERE ARE JEWELS OUT THERE JUST WAITING TO BE STOLEN, MON AMI!

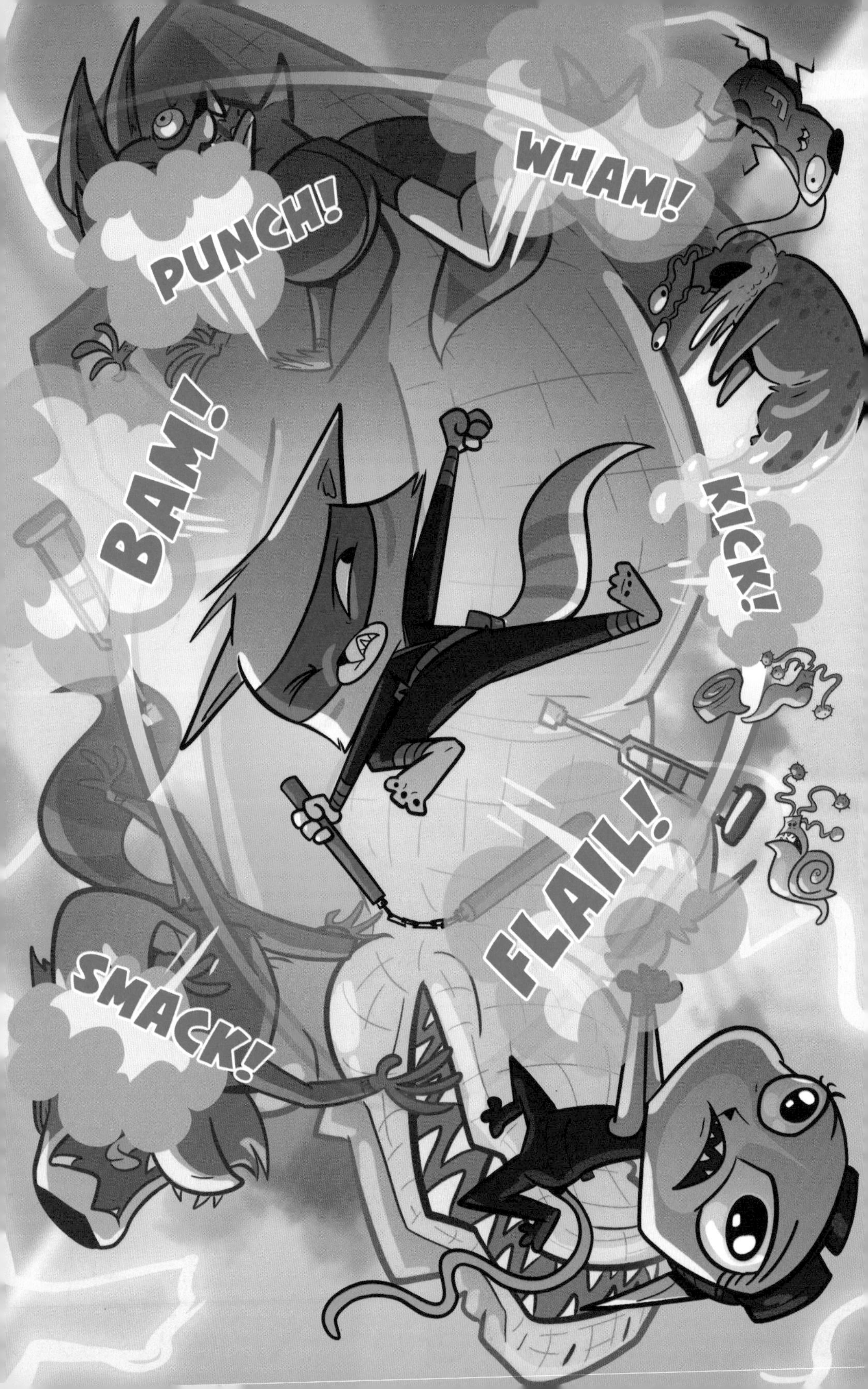
PUNCH!
WHAM!
BAM!
KICK!
FLAIL!
SMACK!

WHUMP!

THUD!

SPLAT!

IMPRESSIVE. BUT ALSO *ANTICIPATED.*

ADONIS!

BRING ME THE HOSTAGES!

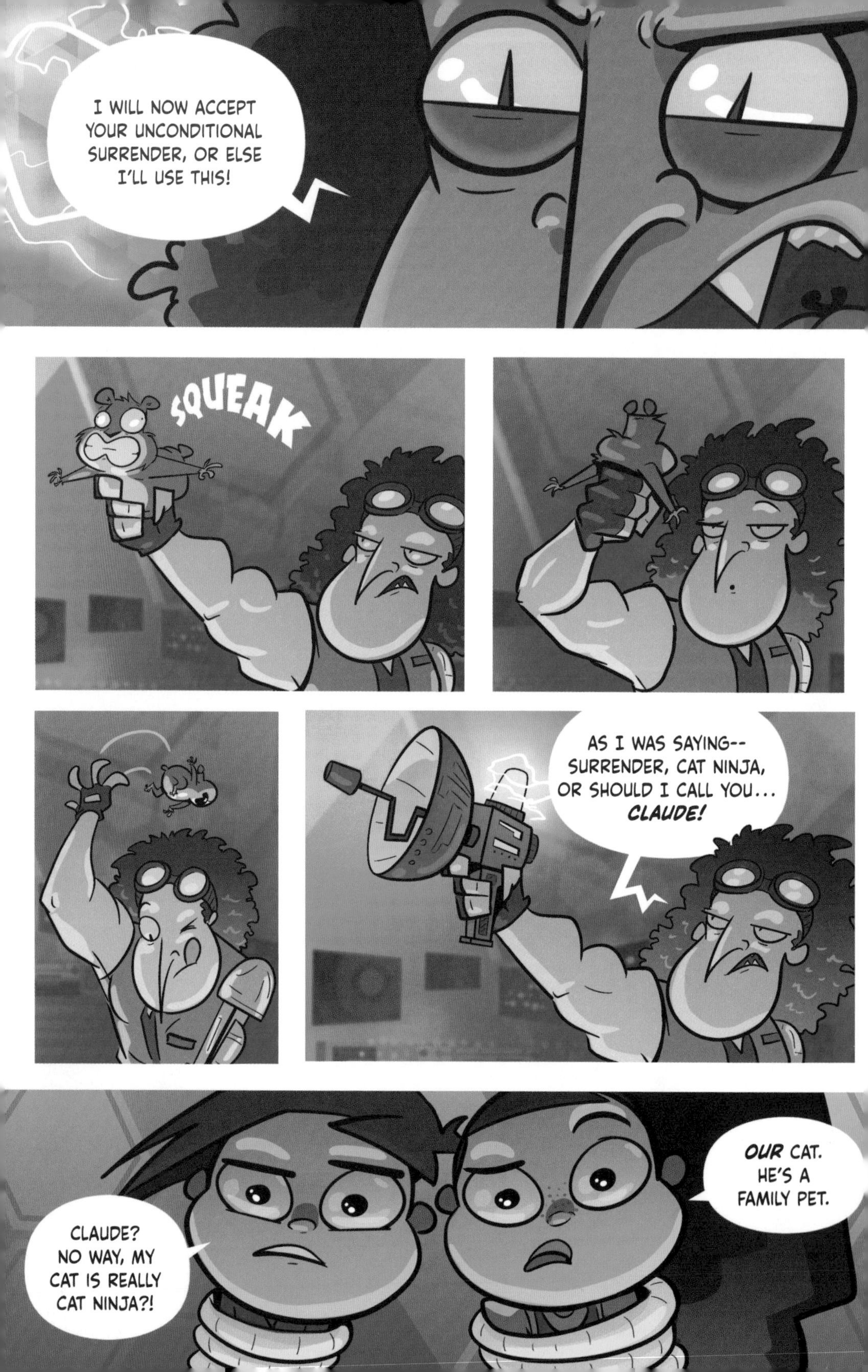
I WILL NOW ACCEPT YOUR UNCONDITIONAL SURRENDER, OR ELSE I'LL USE THIS!
SQUEAK
AS I WAS SAYING-- SURRENDER, CAT NINJA, OR SHOULD I CALL YOU... *CLAUDE!*
CLAUDE? NO WAY, MY CAT IS REALLY CAT NINJA?!
OUR CAT. HE'S A FAMILY PET.

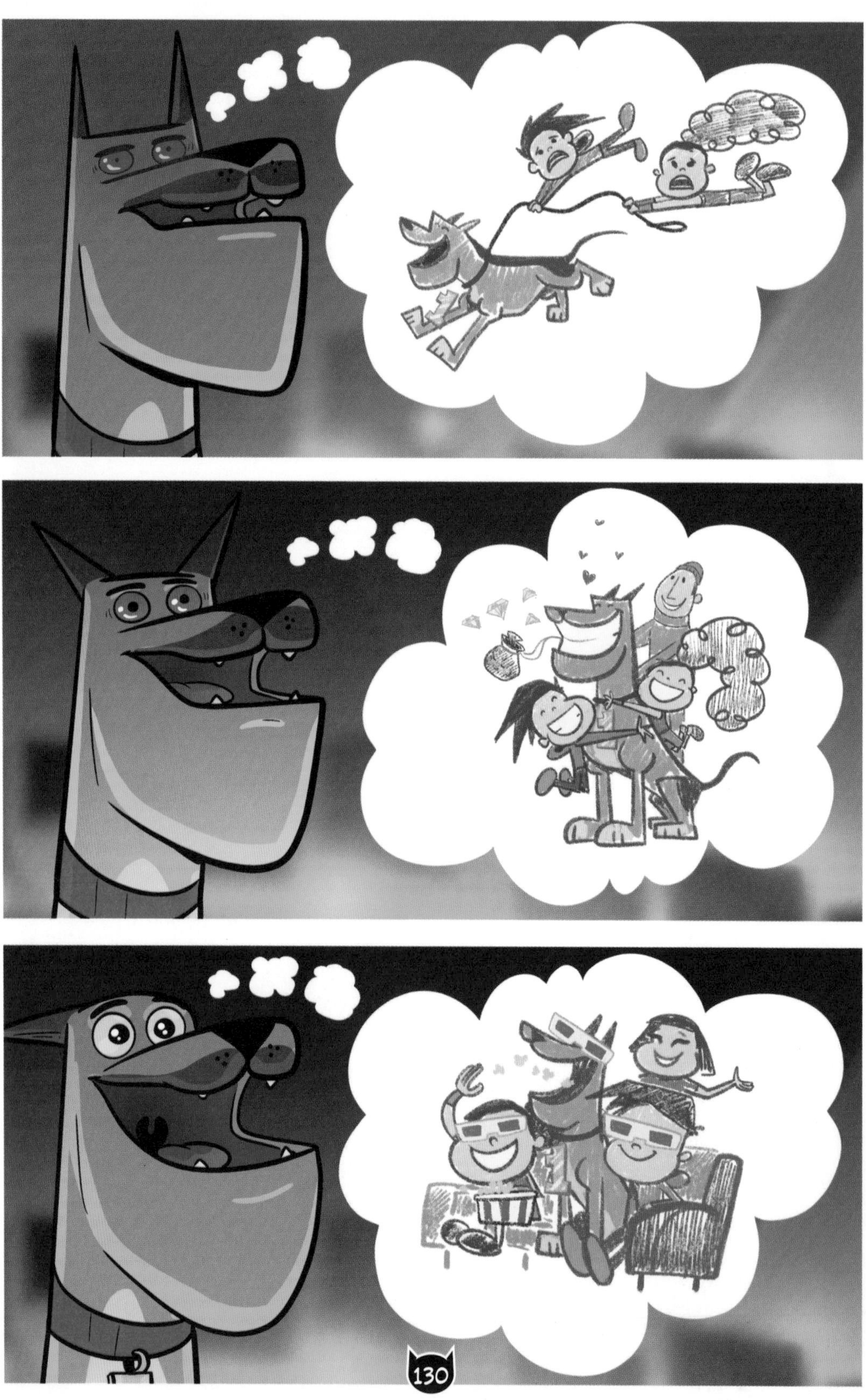

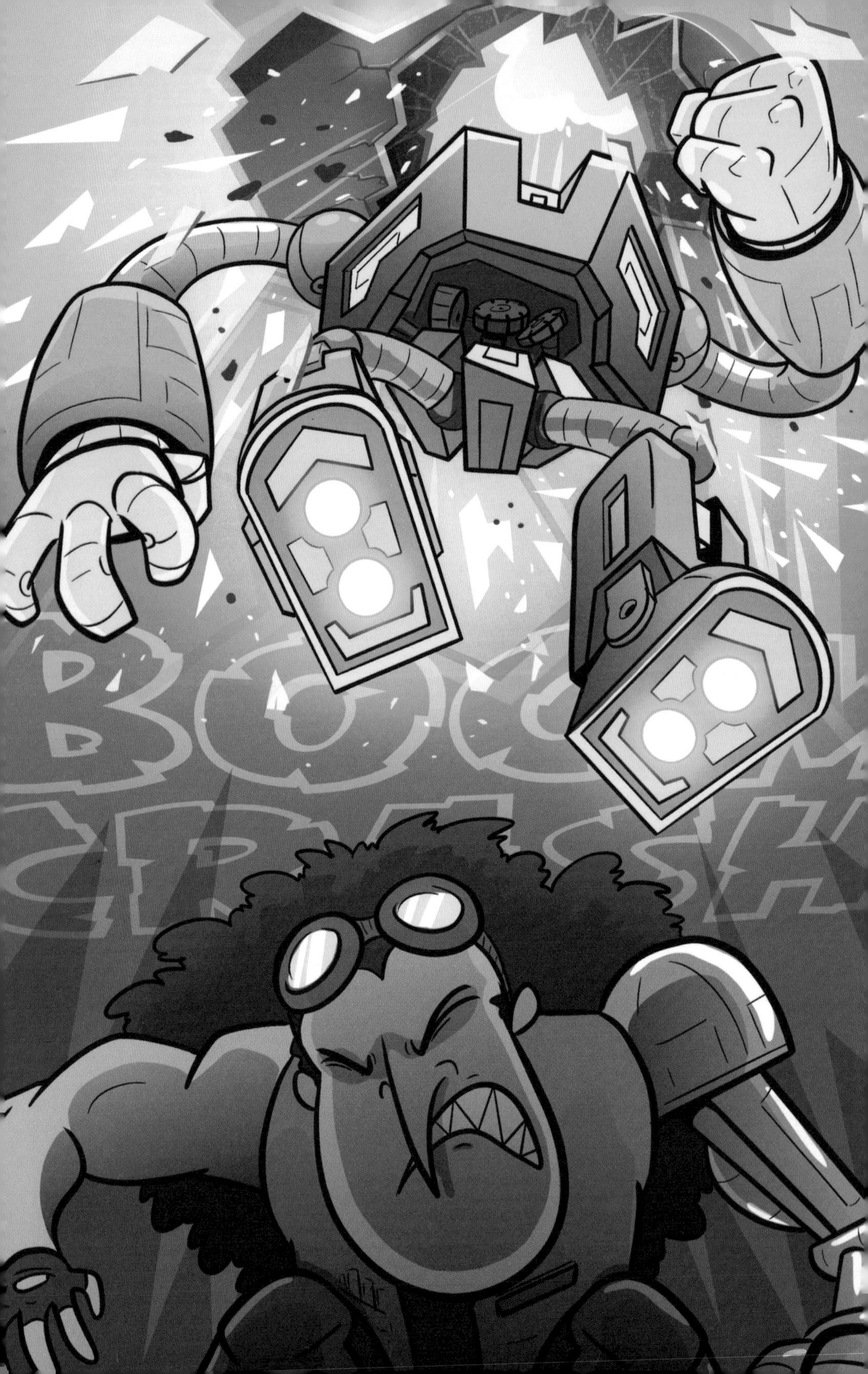

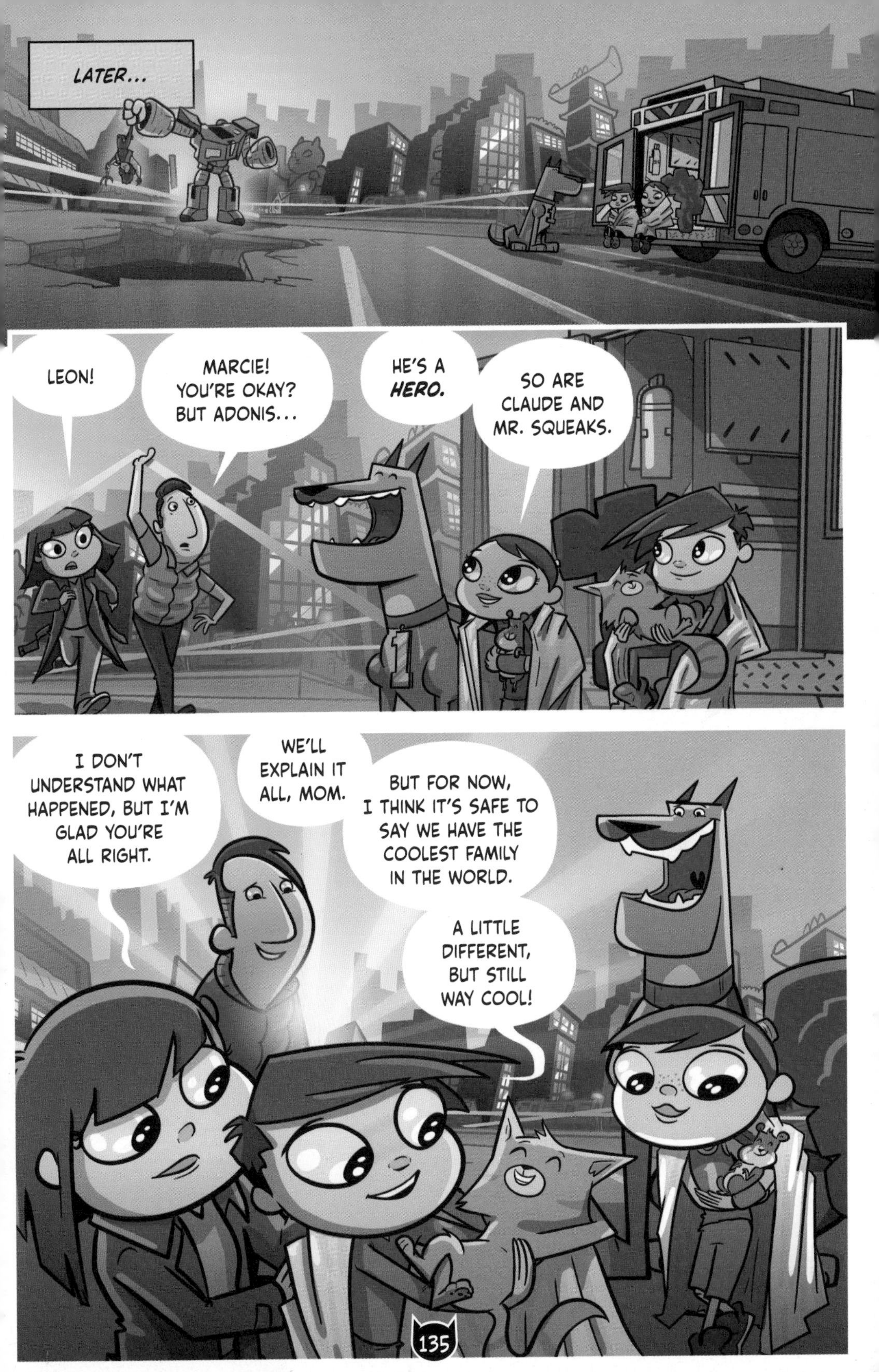
LATER...
LEON!
MARCIE! YOU'RE OKAY? BUT ADONIS...
HE'S A **HERO.**
SO ARE CLAUDE AND MR. SQUEAKS.
I DON'T UNDERSTAND WHAT HAPPENED, BUT I'M GLAD YOU'RE ALL RIGHT.
WE'LL EXPLAIN IT ALL, MOM.
BUT FOR NOW, I THINK IT'S SAFE TO SAY WE HAVE THE COOLEST FAMILY IN THE WORLD.
A LITTLE DIFFERENT, BUT STILL WAY COOL!

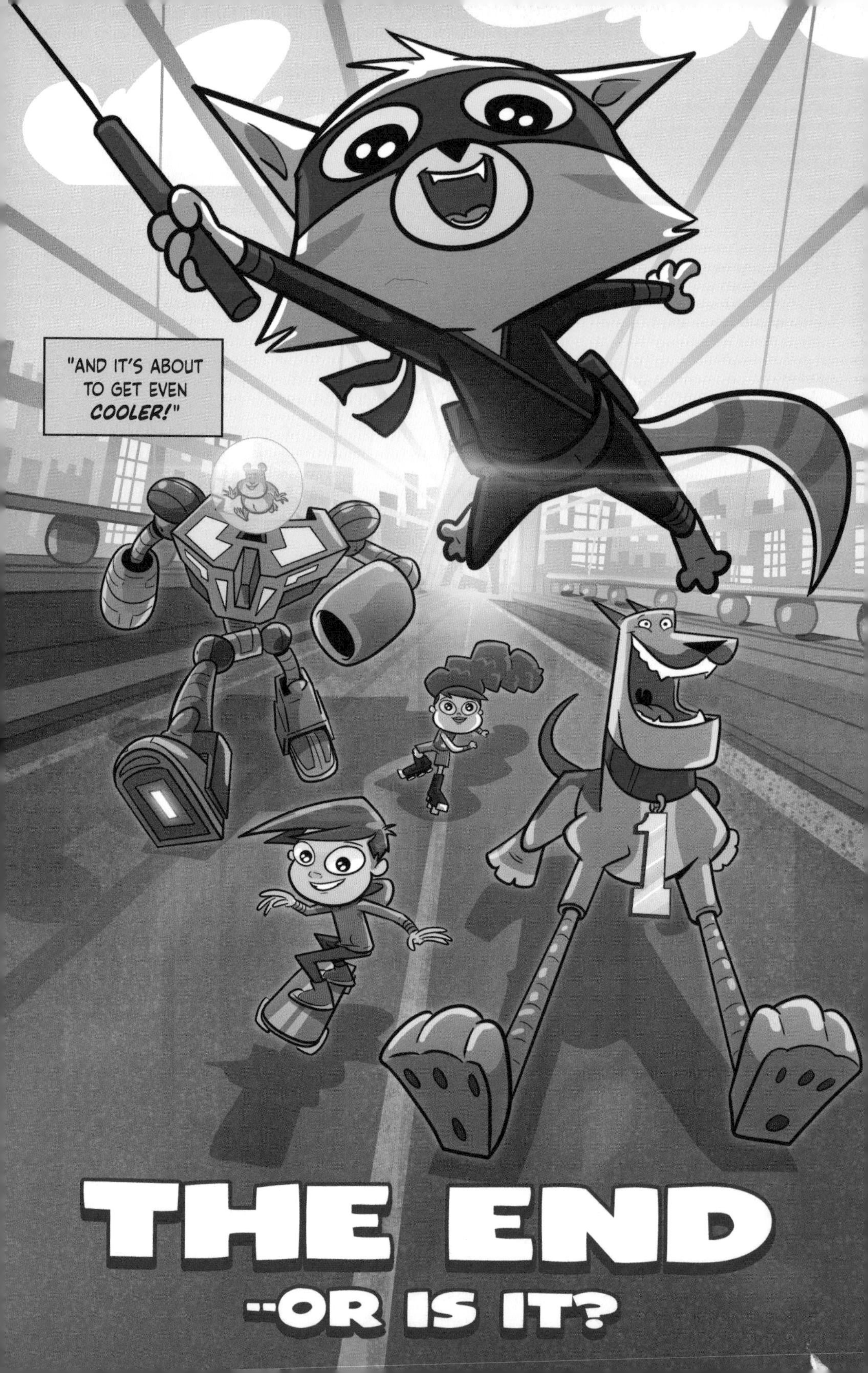
"AND IT'S ABOUT TO GET EVEN COOLER!"
THE END
--OR IS IT?

About the Author

MATTHEW CODY is the author of several popular books, including the award-winning *Supers of Noble's Green* trilogy: *Powerless*, *Super*, and *Villainous*. He is also the author of *Will in Scarlet* and *The Dead Gentleman*, as well as the graphic novel *Zatanna and the House of Secrets* from DC Comics. He lives in Manhattan with his wife and son.

About the Illustrator

YEHUDI MERCADO was born in Mexico City and raised in Houston, Texas. He is a former Disney art director turned successful graphic novelist. His graphic novels as writer-illustrator include *Buffalo Speedway*, *Pantalones, TX*, *Rocket Salvage*, and *Sci-Fu: Kick it Off*. He is currently showrunning a narrative podcast based on his graphic novel *Hero Hotel*.

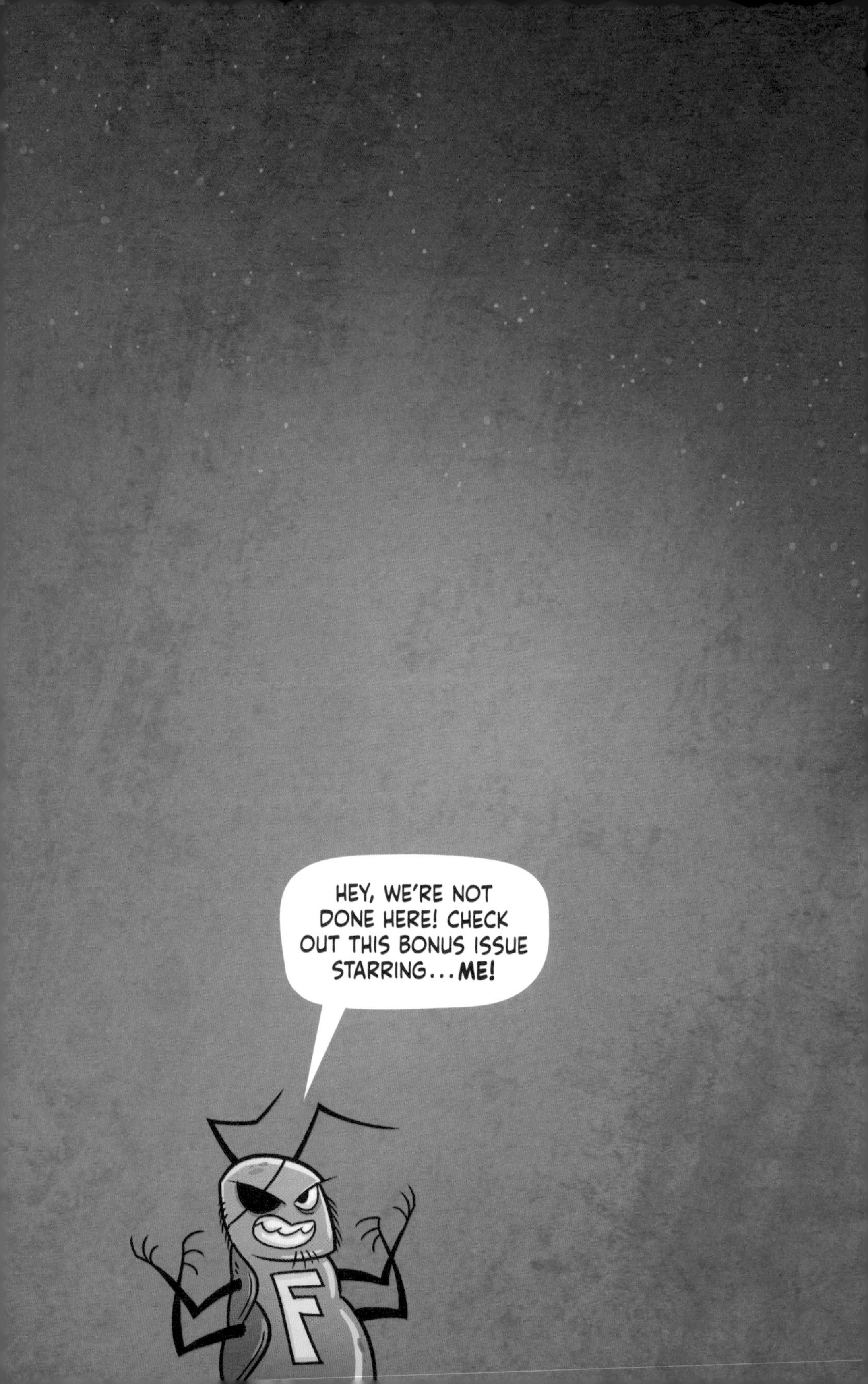
HEY, WE'RE NOT DONE HERE! CHECK OUT THIS BONUS ISSUE STARRING...ME!

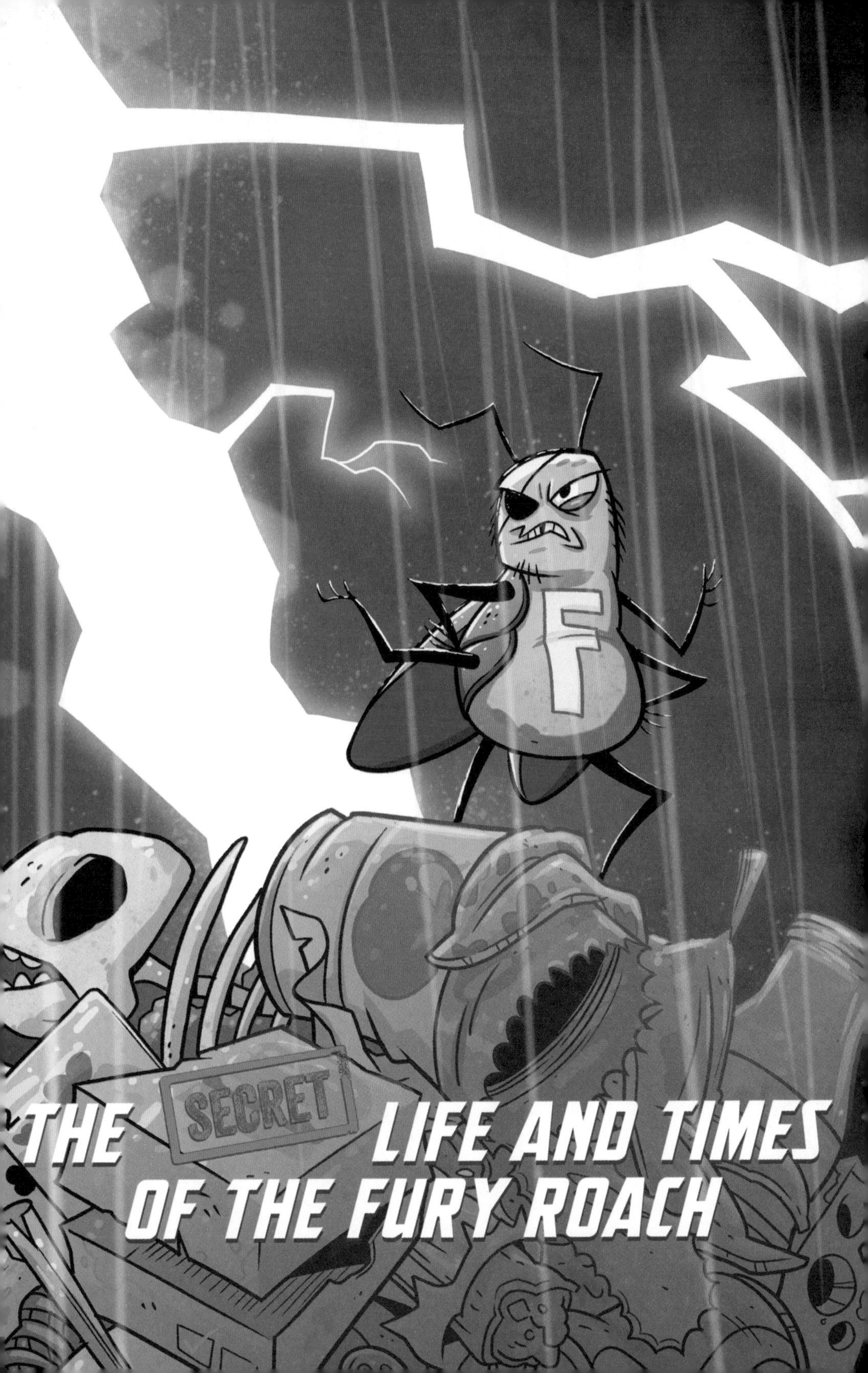
THE SECRET LIFE AND TIMES
OF THE FURY ROACH

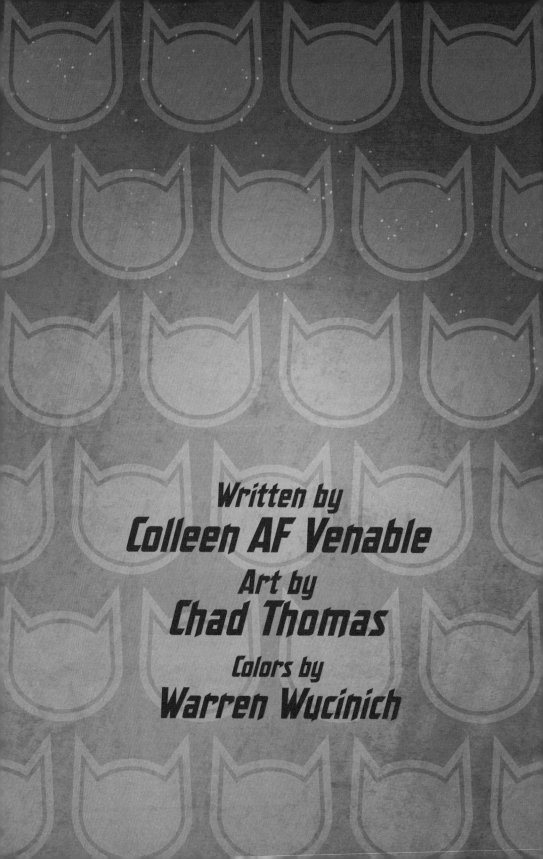

Written by
Colleen AF Venable
Art by
Chad Thomas
Colors by
Warren Wucinich

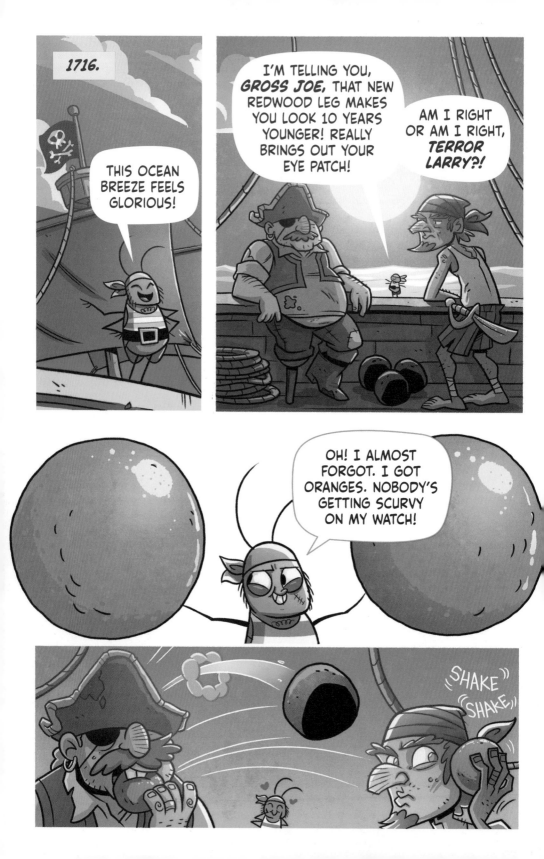

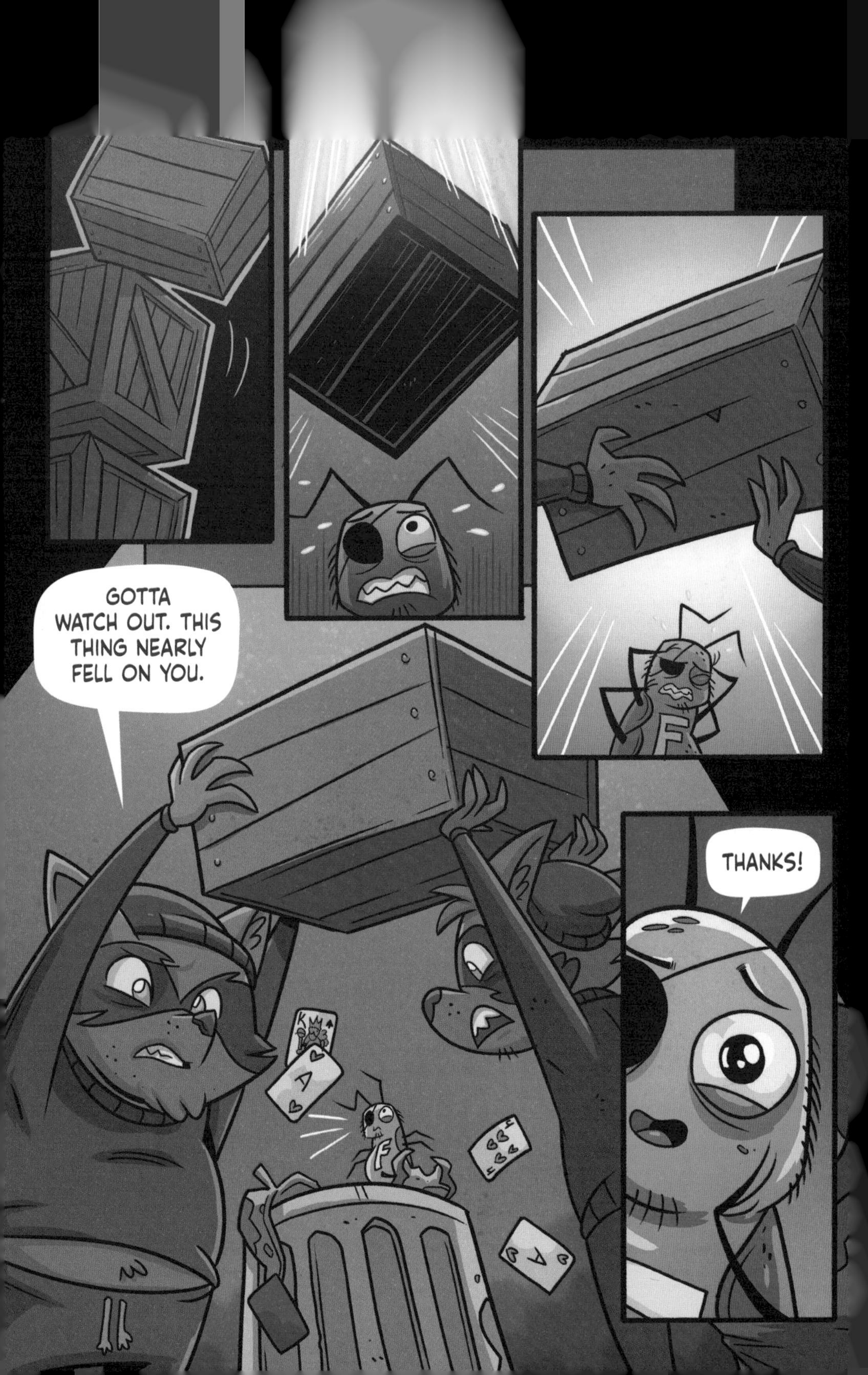
GOTTA WATCH OUT. THIS THING NEARLY FELL ON YOU.
THANKS!

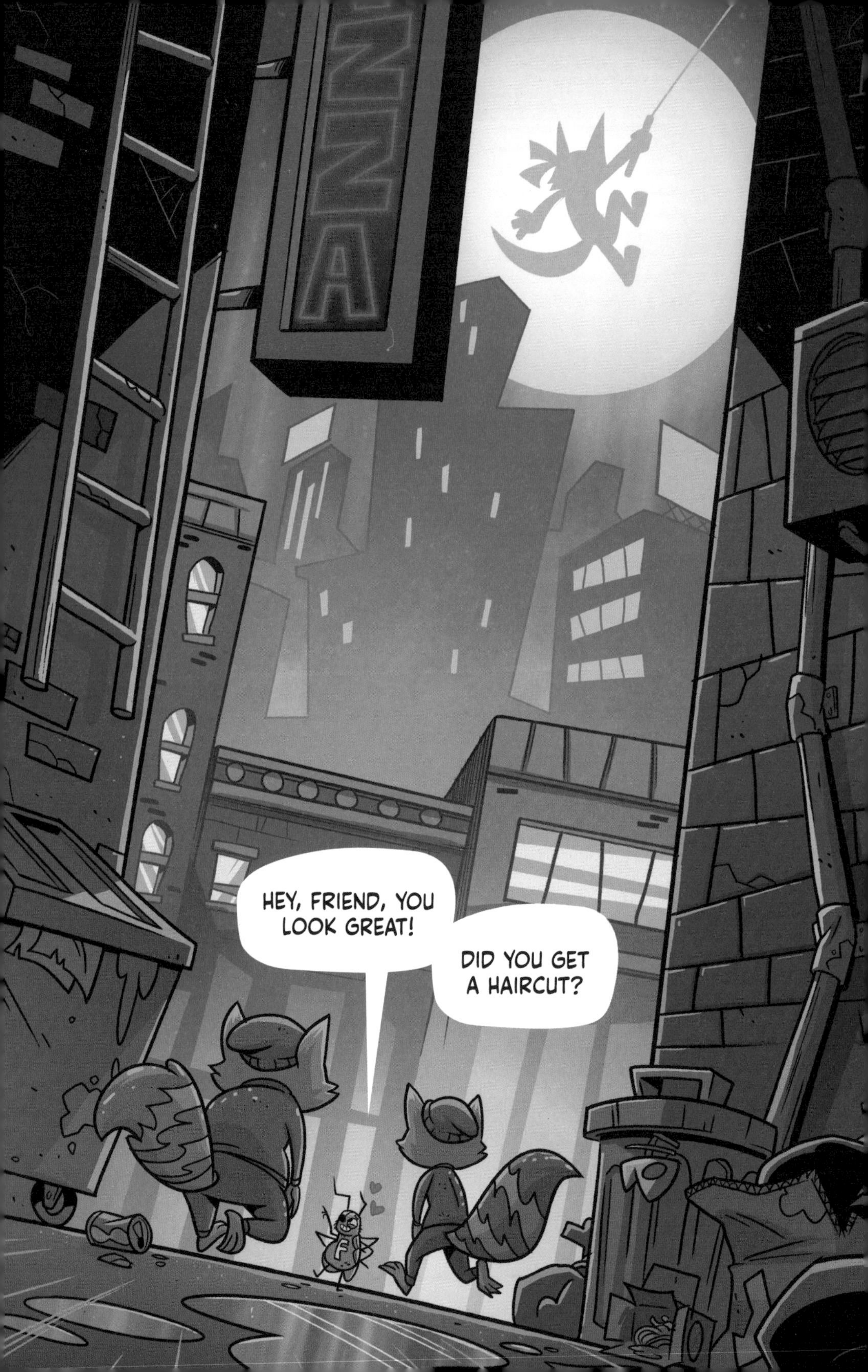
HEY, FRIEND, YOU LOOK GREAT!
DID YOU GET A HAIRCUT?

Is Your Pet a Superhero or a Supervillain?

Answer the following questions and then tally up your responses to find out. (If you don't have a pet, use your favorite houseplant instead!)

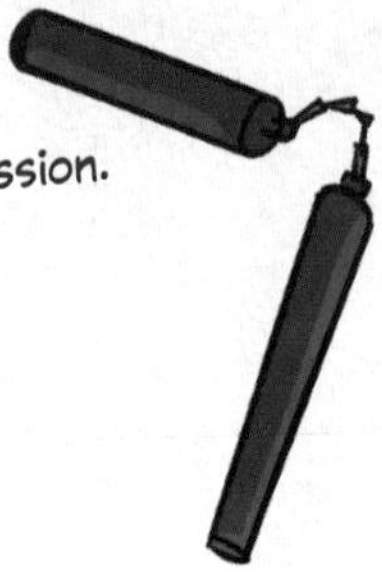

1. When I want to snuggle with my pet, they:
   A. Stash their nunchucks and curl up next to me for a cuddle session.
   B. Stare at me blankly, then ask for more yum-yums.
   C. Sometimes want a head rub and sometimes just walk away.

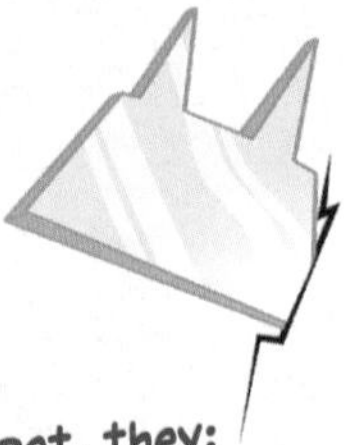

2. My pet's favorite toy is:
   A. A throwing star.
   B. A brand-new freeze ray.
   C. A ball.

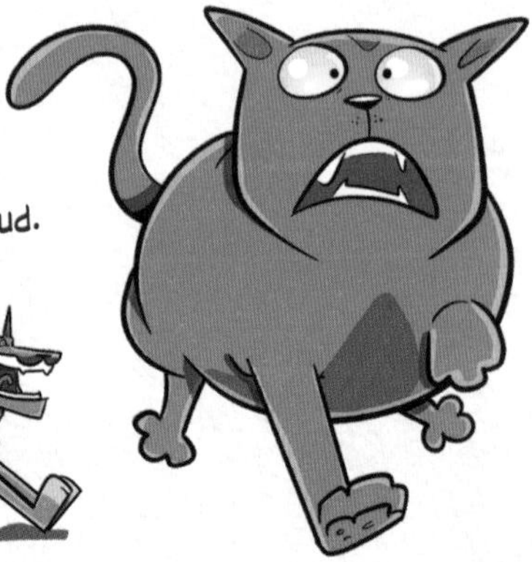

3. When my pet sees another pet, they:
   A. Always seem happy to make a friend--or ally.
   B. Hiss, bark, or glare like they have a secret feud.
   C. Don't even notice them.

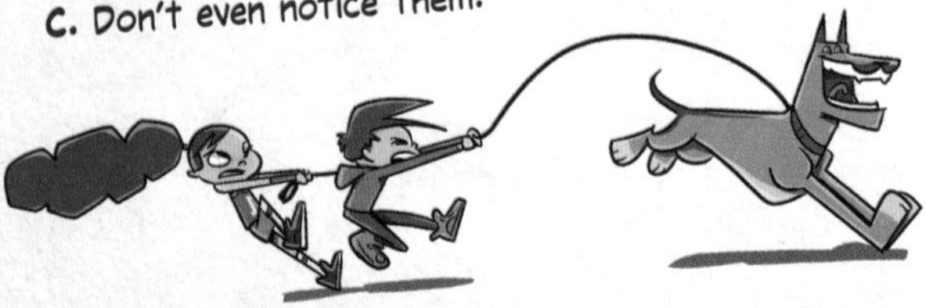

4. My pet is strong:
   A. At surprising moments--like when I get captured by an evil scientist's minions.
   B. All the time. It's almost like they have robot strength!
   C. I'm not really sure. I've never tried arm wrestling my pet.

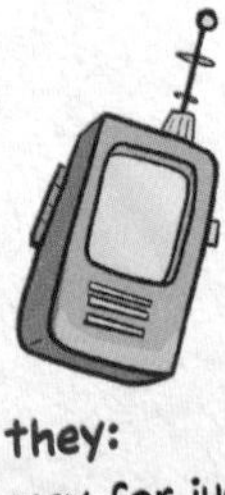

5. My pet's special hiding spot contains:
   A. Ninja gear.
   B. Weird electronic gadgets.
   C. Chewed-up shoes.

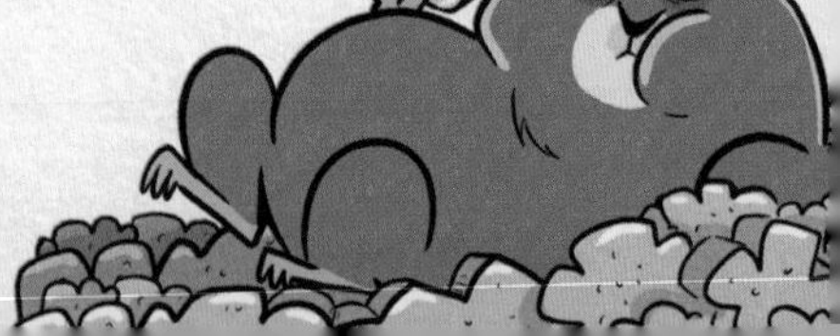

6. When I offer my pet special treats, they:
   A. Take just enough to keep up their energy for justice.
   B. Grab as many as they can fit into their mouth. Need more yum-yums!
   C. Nibble a few? Eat the whole bag? It depends on the day.

7. **When a giant robot messes up the city, my pet:**
   - **A.** Puts on a mask and mysteriously disappears.
   - **B.** Snorts because they know they could've done better.
   - **C.** Snores on the couch.

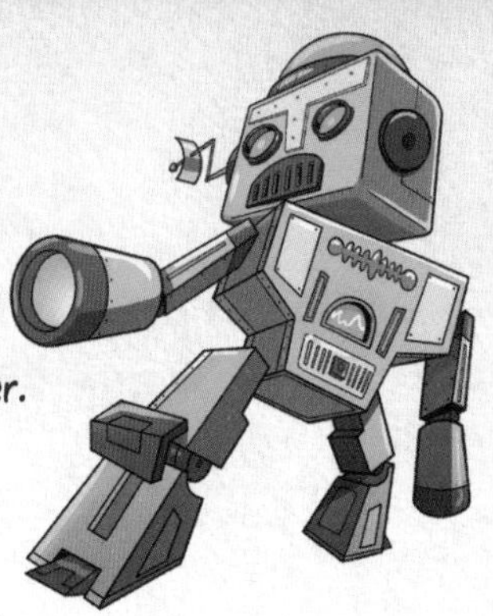

8. **When I talk to my pet about a problem, they:**
   - **A.** Always listen to my troubles and give me extra love.
   - **B.** Stare right through me. Sometimes their eyes even...glow?
   - **C.** Keep on snoring.

9. **When I wake up in the morning, my pet:**
   - **A.** Seems tired, but content, like they spent the night foiling crimes.
   - **B.** Seems grumpy, like they spent the night watching their crimes get foiled.
   - **C.** Is still snoring. Seriously, how much can one animal sleep?

10. **My pet came from:**
   - **A.** A rescue group run by a wise old ninja master.
   - **B.** A championship breeder (who may or may not be an evil scientist).
   - **C.** Who knows? They just showed up at my house one day!

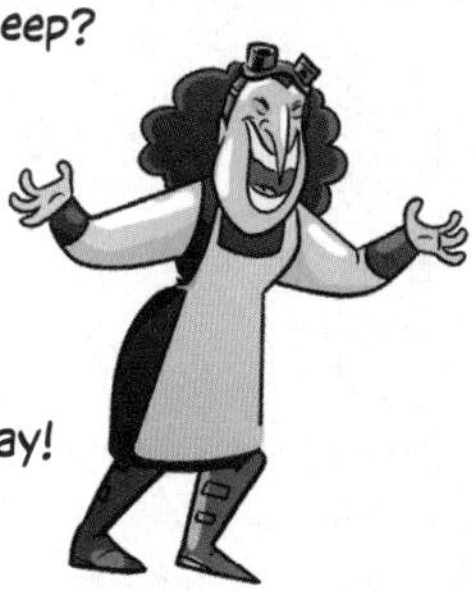

If your answers were...

Mostly A's:

You've got yourself a superhero pet! You spend all day snuggling with your pet, but when the sun goes down, and you're fast asleep in your bed, your stealthy pet springs into action and defends your neighborhood from dastardly foes! Well done, superpet!

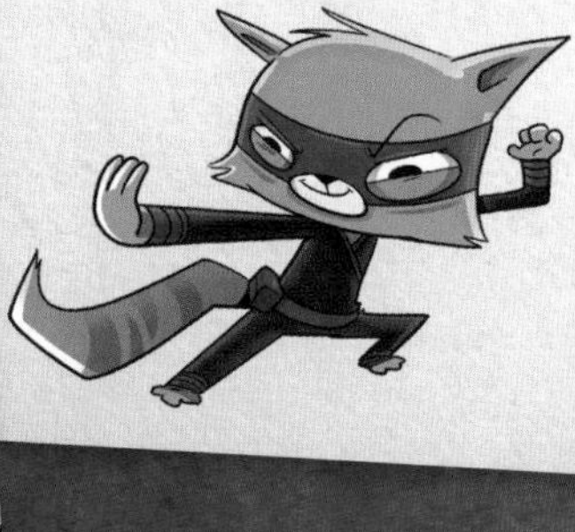

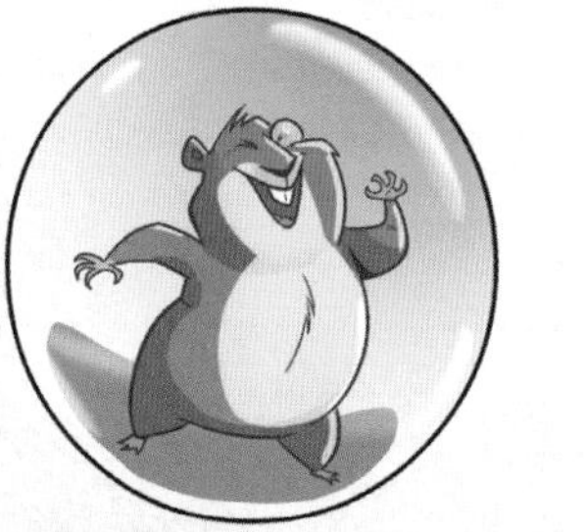

Mostly B's:

Your cuddly ball of fur is actually a supervillain! When your head hits the pillow, your innocent-looking pet is probably setting an evil plan in motion to take over the entire neighborhood! Whatever you do, don't get on your supervillain pet's bad side.

Mostly C's:

It may be too soon to tell whether you're dealing with a superhero or a supervillain. Look for clues that might lead you more in the superhero direction of saving neighbors or the supervillain direction of plotting mass chaos in the local park.

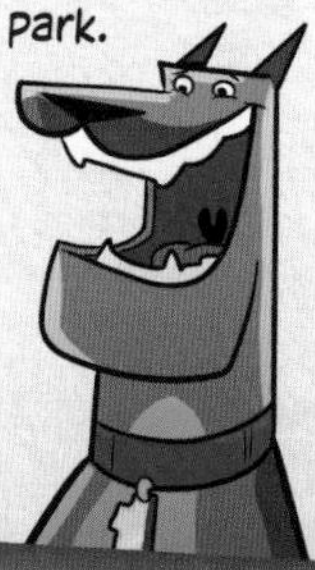

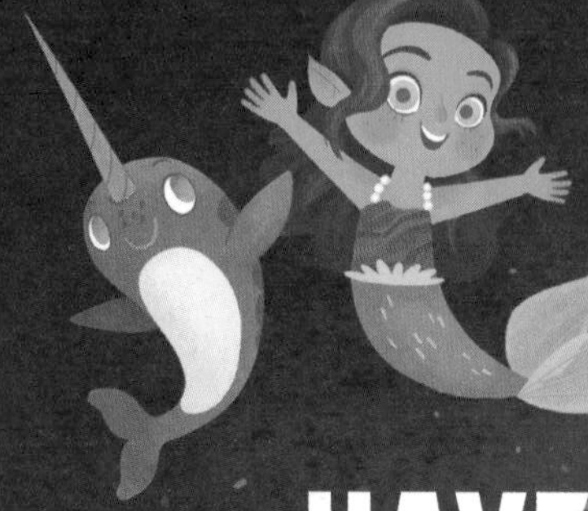

HAVE YOU HEARD ABOUT epic! YET?

We're the largest digital library for kids, used by millions in homes and schools around the world. We love stories so much that we're now creating our own!

With the help of some of the best writers and illustrators in the world, we create the wildest adventures we can think of. Like a mermaid with a narwhal who solve mysteries. Or a pet made out of slime.

We hope you have as much fun reading our books as we had making them!

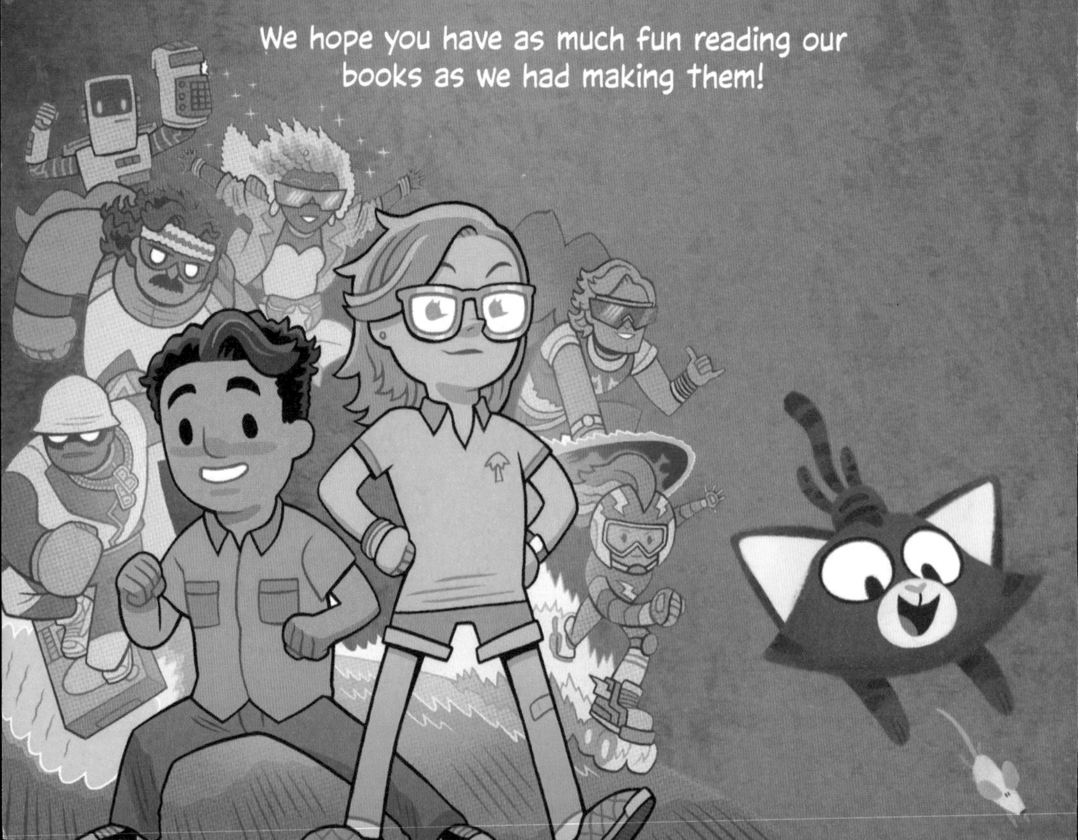

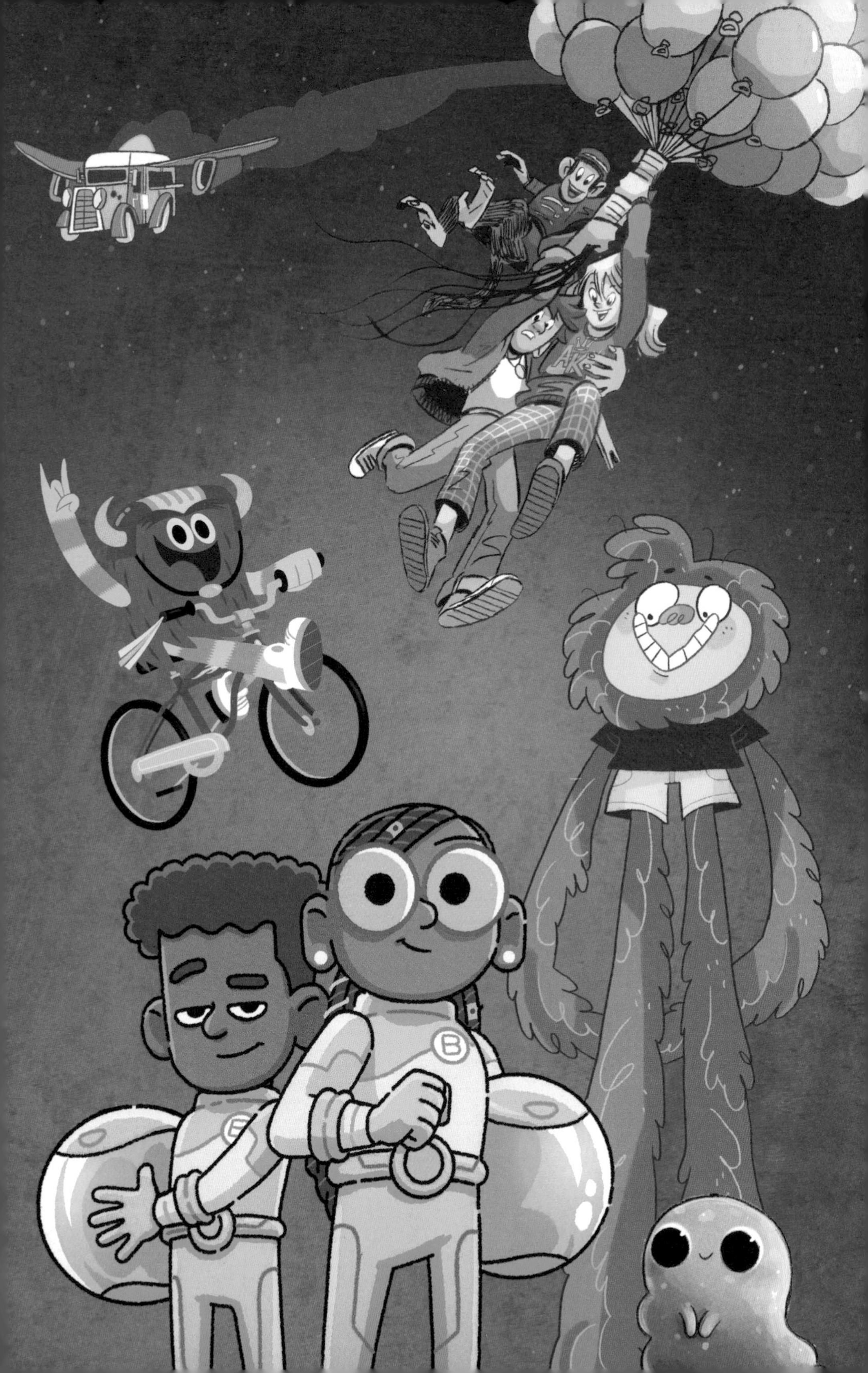

LOOK FOR THESE BOOKS FROM

epic!

epic!originals

OUT OF TIME

LOST ON THE TITANIC

epic!originals

DIARY OF A 5TH GRADE
OUTLAW

epic!originals

My Pet Slime

COURTNEY SHEINMEL **RENÉE KURILLA**

epic!originals

CREATURE CAMPERS

THE SECRET OF SHADOW LAKE

JOE McGEE **BEA TORMO**

AVAILABLE **NOW** AT
getepic.com
AND WHEREVER BOOKS ARE SOLD!